HOMER AND THE

J. V. Luce

Homer and the Heroic Age

Futura Publications Limited

A Futura Book

First published in Great Britain by
Thames and Hudson Limited in 1975

First Futura Publications edition 1979

*Uxori filiisque carissimis
quae mecum troiam viderunt*

ISBN 0 7088 1562 6

Printed in Great Britain by
Hazell Watson & Viney Ltd
Aylesbury, Bucks

Futura Publications Limited
110 Warner Road
Camberwell, London SE5

Illustration Acknowledgements

Pictures 1, 2, 15, 17, 19: Hirmer; 5, 27, 28: J. V. Luce; 6: J. Powell; 8, 10: Peter Clayton; 9, 23: Deutsches Archäologisches Institut, Athens; 11: National Museum, Copenhagen; 12, 13, 16, 22, 25: Princeton University Press and the University of Cincinnati; 18: Staatsbibliothek, Berlin; 21: Maurice Chuzeville; 26, 29, 30, 31: Trustees of the British Museum; 32: Cyprus Museum, Nicosia.

B.C.	EGYPT		GREECE AND THE AEGEAN		B.C.
1600	DYNASTY XVIII	NEW KINGDOM	SHAFT GRAVES		1600
			LATE HELLADIC PERIOD		
				I	
1500					1500
				M IIA	
			Thera eruption		
				Y IIB	
			Greek dynasty at Knossos		
1400				IIIA1	1400
			Palace of Knossos destroyed	C	
	AMARNA EPOCH	Akhenaten	Mycenaean occupation of Zakynthos and Kephallinia		
				E IIIA2	
			Mycenaean occupation of Ithaca		
1300			Troy VI devastated by earthquake	N	1300
	Rameses II Battle of Kadesh	XIX			
			Treasury of Atreus built	A IIIB	
			Final destruction of Thebes		
	Merneptah		Sack of Troy VIIA		
	Libyan invasion		Devastation at Mycenae and Tiryns	E	
1200	Rameses III	XX	Pylos destroyed		1200
	Sea Peoples invasion			A	

Date	Dynasty	Events		Date
		Dorian invasion Aeolian migration begins	N IIIC	
		SUBMYCENAEAN PERIOD		
1100			↑	1100
	XXI (TANITE)			
		PROTOGEOMETRIC PERIOD Transition to Iron Age Colonization of Ionia begins	DARK AGE	
1000				1000
	XXII (BUBASITE)	Ionian cities establishing themselves	↓	
900		GEOMETRIC PERIOD		900
		Dorian colonization of Dodecanese		
	XXIII			
800				800
		Ischia colonized by Euboeans Alphabet introduced from Levant Homer composes Iliad and Odyssey		
700				700

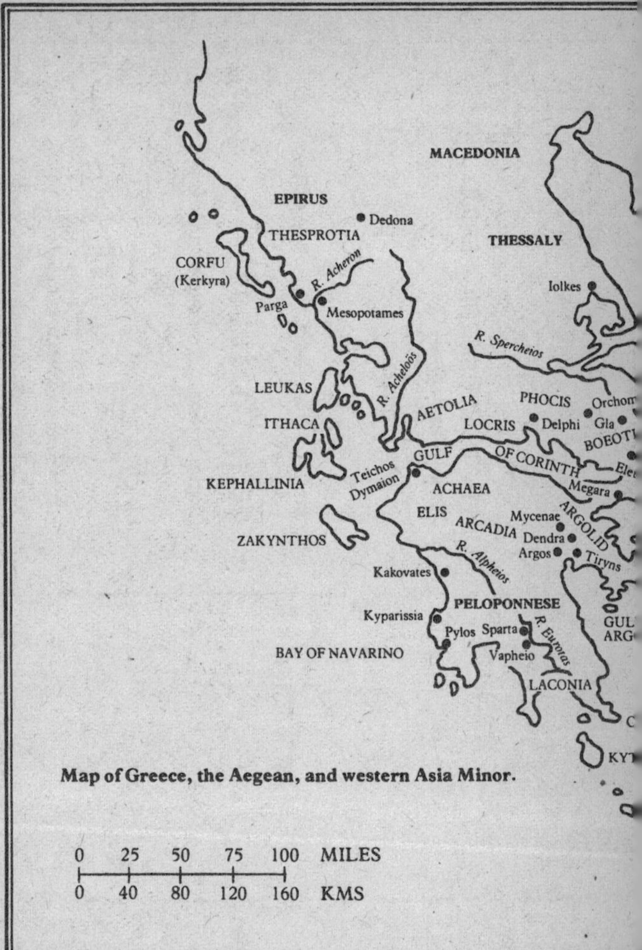

Map of Greece, the Aegean, and western Asia Minor.

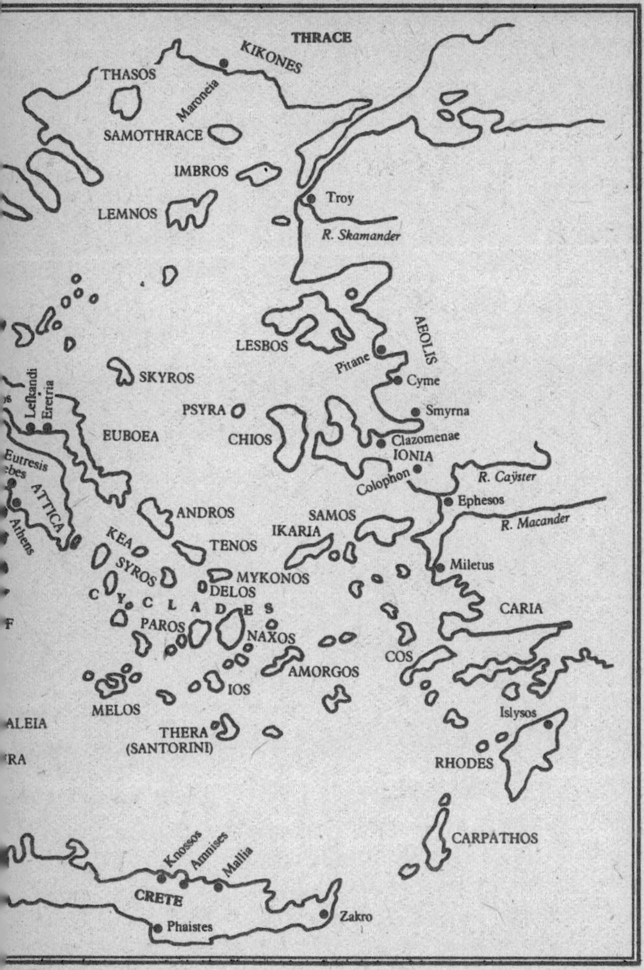
THRACE
KIKONES
THASOS
Maroneia
SAMOTHRACE
IMBROS
LEMNOS
Troy
R. Skamander
LESBOS
AEOLIS
Pitane
Cyme
SKYROS
Lefkandi
Eretria
Smyrna
PSYRA
EUBOEA
CHIOS
Clazomenae
IONIA
Eutresis
ATTICA
Athens
Colophon
R. Caÿster
Ephesos
ANDROS
SAMOS
IKARIA
R. Macander
KEA
TENOS
SYROS
MYKONOS
DELOS
Miletus
C Y C L A D E S
PAROS
NAXOS
CARIA
COS
AMORGOS
IOS
MELOS
Islysos
ALEIA
THERA
(SANTORINI)
RA
RHODES
CARPATHOS
Knossos
Amnises
Mallia
CRETE
Zakro
Phaistes

Preface

A concern for what Byron called the 'authenticity of the tale of Troy' has been my chief motive in this study of the Homeric tradition. I hope that the archaeological data here assembled may prove illuminating to all who read Homer, whether as students, or merely as casual travellers in 'the realms of gold'. Specialists, too, may find something to interest them in my discussion of some of the more recent material from, for instance, Messenia, Dendra, and Epirus. The *List of Abbreviations* provides, in effect, a guide to the standard works on which I have chiefly relied. I have not aimed at comprehensive coverage: for example, no assessment is attempted of Homer's account of dress, jewellery, or shipping. Full and up-to-date information on these and all other aspects of Homeric archaeology is (or soon will be) available in the series of monographs now in course of publication under the general title of *Archaeologia Homerica* (Göttingen 1967–). My aim has been rather to present a sustained argument for the antiquity and reliability of the epic tradition. Homer's picture of the Heroic Age contains, I believe, a significant amount of valid information about events and conditions in the Mycenaean world before 1100 BC. While emphasizing the legacy of the Bronze Age in the *Iliad* and the *Odyssey*, I have tried also to indicate the complexity of the bardic tradition, which went on absorbing cultural elements from earlier centuries down to Homer's own time.

I have been fortunate in being able to draw freely on the Homeric scholarship of my colleague Professor W. B. Stanford. His lectures on the *Odyssey*, which I attended as an undergraduate, first stimulated my interest in the mind and art of Homer. He kindly read my manuscript, corrected a number of errors, and suggested many improvements. Another colleague, Mr Paul Cartledge, also read the work in draft, and I am grateful to him for many helpful comments. I wish also to thank Professor G. L. Huxley, Dr J. N. Coldstream, and Dr J. Chadwick for information and advice on a number of problems.

The following have kindly given permission for quotations: Messrs. Routledge & Kegan Paul for R. Lattimore's *Iliad*; Messrs. Oxford University Press for T. E. Shaw's *Odyssey*; Messrs. Methuen and Co. for E. V. Rieu's *Odyssey*. Where no translator is named, the version is my own.

Trinity College, Dublin
May 1974

Contents

Introduction

The main theme of this book is the impact of archaeological discoveries on the interpretation of the Homeric poems. It is largely a study in what is conveniently called 'Homeric Archaeology'. The term is easier to use than to justify. What, it might be asked, have pots to do with poetry? Archaeology has its own proper techniques of measurement and classification, and these are irrelevant to the study of literature. In reply to this line of argument one might urge that Schliemann would never have made his discoveries if he had adopted such a purist approach. He trusted the evidence of Homer as a guide to where he should excavate, and then used his findings to reflect back light on the Homeric text. Archaeological data become meaningful only when they help us to reconstruct the life and times of vanished peoples. By his excavations Schliemann rediscovered a lost world, the world of Mycenaean Greece. In a sense this world was never lost, for, as we can now see, a picture of it was preserved in Greek myths and legends. The Homeric poems are the earliest source of these legends, and Homer structures his world around the persons named and the events recorded in the legendary tradition. Homer's world is basically the world of Agamemnon and Odysseus, a world of Achaean heroes engaged in warfare and wandering. But such a summary does less than justice to the rich complexity of object and custom embroidered on the basic fabric.

Is Homer's world a simple world, in the sense that it presents a picture of one particular epoch? Or is it a composite world in which elements from different epochs are artificially combined? If the latter, can the overlapping elements be disentangled and assigned to different periods in the history of the Greek people? In general, is it legitimate to treat the Homeric poems as a source for Greek history? Homeric archaeology is concerned with such questions and can, I think, help us to answer them. Homer is poetry, not history: granted. But the poetry is narrative and epic; it tells a story about the past, and it is surely legitimate to enquire how far this story corresponds to what actually happened. Archaeology is not history: granted. But its data can be interpreted to yield historical results. They underpin chronology, and throw light on trade, living standards, cultural interchange, the decline and fall of settlements, changes in weaponry and burial customs. Archaeology provides an essential background for the understanding of the Homeric poems in their historical aspect as a record of one or more stages in the development of Greek civilization.

There are no easy or undisputed answers to the problems that arise when we try to relate Homer and history. We may admire the simple faith of Schliemann in identifying a gold burial mask as the face of Agamemnon, or a hoard of precious objects as Priam's treasure. But we now know that he was mistaken. If Agamemnon is a historical figure he must be dated to the thirteenth century BC, but the gold mask is three centuries older. If Priam is a historical figure he must be contemporary with Agamemnon, but the treasure of Troy dates from the third millennium. Schliemann's chronology was faulty, but this does not upset the essential validity of his approach. The Shaft Grave goods must somehow be related to the epic tradition of Mycenae 'rich in gold'. The long history of Troy must somehow be linked with the Mycenaean world as documented by archaeology and sung by Homer.

In his book *Homer and his Critics*, the late Sir John Myres began with the reflection that 'it is not easy to say anything new about Homer'. It is also true that it is risky to say anything about Homer! 'No statement about Homer is incontrovertible.' There is always the bugbear of the 'remotely conceivable alternative'.[1] If one is to begin to write about Homer, one must make assumptions, and mine had better be stated at the outset.

I assume that the *Iliad* and the *Odyssey* were composed by the same poet, a man called *Homeros*.[2] I assume that he was a singer of tales (*aoidos*, a bard), and that he inherited a long and rich tradition of heroic poetry. I assume that he composed the two great poems with the help of techniques and materials developed in the course of the tradition of many previous singers. I assume that his poems have come down to us substantially in the form in which they were composed. I accept that the text has suffered some modifications from the activities of reciters, editors and copyists in the ancient world, but I believe that changes and interpolations are often detectable and always of minor importance in the poems as a whole. I should be prepared to argue that there have not been any substantial interpolations, but if anyone insists on excluding Book 10 of the *Iliad* or a portion of Book 11 of the *Odyssey* (565–627) as post-Homeric I should not fight hard to retain them. I believe that Homer composed the poems without the aid of writing, that he gained great kudos through their recitation, and that to ensure their preservation he either wrote or dictated a definitive version of them. This implies, of course, that writing was practised in the community in which he lived, and this in turn implies that he lived not earlier than *c.* 750 BC. I believe that his *floruit* falls in the second half of the eighth century, and that he was a native of Ionia. The places with the best claim to be his birthplace are Chios and Smyrna, but I have no doubt that he travelled extensively about the Aegean, and I think it probable that he visited both the Troad and Ithaca. I assume that he was not blind.

It would take several more volumes to argue out the above assumptions and beliefs. Here I can only say that they have not been adopted without much consideration, and they are, of course, quite respectable in the sense that many scholars might accept some, or even most, of them. But few would agree with all of them, and some would reject all of them – such is the potential *odium* of the *quaestio Homerica*. One good reason for listing them is that they at least make clearer what I imply by statements like 'Homer admired the aristocratic ethos', or 'The Homeric poems preserve the memory of a vanished world.' My main concern is not with questions of multiple authorship, or the date of Homer, or how the text was transmitted. In most contexts I make little or no distinction between 'Homer' and 'the Homeric poems' (*i.e.*, the *Iliad* and *Odyssey*). Sometimes, however, I think it permissible to speculate about how Homer viewed the material he was handling, and then it is necessary to date and place him. In such cases my assumption that he was a late eighth-century Ionian comes into play. Generally, however, I am more concerned with Homer as the mouthpiece of a tradition that greatly transcended the individual bard in time and space.

My aim is to present and analyze the Homeric tradition in the light of archaeological discoveries made during the last hundred years. The most relevant discoveries are those made on the Greek mainland and islands, and on the western coast of Turkey. Finds from a wider area are also taken into account when they appear relevant to Greek history or the Homeric poems. As a result of these discoveries we now have a much clearer conception of how the Greeks developed and what they achieved between *c.* 1600 and 700 BC, that is to say, in the Late Bronze Age and the Early Iron Age. The history of these nine hundred years is not a history that can be closely dated and presented in terms of named individuals. It is rather the history of the rise and fall of different centres of power and schools of art, of changes in architecture and pottery styles, of evolution in burial customs and technology, of objects that became obsolete and skills that were lost and regained. Most importantly, it is the history of the Greek-speaking tribes as they explored, expanded, conquered, traded, prospered, declined, migrated, and colonized. Their restless energy brought them originally from the plains of eastern Europe or southern Russia to the shores of the Aegean. There they were drawn into contact with the older and higher civilizations of Crete, Egypt, and the Levant. Responding to the stimulus of the Orient (as their successors were to do nearly a thousand years later) they developed a new form of writing, new types of building, and became most skilful fabricators of weapons and pottery. They took to the sea and spread their sphere of influence from Sicily to Syria. Their persistent aggressiveness brought them great prosperity for some centuries, but later involved them in catastrophe and fragmentation at the close of the Bronze Age. But an ingrained tenacity and resourcefulness enabled them to survive, to regroup, and slowly to rebuild a new world on the ruins of the old.

Through all their vicissitudes the Greeks maintained their language and clung to their cults, and they never, it seems, gave up the art and practice of heroic song. The essential continuity of Greek civilization ensured that a legacy of legends from the Bronze Age was handed down from generation to generation. Legends are to be distinguished from myth on the one hand and folktale on the other. Myths are the primitive equivalent of science in so far as they attempt to provide an explanation of the origin and ordering of the world. Folktales are the primitive equivalent of plays or films in so far as their function is to provide popular entertainment by amusing, clever, and fantastic stories. Legends are the stories that a nation tells and believes about its past. Such legends often contain a large admixture of myth and folktale, but in essence they constitute the record of the heroic achievements or marvellous adventures of historical characters. If recorded in prose they are technically sagas. If recorded in verse they are often called lays or ballads.

The earliest extant Greek legends are contained in the poetry of Homer. The Greek term for composing or reciting in Homeric fashion was 'singing the famous deeds of men' (*e.g.*, *Iliad* 9, 189). The men were kings and warriors believed to have lived in a 'Heroic Age' at the end of the Bronze Age, and the deeds were mainly related to two major enterprises, a war against Thebes and a war against Troy. This book treats the narrative content of the Homeric poems as legend in the sense defined. It assumes that the poems are what they claim to be, traditional stories about former war heroes, and attempts to assess how much historical truth they contain.

1 Homer and the archaeologists

How reliable is the tradition embodied in the Homeric poems? Their basic historicity was widely accepted in the ancient world. Territorial claims could be supported by an appeal to the epic tradition, as was done, for example, by the Athenians when they annexed Sigeum in the Troad soon after 600 (Herodotus, 5, 94). Thucydides and Plato used Homeric data in reconstructing early Greek history. Believing himself to be descended from Achilles, Alexander the Great went to sacrifice in the temple of Athena at Ilion before starting another phase of the ancient conflict between Europe and Asia.

It was not until the first century AD that systematic attempts were made to undermine Homer's credibility.[1] Dio Chrysostom in his *Trojan Discourse* argued that the Greeks lost the Trojan War. Two chronicles were also published by unknown writers, claiming to have recovered the authentic story of the war from records made at the time by one Dictys of Crete, and by an equally fictitious Dares of Phrygia. Needless to say, these third-rate narratives were entirely spurious, but they appealed to the taste of the time, and won a reputation for veracity that lasted all through the Middle Ages. They were not finally discredited until early in the eighteenth century.

Dictys and Dares passed into limbo, but 'deep-browed Homer' remained, an inspiration to poets but a source of grave perplexity to critics. In the nineteenth century the unity and credibility of Homer came under severe and sustained attack. George Grote, in his *History of Greece*, expressed a representative view when he drew a sharp distinction between 'legendary' and 'historical' Greece; for him Greek history began with the first Olympiad in 776.

Persons and events such as Homer described were 'not to be regarded as belonging to the province of real history'. He allowed that the poems were 'full of instruction as pictures of life and manners', but the life and manners were those of the poet's own contemporary society.

This was a sensible, if negative, approach to the problem of Homer as history. But some of the higher critics showed less restraint. By the mid-nineteenth century it had become fashionable to regard myths as symbolic accounts of natural phenomena. 'Myth' was understood in an all-embracing sense as covering all stories told about the past, present, or future state of the world. No distinction was drawn between 'historical' saga and 'religious' myth. In this theory the major personages of Greek legend were interpreted as symbols or personifications of the heavenly bodies, and the Trojan War was written off as a 'solar myth'. Achilles, for example, stood for the sun, his quarrel with Agamemnon represented a solar eclipse, and Hector and the Trojans were clouds scattered by the rays of the sun.

Such aberations were not untypical of Homeric criticism between 1850 and 1870. It is true that William Gladstone, in his *Studies in Homer* (1858), had maintained the basic historicity of Homer's account of the Trojan War, but his belief was unsupported by any external evidence, and was discredited by professional classicists.[2]

It was at this moment that Heinrich Schliemann (1822–90) burst upon the scene.[3] His personality was a remarkable blend of romanticism and practical efficiency. When he was seven years old his father gave him as a Christmas present a copy of Dr George Ludwig Jerrer's *Universal History for Children*. This book contained a picture of the capture of Troy which fascinated him. As he gazed at Aeneas leaving the burning city he formed a resolve that some day he would search for and uncover its remains. But that day was long in coming. His father could not afford to prolong his schooling, and he was set to work in a grocer's shop. Then occurred a memorable incident, vividly described by Schliemann himself in the autobiographical essay prefixed to his *Ilios*. A student had been expelled from the Gymnasium of Neu Ruppin for bad conduct. Forced to become a miller's apprentice, he had taken to drink, and one day he wandered into the shop in an intoxicated state and began to recite Homer. Then, as Schliemann tells it:

> Although I did not understand a syllable, the melodious sound of the words made a deep impression on me, and I wept bitter tears over my own unhappy, uneducated fate. Three times over did I get him to repeat to me those divine verses, rewarding his trouble with three glasses of whisky, which I bought with the few pence that made up my whole fortune. From that moment on I never ceased to pray to God that by His grace I might yet have the happiness of learning Greek.

Schliemann was not destined to remain a grocer's apprentice. To improve his health – he was troubled with tuberculosis – he decided to go on a sea voyage to South America, was wrecked off the Dutch coast, and ended up in Amsterdam where he became a clerk. He prospered in business, taught himself English, French, and Russian, and by 1846 was the Russian agent for the firm of Schröder and Co. Setting up on his own, he went to the USA in 1850 and made $350,000 in the Californian gold rush. Returning in 1852, he married Ekaterina Lyschin, a Russian lady of good family, and in due course three children were born. Over the next fifteen years Schliemann improved his fortunes to the point where he could plan the fulfilment of his boyhood dreams, but his marriage became increasingly irksome as Ekaterina could not bring herself to share his passion for travel nor his enthusiasm for ancient Greece. Finally a divorce was arranged, and Schliemann turned all his energies to an exploration of the principal Homeric sites. After making preliminary soundings in Ithaca, the Peloponnese and the Troad in 1868, he decided that he needed the companionship and inspiration of a Greek wife. He wrote to his friend Archbishop Vimbos of Athens, asking him to find him a Greek girl to wed, and specifying that she must be intelligent, unsophisticated, of pure Greek ancestry, and resembling Helen of Troy. The Archbishop sent suggestions backed up by photographs and after studying these Schliemann wrote to his father: 'I shall go to Athens and marry Sophie.' Sophie was Sophia Kastromenos, seventeen years old and still at the Arsakeion school in Athens. After seeing her in class, and hearing her recite Helen's lament for Hector 'without affectation or elaborate gesture', Schliemann was well satisfied that he had made a good choice. So were the family. Only Sophie had reservations about this brisk and balding business man of forty-seven who was paying such purposeful attention to her. After a short and somewhat stormy courtship they were married, and early in 1870 they made their way together to the Troad.

Here Schliemann was fortunate in securing help and advice from an Englishman named Frank Calvert. Calvert was acting as United States Vice-Consul at the Dardanelles; he knew the Troad well, and actually owned part of the hill of Hisarlik. The hill was known to be an ancient site, but was not regarded as the probable location of Troy. Most scholars favoured the claims of Balli Dagh, a much more impressive hill commanding the river Menderes at the point where it enters the Trojan plain (see below, pp. 142ff). Schliemann had made soundings on Balli Dagh in 1868, but with such poor results that he was ready to look elsewhere for Troy. Calvert suggested further work at Hisarlik, and Schliemann took up the proposal with his usual headlong enthusiasm. Though his official permission to excavate had not been cleared by the Turkish authorities, he brought two workmen to the site on 9 April 1870 and directed them to sink a trench on the hilltop. He wrote that evening in his diary that he 'could see the handsome Paris and fair Helen landing at this spot in their flight from Sparta . . .

Although it was morning, with the sun rising high, to me it was night and I saw flames leap into the sky as they did in Jerrer's book read at age seven. I was filled with intense desire to begin my digging and lay bare for the world to see the city of Priam and the war recorded by Homer.'

This was the prelude to the great seasons of 1871 and 1872 with their discovery of innumerable artefacts and the remains of city buried under city. In 1873 Heinrich and Sophie, digging together on a flagstone floor near one of the very ancient walls of the citadel, personally uncovered the great treasure that was to ensure the widest publicity for the excavations. As soon as he detected the hoard, Schliemann proclaimed a holiday for the workmen, ostensibly to celebrate his birthday. Then he and Sophie set to work to dig out the precious objects, which included gold cups, gold jewellery, and silver vases. They carried all the items to their house on the site, whence they were secretly transferred to Greece. Schliemann incurred the wrath of the Turkish authorities, who sued him for illegal removal of the finds. A Greek court finally ruled that he might keep them subject to payment to the Turkish government of an indemnity of 10,000 gold francs.[4] This he sent, adding a gift of 40,000 francs for the Imperial Museum at Istanbul, and he was able to secure permission to continue his excavations at Hisarlik by April 1876.

Schliemann completed seven seasons' digging at Hisarlik up to his death in December 1890, and published his results in three major books, *Troy and Its Remains* (1875), *Ilios* (1880), and *Troja* (1884). He identified seven 'cities' piled one on top of the other to a depth of nearly fifty feet. To the end of his life he maintained that the second lowest of the cities (and the one in which he found the treasure) was Priam's Troy. In this he was mistaken, as was shown by his assistant Wilhelm Dörpfeld, who continued the excavations in 1893 and 1894, and revealed the massive walls and great houses of the sixth stratum. Imported pottery found in this stratum showed that the later stages of Troy VI were contemporary with the heyday of the great strongholds of Mycenae and Tiryns on the Greek mainland.

But this error detracts little from the magnitude of Schliemann's achievement. He had realized his boyhood dream of finding Troy. Against the scepticism of professional scholars he had demonstrated that the Troy of Greek tradition could plausibly be identified with the hilltop site at Hisarlik. Homer's Troy was an ancient stronghold, protected by a notable ring of walls and towers, and the seat of a royal dynasty dominant in north-west Asia Minor. Schliemann found just such a citadel, strategically placed to dominate one of the important land-routes of the Troad, and close to the entrance to the Hellespont. The site fits well with the general topographical indications given by Homer (see chapter 6). Some detailed features, notably the hot and cold springs placed near the walls by Homer, cannot be traced, but such discrepancies should not be allowed to obscure the large positive gain made by Schliemann in identifying by excavation the focal point of the Trojan War. As Professor Blegen has written: 'There is no alternative site. If there ever was a Troy (and who can really doubt it?), it must have stood on the hill at Hissarlik.'[5]

Blegen and Professor W. T. Semple directed a meticulous new investigation of the site in seven campaigns from 1932 to 1938. A great deal of new evidence was recovered, and valuable contributions made to the problems of stratification, dating, and culture development. The results published in the four volumes of *Troy* (1950–58) present a definitive account of the site that is unlikely ever to be superseded.

For students of the Homeric tradition the crucial phase in the history of the site comes in the stratum known as VIIa. Troy VI and its powerful fortifications were severely damaged by an earthquake at a date not far from 1300 BC. Repairs were made, and life continued without a culture break into Troy VIIa, but there are significant changes in the lay-out of the buildings. Mean, hastily built houses now adjoin the walls and cover what had formerly been wide open spaces inside the citadel. Large storage jars suitable for holding oil and grain were sunk into the floors of many of these houses. One gets the impression that the inhabitants of Troy VIIa felt far less secure than their predecessors in Troy VI, and had crowded into the citadel for protection. If so, their fears were well-founded, for their city met its end in a great conflagration. An arrowhead of mainland Greek type and some fragments of human skulls were found in the streets – a strong indication that the city was sacked and burnt by invaders. The archaeological evidence is entirely consistent with Greek traditions about the Trojan War, and it is now widely accepted that Priam's Troy is to be identified with city VIIa at Hisarlik.[6]

In addition to his work at Troy, Schliemann opened up a whole new field of prehistory by his pioneering work in mainland Greece. The very term 'Mycenaean civilization' derives from his remarkable discoveries at Mycenae in 1876. Unlike Troy, the site of Mycenae had never been in doubt. Its 'Cyclopean' walls and Lion Gate had always remained visible. What Schliemann did was to confound the pundits by digging for, and finding, a group of rich royal tombs *within* the circuit of walls. With his usual faith in ancient tradition, he simply followed up the statement of Pausanias that graves reputed to be those of Agamemnon and his companions lay inside the walls. When Schliemann dug down in the area now known as Grave Circle A, he found six shaft graves where interments had been made with a wealth of gold and other precious objects, including gold masks over the faces of some of the deceased. In the excitement of this discovery he dispatched his famous telegram: 'TO HIS MAJESTY KING GEORGE OF THE HELLENES, ATHENS. With extreme joy I announce to Your Majesty that I have discovered the tombs . . . of Agamemnon, Cassandra, Eurymedon and all their companions . . .'. He had jumped to the conclusion that such splendid finds must date from the heroic generation that fought at Troy, but here, as at Troy, his chronology was faulty. The graves in fact date from the sixteenth century, and testify to the wealth of Mycenae at least three centuries before the Trojan War.

In 1884 Schliemann turned his attention to Tiryns, and soon laid bare the ground plan of a complicated palace inside the massive fortifications. The remains of a pillared portico with a carved stone dado and halls with figured frescoes indicated that the palace had been a rich and finely wrought structure. Here was a Bronze Age building that answered well to the description of palaces in the Homeric epics. Yet the associated pottery seemed to date the palace later than the structures he had found at Mycenae and Troy. Reluctantly he came to admit that his earlier identification of Agamemnon's grave might be open to question. In 1890 he returned to Troy, and here too the progress of excavation would soon have forced him to reconsider his views, but death cut short his labours before the end of the year.

The task was now to consolidate Schliemann's pioneering work and to establish the chronology of his finds. This was done by worthy successors like Dörpfeld (his assistant at Tiryns and Troy), Tsountas (who located the palace at Mycenae) and, in the present century, Wace, Blegen, and Mylonas. They have traced the relationship between Troy and Mycenae, and have shown that Mycenae was a key point in a major civilization that flourished in Greece in the Late Bronze Age. The study of this civilization in relation to the *Iliad* and *Odyssey* has added a new dimension to Homeric criticism. For better or worse, Homer and history are now indissolubly bound together. Many of the threads that link the epic tradition with Bronze Age Greece have been revealed by the progress of Aegean archaeology. Schliemann illuminated the old legends by uncovering the reality of 'well-walled Troy' and 'Mycenae rich in gold'. His successors have so widened our knowledge of the Mycenaean world that by

1932 Martin Nilsson was able to demonstrate that its areas of major importance coincided with the places that had always been most rich in legendary associations.[7] In this way a factual basis was established, not merely for the tale of Troy, but also for the other main cycles of heroic legend including the saga of the Argonauts and the story of the Seven against Thebes.

Among the heroes who fought at Troy, tradition gave great prominence to King Nestor of Pylos. His palace is the setting for an important episode in the *Odyssey*. Its location was the subject of much controversy in the ancient world, but there is now good reason to suppose that the problem has been solved. Blegen's excavations at Ano Englianos in Messenia, begun in 1939 and continued from 1952 to 1963, constitute another major chapter in the history of Homeric archaeology. His findings are being published in the splendid volumes of *The Palace of Nestor at Pylos in Western Messenia* (1966, 1969, 1973).

The title expresses Blegen's conviction that he has indeed located Homeric Pylos, and there are strong arguments to support the identification. There can be no doubt that the site was that of a palace. In size and splendour the complex of buildings does not fall short of the palaces of Mycenae and Tiryns, and the central block conforms to the same general plan at each site. In his initial campaign Blegen located the archives room and recovered over six hundred clay tablets written in the Linear B script previously known from Knossos. The publication of a preliminary transcript of these tablets by Bennett in 1951 led directly to the decipherment of the language as a form of Greek by Michael Ventris in 1952.[8]

This was another great advance in Bronze Age archaeology. Since the Knossos tablets dated to *c.* 1400,[9] it followed that a Greek dynasty was ruling at Knossos in the latter part of the fifteenth century. This Greek takeover of Minoan Knossos was just one part of the expansion of Mycenaean power, and it meant that the achievements of the Mycenaeans were the achievements of Greek-speaking peoples. There is, therefore, linguistic continuity between Mycenaean and classical Greece. This had been generally, but by no means universally, assumed, but the Ventris decipherment has now put the matter beyond reasonable doubt.

The Englianos tablets date from *c.* 1200, and show that the palace was the administrative centre of a populous and extensive kingdom. Much the commonest place-name on them is pu-ro, *i.e.*, Pylos; it occurs over fifty times and lends very strong support to the identification of the site with Nestor's Pylos. By comparison the site at Kakovatos in Triphylia, favoured by Dörpfeld as the best candidate for Homeric Pylos, appears as no more than a district centre. Field surveys of the south-west Peloponnese carried out by McDonald and Hope Simpson have shown that Mycenaean sites cluster most thickly to the north and east of the Bay of Navarino, with Englianos as their focus.[10] The surveys have also shown that the whole area was one of the most populous parts of the Mycenaean world in the thirteenth century. In the light of these findings it is interesting to note the Homeric tradition that the Pylian contingent was the second largest at Troy, numerically little inferior to the force mustered by Agamemnon of Mycenae.

The progress of archaeological discovery has provided all the leading Homeric heroes with at least some sort of Mycenaean background. Not all of them can be located in impressive palaces like Agamemnon at Mycenae and Nestor at Pylos. The material remains so far noted from the territories assigned to two of the greatest warriors, Ajax in Salamis, and Achilles in the valley of the river Spercheios, are indeed scanty. But, as Thucydides has warned us, we cannot safely infer the former power of the city-states from the scale of their public buildings. At least, Mycenaean sherds of the appropriate date have been found in all the areas reported to have sent contingents to fight at Troy. If they could not all boast of great palaces, they at least had towns and villages, and the personal prowess of their leaders must have counted for a great deal in the conditions of warfare at the time.

We may suppose this to have been particularly true of Odysseus. If tradition can be believed, his daring and resourcefulness contributed decisively to the success of the expedition. Yet he came from an outlying island kingdom, and brought with him only twelve ships, one of the smallest contingents to muster at Aulis. Ithaca was carefully investigated by a British archaeological expedition between 1931 and 1939, and the findings were gratifyingly consistent with the Homeric evidence.[11] There had been a Mycenaean occupation of the northern part of the island during the latter part of the Late Bronze Age. A cave shrine and at least one substantial mansion were identified, and a considerable quantity of Mycenaean pottery was recovered from a number of sites in what is still the most fertile and best watered district of the island.

In the 104 years since Schliemann's first soundings at Hisarlik, archaeological investigations in Greek lands and on the Aegean coast of Turkey have been very numerous and productive. Only the highlights have been touched on above. Perhaps the single most important result of all this activity has been the establishment of a firm factual basis for the Greek heroic legends. We know now that there was a Greece before classical Greece that excelled in some of the same characteristic ways, in building with unmortared stone, in the manufacture of fine painted pottery, in overseas trade and colonization, and in the arts of war. It is no longer possible to draw a firm line between Greek history and prehistory, and to dismiss all events before the eighth century as mythical.

Mycenaean civilization declined from 1200 onwards, and was virtually extinct by 1100. Many sites were destroyed and abandoned. There was catastrophic depopulation. The art of writing disappeared with the palaces which had fostered it. But a few survivors continued to occupy some of the old sites, and many more migrated eastwards over the Aegean to found new communities.

Though Greece entered a Dark Age of poverty and isolation, there was continuity in language and cult. Memories of the great past were enshrined and transmitted in legend.

By 800 Greece was again beginning to prosper and expand, and the century that followed saw the introduction of the alphabet and the revival of literacy. This was also the century in which epic poetry reached its acme, and the *Iliad* and *Odyssey* took shape substantially in the form in which we have them. They are poems about the Trojan War and the wanderings and trials of a major hero returning home from that war. In the light of the archaeological advances it can hardly be doubted that some history underlies them. But we also have a clearer appreciation of the long time-gap that separates Homer from the destruction of Priam's Troy. Assuming that Priam's Troy is Troy VIIa, then its fall is to be dated between *c.* 1260 and 1180. Some experts favour a date nearer the upper limit, others nearer the lower, but the disagreement is confined within a range of some eighty years (see p. 149). A majority of scholars would also agree to an eighth-century dating for the *Iliad* and *Odyssey*. On these datings there is a gap of four to five hundred years between Homer and the central event with which his poems are concerned.

It is no longer acceptable in the light of modern knowledge to prolong the Bronze Age and to up-date Homer so that the time-gap between them becomes quite short. Homer is a distant witness to the Mycenaean world, and the intervening centuries saw great changes in Greece and the Aegean. These centuries also left some mark on the bardic tradition. So the tradition represented by the Homeric poems is composite, with some elements dating back to the period of the Trojan War and even further back into the Mycenaean Age, some elements originating in the so-called Dark Age between 1100 and 800, and finally some elements that reflect life in Homer's own day.

Before attempting to analyze these different elements,

I propose to survey in more detail the period from the heyday of Mycenae before 1200 to the renaissance of Greece in the eighth century.

2 From Mycenae to Homer

In the Late Bronze Age the heartland of Mycenaean civilization lay in the Peloponnese, with the main focus of power in the Argolid.[1] There were important centres also north of the isthmus of Corinth, notably in Attica and Boeotia. The cultural unity of these areas is evidenced in their art, architecture, and pottery. They constituted a Mycenaean world which showed its vitality by successive extensions of its power beyond the confines of mainland Greece. It is not possible to give a connected political and economic history of Mycenaean expansion, but the main stages are clear enough in outline. Before 1500, Minoan culture, backed up, it is generally thought, by sea power, was dominant in the Aegean, but in the course of the fifteenth century the balance of power tilted sharply in favour of the Greek mainland, and a Greek dynasty installed itself at Knossos, perhaps as early as 1450. The palace at Knossos was destroyed by fire soon after 1400, and simultaneously Greek power and influence spread out over the Aegean to embrace the Cyclades and Rhodes, and to secure a foothold on the coast of Asia Minor at Miletus. Westwards the bearers of Mycenaean culture were also expanding into Zakynthos, Kephallinia, and Ithaca, but the 'drive to the East' was more significant and lucrative. It seems probable that the Mycenaeans took over the trade between the Aegean and the Levant that had previously been handled by the Minoans. Cyprus, with its valuable copper deposits, now comes into the Mycenaean orbit, and contact with Egypt is proved by considerable quantities of Mycenaean pottery found at Tell el-Amarna, site of Akhenaten's short-lived capital in Middle Egypt. These finds (of IIIA 2 type) provide an important synchronism, for the city was occupied for only about fifteen years (*c.* 1375 to 1360). The energy of Mycenaean trading after 1400 is also confirmed by Mycenaean pottery (of IIIA and IIIB type) found at about ninety other sites in the Levant from Syria down to the Negev, and up the Nile valley as far as Nubia.

Recent analysis of the chemical composition of Mycenaean pottery indicates that the bulk of it was manufactured in the Peloponnese, but that there were also local centres of production, in Euboea, for example, and in Crete and Rhodes.[2] The minor centres reproduced the standard shapes and decorative patterns with great fidelity, working, it seems, in artistic subservience to the Argolid, and to Mycenae in particular. This evidence points strongly to the existence of a trading nexus centred on the Argolid, and presumably backed up by the military and naval power of the rulers of Mycenae.

In this thirteenth century the cultural uniformity of the Mycenaean world is so marked that some scholars have talked in terms of an 'empire' centred on Mycenae. They have pointed to the traces of a network of well-built roads radiating from Mycenae as evidence of the sort of imperial control from the centre that was later to be associated with the Roman empire.[3] But such a concept of a 'Mycenaean empire' could be misleading and anachronistic. A better parallel is probably to be found in the state of Greece in the fifth century BC, when Athens dominated the Aegean through her naval power and led the other Greeks in commercial enterprise, but was by no means all-powerful on land. The size and wealth of the palace by Pylos suggest that it was the centre of an independent kingdom, and political independence may also be claimed for Attica, and for Boeotia until the final destruction of the palace at Thebes. It is in fact a conjecture to say, as does the revised *Cambridge Ancient History*, that in the Mycenaean period the other Greek rulers 'acknowledged a single overlord'. Nevertheless, by 1250 Mycenae had probably emerged as the strongest kingdom, partly by successful aggression, and partly by intermarriage with other dynasties (on the pattern of Menelaos's marriage into the Spartan royal house).

What lay behind this rise to pre-eminence? Already as early as the sixteenth century Mycenae was a conspicuously wealthy centre.[4] The evidence was found in two circles of Shaft Graves, Circle A discovered by Schliemann in 1876, and Circle B discovered and excavated by Papdimitriou and Mylonas in 1951–54. The graves were cut down into the rock, in some cases to a depth of four metres, and the shafts were roofed near the bottom with wooden beams to prevent the earth fill from pressing directly on the interments. They represent a development of the simple cist graves of the Middle Helladic period. Their regal and dynastic character is indicated by the rich grave goods and multiple burials. They were set apart from the common cemetery by the circular wall retaining the earth that covered them and by the provision of grave-markers in the form of carved slabs. N. G. L. Hammond views them as a development of the tumulus burials of Epirus and Illyria.[5] If he is correct, we may see them as evidence that chieftains with northern connections had established themselves at Mycenae, and were acquiring great wealth by their prowess in warfare and enterprise in trading. Mycenae has no outstanding natural resources, but it stands at the point where the road from the isthmus of Corinth cuts through the mountains on to the fertile plain of Argos with its great eastward-facing bay. In its situation lies the clue to its importance in the Helladic world of the Bronze Age. It was strategically placed at the point where migrants from the Balkans found opening out before them a natural route across the Aegean to the ancient civilizations of Crete and Egypt. G. Mylonas believes that the rulers of Mycenae at this time 'seem to have become acquainted with the elaborate and magnificent burials of the Pharaohs and their nobles and, in a new-found prosperity, tried to imitate them'. Mycenaean pottery was finding its way to Egypt at this time, and Egyptian influence may be detected in the gold death masks, and an inlaid dagger with a scene of cats hunting through papyrus thickets on a river bank. There is even the possibility that one of the bodies in Grave V was embalmed. Greek legend preserves a memory of this Egyptian influence in the story of the daughters of Danaos wooed by the sons of Aegyptos.

A later stage in the story of Mycenae is represented by the *tholos* tombs which succeeded the Shaft Graves as royal sepulchres. Nine of these tombs have been found on the site, all showing the distinctive feature of a round chamber (the *tholos*) with a roof corbelled in to a pointed apex. Access was by a horizontal passage (the *dromos*), cut into the slop of the hillside where space for the lower part of the chamber had been hewn out of the rock. The series spreads over quite a long period of time, but dating is difficult because none was left unplundered. A steady improvement can be traced in the quality of the stonework of the vaults and passages, and in the later examples sophisticated devices like relieving triangles are introduced over the lintels of the great doorways. Wace assigns them to the two centuries from 1500 to 1300, but Mylonas would bring the lower limit down to *c.* 1220. All agree that the series culminates in the so-called Treasury of Atreus, one of the most impressive monuments of the ancient world. It seems likely that this massive and ornate tomb dates from *c.* 1250, not more than two generations before the first destruction of the citadel. Its size and grandeur indicate that the might of Mycenae was at or near its zenith when the king gave orders for its construction. Homer in the *Iliad* (2, 105–8) lists three predecessors of Agamemnon, Pelops, Atreus, and Thyestes, and says that Thyestes bequeathed the sceptre to Agamemnon to carry and 'to be ruler over many islands and all Argos'. If this is a genuine tradition about the dynasty that presided over Mycenae at the height of its power, we shall probably not be far wrong if we attribute the great *tholos* to the generation of Atreus. Homer does not associate any other dynasty with Mycenae, but in later Greek tradition the

Pelopids are represented as taking over power from the Perseids, descendants of Perseus, the founder of Mycenae. The tradition does not record enough names to cover the whole period of Mycenae's greatness from 1600 on. The chronology appears to have been telescoped – a not infrequent happening in the myth-history of Bronze Age Greece. But it is possible that the recorded change of dynasty is related to the transition from Shaft Grave to *tholos* tomb.

The Lion Gate provides further testimony to the power of the Pelopids, for Mylonas appears to have shown conclusively that it dates from *c.* 1250. With the stretch of Cyclopean wall enclosing Grave Circle A it represents the climax of military and monumental construction at Mycenae. Some of the great blocks are carefully squared, more are just boulders, unhewn or very roughly shaped, but all exude an air of impregnable authority. Fortifications on this scale must have taken many years to complete, and can only have been accomplished by a large labour force under the direction of a strong central authority. The only weakness in the fortress was the absence of an assured water supply. This was remedied by the construction of an underground cistern deep under the north-east corner of the enceinte to store water piped from the hillside outside the walls. It was the last major piece of military engineering at Mycenae. Less than a generation later, *c.* 1200, a major disaster overtook the citadel with destruction and burning of buildings including the palace.

The sack of Mycenae was part of a wider pattern of aggression and catastrophe.[6] In the course of the thirteenth century the principal Mycenaean centres had all set about strengthening their defences. Strong fortresses were built at Gla in Boeotia and Teichos Dymaion in Achaea. The fortifications of the Athenian acropolis were improved, and here, as at Mycenae and Tiryns, elaborate works were undertaken to ensure a supply of water for the citadel. Most significant of all, a wall with projecting towers was constructed across the isthmus of Corinth, evidently to secure the Peloponnese against invasion from the north. The Mycenaean world was concerned about its security, and a series of tablets from Pylos lists detachments of troops under the heading: 'Thus the watchers are guarding the coastal regions.'

The preparations were in vain. Disaster struck the main power centres around 1200 BC. The fortresses at Gla and Teichos Dymaion fell and were not restored. The palace at Pylos was looted and burnt, and not rebuilt. Not even the great walls of Tiryns and Mycenae could protect their palaces from destruction by fire. Athens was the only major Mycenaean citadel to survive intact.

The Peloponnese seems to have suffered most. Pylos was not reoccupied; Mycenae and Tiryns managed to weather the catastrophe and continued in occupation for much of the twelfth century, but the Mycenaean world of the IIIC period was greatly changed and weakened. Comparative statistics have been compiled for Peloponnesian sites occupied in the thirteenth and twelfth centuries respectively, and the figures convey something of the extent of the disaster:[7]

District	*Number of inhabited sites known from the thirteenth century*	*Number of inhabited sites known from the twelfth century*
Messenia and Triphylia	150	14
Laconia	30	7
Argolid and Corinthia	44	14

A similar pattern is found in districts north of the isthmus. In Boeotia the number of sites is reduced from 27 to 3, in Phocis and Locris from 19 to 5. Even in Attica, where the Athenian acropolis remained unsacked, the number was halved from 24 to 12. The actual figures just given will be subject to revision as more intensive surveys are carried out in remoter areas, but the ratio of the totals will in all probability continue to attest a dismal pattern of disaster. On average, where five sites flourished in these areas before 1200 only one survived to continue the Mycenaean way of life into the twelfth century.

Before 1200 the Peloponnesian sites in particular convey the impression of a highly organized and sophisticated civilization centred on royal citadels at Mycenae, Tiryns, Pylos, and, presumably, Sparta (though no palace has yet been found in Laconia). The Pylos tablets reveal something of the extent to which the whole economy was palace-centred. Seed-corn and copper were issued from the palace storerooms, and contributions were assessed and exacted from the surrounding towns and villages. Overseas trade was presumably also controlled by palace officials, and on it the metal-workers and ivory carvers depended for their raw materials. Fine arts like fresco painting must also have depended largely on palace patronage. As Desborough has written: 'All the evidence indicates that the population was large and fairly prosperous, an orderly community controlled by the kings and their all-pervasive bureaucracy.'

When the palaces were sacked, this orderly word fell apart. One can picture the centralized economy foundering once bureaucratic control was removed. Herds would be slaughtered, and fields left untilled. Grain ships would no longer arrive to replenish the royal granaries. It is easy to imagine famine and pestilence in the land. Only a major social and economic disruption can account for the devastation and depopulation so apparent in the Peloponnese. It seems that the fabric of Mycenaean life had come to depend too much on the royal dynasts, and when this support was removed the delicate and top-heavy structure collapsed.

The cause of the catastrophe is unknown.[8] There seem to be three main possibilities: internecine warfare and civil strife within the Mycenaean world; barbarian incursions from outside the Mycenaean world; persistent drought in the Argolid leading to famine and popular uprisings. Rhys Carpenter has argued ingeniously for climatic factors as the main cause of the catastrophe, but his theory appears to conflict with the evidence of pollen analysis from Messenia and is not as yet supported by any firm and specific scientific evidence.[9] The hypothesis of barbarian incursions is largely based on the alleged intrusion of new weapon types and the 'violin-bow' fibula from central or eastern Europe at the start of IIIC. But, as Snodgrass points out, some of the material was already present in Greece in IIIB, and it is by no means clear that invasion is the best explanation of its dissemination. Furthermore, if victorious incursions of new peoples occurred, one would expect some of the destroyed and reoccupied sites to show new cultural elements, but none does so. This difficulty has been met by the neat but nebulous supposition of a sudden destructive raid with the invaders withdrawing as rapidly as they came.[10] On the whole it seems most likely that dissensions within the Mycenaean world provoked the catastrophe. Later Greek tradition indicates that there was much tension and strife even before the Trojan War. In addition to the struggle between Argos and Thebes, there were legends of feuds between the Perseids and Pelopids, between Herakles and Nestor, and between Eurystheus and the Heraclidae. Hyllos, son of Herakles, it was said, attempted to invade the Peloponnese, but was defeated in single combat by Echemos of Tegea (Herodotus 9, 26). The long and costly Trojan expedition presumably aggravated the tensions. Thucydides (1, 12) assigns 'widespread civil strife' to the period immediately after the fall of Troy. In legend, Mycenae was notorious for the feuds in its royal house. Its dynastic quarrels could have so weakened it that it fell before a plunder raid from one of the more outlying Achaean kingdoms. There may well have been a fundamental division in the Mycenaean world between a wealthier south and a more warlike north, and strife between the two areas could have precipitated the political and economic collapse at the end of IIIB.

Whatever the cause, the effects were most marked in the most highly developed areas, that is to say, the provinces of the Peloponnese and central Greece north of the isthmus.

Outlying areas received an influx of refugees, and in some districts, notably Achaea, Mycenaean sites actually increased in number after 1200. There was a westwards migration to Kephallinia, but most of the fugitives who took to the sea made their way eastwards, to Crete, to Chios (where a new settlement was founded at Emborio), and to Cyprus. The dispersion brought new life to parts of eastern Attica and Euboea, and there are indications of active trading round the coasts and islands of the Aegean. Pottery of some liveliness and much originality was produced in a number of centres, at Perati and Lefkandi, for instance, and in the Cyclades. Twelfth-century Mycenaean pottery shows a diversity of style that is in marked contrast to the previous uniformity, and reflects the loss of political cohesion after the great disasters of *c.* 1200. There is even some evidence of partial recovery in the Argolid. Mycenae and Tiryns were re-inhabited, and produced competent, even lively, pottery for a time. One feels that, given peaceful conditions, the Mycenaean civilization might have climbed back to something like its old levels of achievement in art and architecture. But it was not to be; there was too much instability and insecurity on land and sea. It was an age of migrations and sea-raiding, and renewed destructions depressed living standards still further. The palace at Iolkos, which had escaped the earlier wave of catastrophes, was burnt *c.* 1150. Towards the end of the century the community at Emborio was wiped out, and the long-established settlement at Miletus came to an end. Mycenae was sacked again *c.* 1120 (by the Dorians according to Mylonas), and settlement there, and at Tiryns, dwindled almost to nothing. By 1100 Mycenaean civilization was virtually extinct, and the Greek world had sunk into a deep trough of poverty and isolation. Restored and newly founded settlements alike had faded and foundered, and after 1100 the opulence of the Mycenaean kingdoms remained only as a bright memory in a darkened Greece.

The Greek Dark Age is 'dark' in comparison with the splendours of the Mycenaean world down to *c.* 1200, and 'dark' too in comparison with the economic and political advances of the eighth and seventh centuries. It is 'dark' also in the sense that the Greeks knew very little about its history. It was an age deficient in legend and devoid of written records, and we have to rely mainly on the comparatively scanty data of archaeology when we try to pierce the shadows. How dark an age was it? Was it dark to those who lived through it? Thanks to the excellent recent surveys by Desborough and Snodgrass we can make a reasonable attempt to answer such questions objectively without either exaggerating or minimizing the hardships and deprivations then endured.

When the first half of the eleventh century is compared with the period before 1200, it is apparent that a major deterioration has occurred in the quality of life in the Greek lands. By 1100 the population was perhaps as little as one-tenth of what it had been a hundred years earlier.[11] Figures based on Hope Simpson's *Gazetteer of Mycenaean Sites* indicate that of 320 sites occupied in the thirteenth century only about 40 continued to be occupied in the eleventh century. Important skills had been lost: the ability to build with large blocks of well-cut stone, the ability to produce fine jewellery and metal-work. Fine arts like fresco painting, gem-cutting, and ivory carving had disappeared with the palaces. Literacy had apparently been confined to the palace scribes, and vanished with them. The very undistinguished Submycenaean pottery makes a sorry contrast with LH IIIB ware. It was a time of isolation when all contact with the Levant and Egypt was lost. The furnishing of the graves indicates a very marked decline in living standards. Cheaper materials were in use, clay for beads and obsidian for knife blades. By all these criteria the first half of the eleventh century was indeed a 'dark' period after an age of great achievement.

No progress is apparent for two generations or so, but after *c.* 1050 the darkness begins to lift a little in certain areas. Signs of revival can first be detected in Athens. Stimulated by renewed contacts with Cyprus, the Athenians had the resilience and the enterprise to pioneer a revolution in pottery style. Using the fast wheel and a new technique of painting with a multiple brush, the Athenian potters developed the Protogeometric style with new shapes and a sparing but effective use of abstract decoration. The new style spread rapidly south into the Argolid and north to Thessaly, and was carried across the Aegean to Miletus. This was a turning point in Greek history, and one can sense that the tide of civilization was beginning to flow again. The beginning of the Greek Iron Age is also dated to about this period. The required techniques were introduced to the Aegean from the east, probably from Cyprus. In the Argolid, Attica, and Euboea iron deposits were located and mined, and an iron industry was established.

The most significant feature of the Dark Age was the movement of Greeks eastwards across the Aegean, and their settlement on the coasts and offshore islands of Asia Minor.[12] In its earliest stages this was a refuge rather than a colonial movement. Necessity drove the migrants to band together, to choose leaders, and to leave the impoverished shores of Greece in search of new homes overseas. The eastwards drift first set in under the pressure of less civilized tribes emerging into the plains of Thessaly and Boeotia from the north and west, and then flooding on down towards the Peloponnese, the so-called Dorian invasion. The most northerly group of migrants, traditionally known as Aeolians, moved across to Lesbos and the stretch of coast between Cyme and Pitane. Somewhat later, and well to the south, Dorians occupied Melos and Thera and spread gradually across to Rhodes and Cos and into the peninsulas of western Caria. The fortunes of the Dorians do not concern us for they contributed nothing to the development of epic poetry. Into the sector of coast between them and the Aeolians came the Ionians, destined to play a leading role in the transmission and development of the Bronze Age heritage of song and legend. Tradition represented Attica as an important assembly area, and

Athens as the chief springboard, for the Ionian migration. This is consistent with the archaeological picture of Athens as comparatively well-settled and progressive in the second half of the eleventh century. In successive waves, detachments moved through the Cyclades and established themselves in Samos and Chios and on the coast from the Gulf of Smyrna south to the Bay of Latmos.

It is difficult to determine the dates at which sites were first occupied but the trend has been to revise earlier estimates upwards. In the last twenty years important finds of Protogeometric pottery have been made at key sites like Miletus and Old Smyrna. We can now be reasonably sure that Aeolians were quite well established at Old Smyrna early in the tenth century. At Miletus some elements of the Submycenaean style have been detected in the earliest Protogeometric pottery, which would put the first Ionian settlement there back before 1050.[13]

It is interesting to compare this dating with the Greek tradition that Miletus was founded by Neleus, a son of Codrus, king of Athens. Codrus's father Melanthus was one of the Neleids displaced from Messenia by the Dorian occupation of the Peloponnese, which, according to Thucydides, took place eighty years after the Trojan War. If we date the Trojan War close to 1200, the generation of Codrus will fall early in the eleventh century, and his son Neleus could have led an overseas venture before 1050. The findings of archaeology suggest that the tradition is reliable. Herodotus records that, on arrival at Miletus, the Ionians drove out Carians, killing the men and taking the women to wife (1, 146). Neleus then ordered his sons to conquer the Cyclades, a campaign in which Hegetor won much success, but Hippocles could only capture Mykonos.

In this and other legends we can detect something of the dangers and vicissitudes of the early migrations. They were neither so simple nor so clear-cut as summary accounts tend to represent them. The Ionian preference for sites on defensible promontories indicates that native resistance was often stubborn and prolonged. Many foundation legends tell of the forcible ejection of Carians; others speak of accommodations reached and mixed settlements. The founders of Clazomenae tried first to gain a footing on Mount Ida, and then in the territory of Colophon, before finally occupying a site on the south of the Gulf of Smyrna.

Before leaving Attica, the migrants had gathered from many parts of the Greek mainland, from Boeotia, from the Argolid, from Messenia, and from Achaea. They were a heterogeneous group of Hellenes dispossessed by the dying convulsions of the Mycenaean world. The legend of Tisamenus reflects the upheavals of the time. Tisamenus was a grandson of Agamemnon, driven from the Argolid by the Dorians. He led his Achaean followers west to Achaea (which took its name from them), and expelled 'Ionians' who then took refuge in Attica. These 'Ionians' must have included Mycenaeans displaced from the Argolid at the time of the first disasters close to 1200. Desborough has suggested that they may have been the key people who carried memories of the Mycenaean world eastwards to Ionia. But perhaps we should not try to pinpoint any one vehicle for the epic tradition. We should rather recognize that a rich variety of legend and folk memory was carried by all these migrants from all the anient centres of Mycenaean power from Orchomenos to Pylos. A good example of such a memory is the tradition in Mimnermus that his Colophonian ancestors were of Pylian origin, a far from unlikely supposition.

Ionia became the chief matrix of the tradition that culminated in the Homeric poems, but we should not overlook the contribution of the Aeolians. The traditional homes of Jason and Achilles lay in the territories from which they migrated. They had a special link with Boeotia, a region particularly rich in legendary associations. They also claimed that their migrations to Lesbos and Cyme had been led by descendants of Agamemnon, and the name Agamemnon was later borne by a king of Cyme. The Aeolian colonists must have played an important part in preserving and fostering the traditions of the Heroic Age.

The Aeolian sphere of influence overlapped the Ionian between Phocaea and Smyrna. Smyrna was occupied at an early date by Aeolians from Cyme. Later, it was treacherously seized by exiles from Colophon, and became an Ionian city. The date of the takeover is not known for certain, but it must have been before 688. If Homer was a native of Smyrna – and no city had a stronger claim to him – he must have been familiar with an exceptionally varied stock of legends about the past.

As a result of the migrations 'the Aegean became, what it had never been even at the height of Mycenaean power, a Greek sea'.[14] This was the main historical development of the tenth century, a century in which Athens set the pace in art and commerce. Athenian exports in pottery and dress pins (of iron topped by a bronze globe) have been noted over a wide area from Ionia to Crete and Messenia. Though Greek trade was confined to the Aegean, the communities that took part in it began to rise towards a modest level of prosperity. These included the Argolid (which traded with Cos), the growing settlements in Asia Minor (which maintained close links with Athens), and Euboea together with southern Thessaly. By 900 the Dark Age may be regarded as over for these Aegean-centred communities. Their Protogeometric pottery had reached a high standard of artistic achievement, they had developed the production of iron, and they had built up quite a complex network of trading connections. The discovery of a bronze foundry with moulds for casting tripods in the Late Protogeometric settlement at Lefkandi in Euboea proves that copper and tin were again available.

Progress continued in the ninth century. The richly furnished grave found in the Athenian agora in 1967, and dating to *c.* 850, is symptomatic of growing wealth and skill in jewellery manufacture. The excavations at Lefkandi indicate that it was wealthier than Athens at this time. Many of its tombs dating between 900 and 850 contain gold objects. This renewed presence of gold in Greece is an index both of increasing prosperity and of trade with the

Levant. The lavish stocks of gold in the Late Mycenaean world seem all to have been imported from the eastern Mediterranean area. After 1200 the supply diminished, and no gold objects are known between *c.* 1125 to 1075. After that, a few minor items of jewellery reappear (perhaps due to contact with Cyprus in the mid-eleventh century), but generally a dearth of gold continues down to *c.* 900.

When we come to the eighth century we can begin to speak of a Greek Renaissance. The line between Greek history and prehistory is traditionally drawn in 776, the date of the first recorded victor in the Olympic Games. More than four centuries of illiteracy were ended with the introduction of the Phoenician alphabet about 750.[15] This crucial innovation may have been due to the enterprise of merchants from Euboea, who early in the century established a trading post at Al Mina in Syria. At the same time, the Euboeans were penetrating far to the west to found a colony on Pithecussae (Ischia) off the Bay of Naples. The latter post grew rapidly into a prosperous settlement with its own pottery works and iron foundry. The western colonial movement gathered impetus with the foundation of numerous colonies in southern Italy and Sicily from 734 on. The population of the homeland was growing rapidly, and the new cities provided an outlet for surplus manpower.

The eighth century is also the century in which most authorities place Homer. Nothing is known for certain about him as a person, not even that he was a person. Beliefs about him are in effect beliefs about the *Iliad* and the *Odyssey*. The more sceptical one is about the unity of either poem, the less one is inclined to accept the ancient Greek view that one supremely great poet composed both epics. Belief in multiple authorship can take many forms. There is the moderate and reasonable view that the two poems, while unified in themselves, differ so markedly in spirit and outlook that they cannot be the product of a single mind. This amounts to a belief in two Homers, an earlier poet of the *Iliad* and a later poet of the *Odyssey*. But there are much more extreme views: the view that the *Iliad* is a patchwork of short heroic lays consolidated by editorial work at Athens in the time of Pisistratus (mid-sixth century); the view that the *Odyssey* is a compilation of three originally separate poems, one about Telemachos, one about the wanderings of Odysseus, and one about the slaying of the suitors. Such views amount to disbelief in Homer. Instead of the unifying force of a great poetic imagination, they posit the meritorious but minor creativities of many bards at different dates, supplemented by the slipshod activities of anonymous compilers and editors.

In opposition to the Separatist or Analyst school of Homeric criticism, stand the Unitarians who believe in Homer as an outstanding poet and author of the two epics substantially in the form in which we have them. In support of this belief they emphasize the dramatic unity of plot in both poems, the consistency of the characterization of the major heroes, and the uniformity of the poetic diction.

The debate continues, and will continue indefinitely because each side chooses to emphasize one of the two main factors in the genesis of the poems at the expense of the other. The two factors are tradition and design, and they lend strength respectively to the Analyst and Unitarian cases. One must concede to the Analyst that many Homeric phrases, lines, similes and descriptions are of high antiquity, and must have been current far earlier than any date at which one can reasonably place Homer. One must further allow that many of the scenes and incidents that occur in the poems must have been shaped for poetic purposes well before the time when the epics crystallized in the form we know. On the other hand, the Unitarians are on strong ground when they appeal to our aesthetic reactions to a reading of the *Iliad* and the *Odyssey*. Do you not feel, they will ask, that a mind of great sensitivity and creative power has shaped the phrasing, vivified the characters, and co-ordinated the incidents into a narrative of compelling interest, vigour and dignity? In short, can you fail to believe in Homer when confronted with the evidence of such poetic genius?

The claims of tradition and design have now to be assessed in the light of the knowledge that Homeric epic is oral epic. The oral nature of the Homeric style was demonstrated by the American scholar Milman Parry in a series of papers published in the late twenties and early thirties of this century and now collected in a volume entitled *The Making of Homeric Verse* (1971). It is hard to overemphasize the importance of Parry's researches. First, he demonstrated that the *Iliad* and *Odyssey* were composed with the aid of what Kirk calls 'a traditional store of fixed phrases which covered most common ideas and situations'.[16] In the case of formulae of the type 'swift-footed Achilles', 'much-endearing Odysseus', he showed that they constitute a system of remarkable scope and economy. By 'scope' he meant the coverage given by the formulae to the natural divisions of the hexameter (last three-and-a-half feet, last two feet, etc.). By 'economy' he meant the absence of metrical duplication. The system was designed to facilitate the oral improvization of hexameter verse. It was developed over the centuries by a long succession of oral poets. Homer did not create it; he inherited it from his non-literate forerunners. So his composing was done in the time-honoured oral manner, and much that delights us in his phrasing may not be original to him.

Parry's second contribution to the Homeric problem was to study the techniques of oral composition as practised by 'singers' in Yugoslavia. He spent three years (1933–35) in field-work in the Serbo-Croat area, and collected over 12,000 texts, partly by direct recording and partly from dictation.[17] As a result he was able to make illuminating comparisons between the technique of the Yugoslav singers and that of the bards described by Homer. He also gained valuable insights into how an oral tradition is conserved and transmitted.

There is a close connection between oral poetry and the type of culture known as a Heroic Age. G. S. Kirk has listed the main components of such an age as 'a *penchant* for warfare and adventure, a powerful nobility, and a simple but temporarily adequate material culture devoid of much aesthetic refinement'. 'In such conditions,' he continues, 'the heroic virtues of honour and martial courage dominate all others, ultimately with depressive effects on the stability and prosperity of the society.'[18] The main function of an oral poet in relation to such a society is to preserve the memory of the great deeds of its heroes by composing and transmitting in song a narrative of their exploits. The songs originate at the time of the exploits, and are progressively elaborated as the Heroic Age fades away into the past. It is a striking fact that cycles of heroic song comparable to the Homeric poems have been preserved from many periods of European history, including *Beowulf* and the *Nibelungenlied* from the Anglo-Saxon and Teutonic Heroic Ages respectively, the *Chanson de Roland* from the time of Charlemagne, poems and sagas from the Viking age, and Russian and South Slavic oral poetry which has been developing from the twelfth century down to our own day. The bard or minstrel is an honoured figure at the court of the hero king, and comparative study has shown that Phemios and Demodokos in the *Odyssey* are typical of the class of professional 'singers' (*aoidoi*) of heroic lays. Such singers need to have a wide knowledge of the national heritage of legend and a ready mastery of the technique of composition by formula. When called upon to perform they retell one of the old stories in general conformity with the tradition shared by themselves and their audience. The skill of the singer is shown in his ability to ornament and elaborate a traditional tale. The audience also appreciates an orderly presentation of the narrative. These are two respects in which Homer displays a virtuosity amounting to original genius.

The traditional materials of Greek epic derive from a Heroic Age, which is placed by Hesiod between the Age of Bronze and the Age of Iron. The heroes of this age, he says, fought at Thebes and Troy (*Works and Days* 161–5).

This account accords well with modern reconstructions of the final phases of the Mycenaean Age. The final destruction of Thebes is now believed to have occurred not more than a generation before the burning of Troy VIIa, and both events may be dated in the second half of the thirteenth century. If the exploits of Hesiod's heroes are to be related to these events, the Heroic Age as the Greeks conceived it will coincide with the period when Mycenaean power reached its apex and began to decline. We may conjecture that the principal military enterprises of the period were celebrated in song at the time, and that lays about the heroes who fought in these wars were incorporated in the oral tradition. The exploits came towards the end of an era, and were not surpassed by any later achievements. The last Mycenaeans might well cherish the memory of them as their prosperity waned and their world disintegrated.

Sir Maurice Bowra has analyzed various ways in which nations and peoples are led to view their past as a heroic age.[19] This may happen when a people is conquered and overrun and 'console themselves for lost grandeur by exalting the past to a special glory'. This cause operated in the case of the Russians after their crushing defeat by the Mongols at the battle of Kalka in 1228, and in the case of the Serbs after the Turkish victory at Kossovo in 1389. Again, when a people decides to leave its homeland and seek a new home overseas, it often 'keeps touch with its past by glorifying it in legends'. Striking examples of this are to be found in the sagas of the Norse colonists of Iceland and Greenland, and of the Maoris in New Zealand. 'A third cause is when a political system disintegrates, and success and dominion give place to dissolution and decay.' Bowra illustrates this from the glamorized picture of the reign of Charlemagne which developed after his death. This cause must also have operated strongly in the formation of the Greek belief about their Heroic Age, and led them to cherish and idealize memory of the palace-kingdoms of the thirteenth century BC. Clearly, too, the process will have been reinforced by the second cause, the nostalgia of exiles displaced from the Greek mainland at the time of the early migrations, and forced to cross the Aegean to Aeolis or Ionia. The conjunction of these two causes goes far to explain the strength and persistence of the Greek heroic tradition. The art of song survived the dissolution of the Mycenaean world, and the lore of the past was transmitted by a succession of singers to comfort and inspire the dispossessed survivors.

Formula and list served as the vehicles of history. Old customs became embedded in standard descriptions and were remembered as part of the fabric of the narrative. The spirit of the past was caught and held by well-loved combinations of stock themes. But changing times also made their contribution to the stream of song. The tradition had to be adjusted to take account of new customs, new modes of warfare. These new ways in turn became fixed in formulae. So the tradition was built up layer upon layer, with the remoter past submerged but not always discarded. In content, as in language, the Homeric poems form a complex amalgam of elements derived from different epochs, and artificially welded together by the craft of song that each singer inherited from his forerunners. It will be the task of the next chapter to analyze out some of these elements, and to try to assign them to successive periods in the development of the Greek world from Mycenae to Homer.

3 The overlapping worlds of Homeric poetry

The world of the palaces

The scene is the palace of Menelaos. Telemachos and Peisistratos have arrived at the courtyard gate in their chariot, and one of the courtiers has been ordered to admit them.

> Eteoneus ran off through the hall, shouting to his assistants to look sharp and follow him. They led the horses sweating from the yoke and tied them up at the mangers in the stable, throwing down beside them a feed of spelt mixed with white barley. Then they tilted the chariots against the burnished wall by the gate and ushered the newcomers into the royal buildings. Telemachus and his friend opened their eyes in wonder at all they saw as they passed through the king's palace. It seemed to them that this lofty hall of the sublime Menelaus was lit by something of the sun's splendour or the moon's. When they had feasted their eyes on the sight, they went and bathed in polished baths, and after the maidservants had washed them, rubbed them with oil and dressed them in warm mantles and tunics, they took their places on high chairs at the side of Menelaus son of Atreus. A maid came with water in a beautiful golden ewer and poured it out over a silver basin so that they could rinse their hands. She also drew a wooden table to their side, and the staid housekeeper brought some bread and set it by them with a choice of delicacies, helping them liberally to all she had. Meanwhile a carver dished up for them on platters slices of various meats he had selected from his board, and put gold cups beside them . . . When they had satisfied their appetite and thirst, Telemachus leant towards Nestor's son and whispered in his ear so that the rest might not hear him:
>
> 'Look round this echoing hall, my dear Peisistratus. The whole place gleams with copper and gold, amber and silver and ivory. What an amazing collection of treasures! I can't help

thinking that the court of Zeus on Olympus must be like this inside. The sight of it overwhelms me.'

Odyssey 4, 37–75
(translation by E. V. Rieu)

No palace has yet been found in Laconia, but from the excavated remains of three large Mycenaean palaces in the Peloponnese, at Mycenae, Tiryns and Pylos, we can tell that Homer's evocation of the great house of Menelaos is soundly based in fact. A Mycenaean palace was in Menelaos's own words, 'a well built dwelling full of precious objects' (*Odyssey* 4, 96). The 'amazing collection of treasures' recovered from the Shaft Graves testifies to the opulence of the royal house of Mycenae even as early as the sixteenth century. Vessels of silver and gold must have been in daily use in the palaces. The celebrated gold cups found in a tomb at Vapheio doubtless graced the table of some Laconian monarch. Amber was common in the Mycenaean world, particularly in the period before 1400. Furniture with ivory inlay is attested by the Pylos tablets. The excavators of the Pylos palace found fragments of gold, silver and ivory objects, and scraps of gold foil in many of the rooms. The main rooms were brightly decorated, with painted floors and frescoed walls. The comfort of the palace dwellers was also served by a well-appointed bathroom. All the palaces were destroyed before the end of the twelfth century and nothing like them was ever built again in Greece or Ionia, yet details about their structure, lay-out and decoration were handed down in the epic tradition.[1] Minstrels like the one shown on a fresco fragment from Pylos must have sung in their halls, and so it is not surprising that the descriptions have an authentic ring, for they were originally studied from life. Many details in Homer can be paralleled from the excavated remains. The palaces did contain 'echoing porticoes' with cut stone benches, and pillared halls with central hearths. They did contain basement storerooms, corridors, and upper floors, and there is no certain evidence for any of these features in Early Iron Age buildings in Greek lands. At Pylos there was a lantern-chimney in the roof over the central megaron through which a goddess might make her exit as Athena does from the palace of Odysseus (*Odyssey* 1, 320). There was also a throne set against the east wall, and beside it in the floor two basin-like hollows some two metres apart and connected by a narrow runnel along which liquid could flow. It has been suggested that the purpose of these hollows was to receive libations poured by the occupant of the throne, and we find that Nestor does just this when he returns to his palace (*Odyssey* 3, 389–94). Nestor is also described as coming out from his private apartments and taking his seat 'on polished blocks of stone which stood before the lofty doors' (*Odyssey* 3, 406–7). The blocks are further described as 'white, with an oily sheen'. The description has usually been taken to refer to a bench of *marble*, and the question has been asked whether it was actually polished with oil, or merely looked 'oily'. In fact, marble seems to have been a scarce and semi-precious material at Pylos, used only for ornaments and inlays. But the excavators did find a stone dado in the portico to the Throne Room 'faced with a veneer of limestone *almost like marble*, 0.045 m. thick, *with a smoothly finished surface*' (my italics). They also found a limestone structure, jutting out from the front wall of the palace near the main entrance, which Blegen took to be a 'rostrum' or 'reviewing stand'. Homer emphasizes the formal and ceremonial nature of Nestor's appearance as he sat, sceptre in hand, surrounded by his sons and guests and issuing his orders. It seems possible that the passage preserves a memory of Neleid court ritual combined with the constructional detail of a marble-like veneering used in the palace at Pylos.

In general, Homer gives a stylized and idealized picture of the palaces. This is most obvious in the case of the palace of king Alkinoös in Scheria (*Odyssey* 7, 81 ff.). The building is given the standard lay-out of a courtyard, portico, and pillared hall, but there is a fairytale sound about its bronze walls, silver pillars, and golden doors, not to mention the gold and silver hounds that Hephaistos wrought to guard its entrance. But its imagined splendours include one distinctive touch which can be plausibly related to the actualities of Mycenaean architectural decoration. The great hall is surrounded by a 'frieze of blue enamel (*kyanos*)' (*Odyssey* 7, 87). Blue tiles were found at Mycenae, while at Tiryns the palace was decorated with an alabaster frieze in which the spirals were picked out in blue glass paste. This paste was an Egyptian invention designed as a substitute for lapis lazuli. (In classical Greek *kyanos* designates both lapis lazuli and the paste substitute.) The Mycenaeans, instructed perhaps by Minoans, had acquired the technique of its manufacture, and *kyanos* craftsmen are mentioned on a tablet from Mycenae. It is also interesting that water is apparently piped to the palace (*Odyssey* 7, 129–31) as it was to the palace at Englianos – yet another feature unparalleled from the Early Iron Age in Greece.[2]

The palace of Odysseus figures prominently in the action of the *Odyssey*. A possible site of a Mycenaean palace has been located on Ithaca (see pp. 8–9), but no structural remains have been found *in situ*. We can infer from Telemachos's unbounded admiration of Menelaos's palace that his own establishment was not built or furnished on a very opulent scale. There is an unpretentious air about the dung-heap in the courtyard near the doors of the main hall, not to mention the feeding trough for geese nearby (*Odyssey* 17, 297 and 19, 552–3). Nevertheless it did contain a storeroom for gold, bronze, clothing, and olive-oil, with large jars for the storage of wine ranged along the walls. Storerooms of this kind are known from Minoan and Mycenaean palaces and mansions.

The building is pictured as one of considerable complexity, with rooms on an upper story, and one quarter opening out from another (*Odyssey* 1, 328–30; 17, 266). A distinctive feature of its plan was a small side-door set in the wall of the main hall towards its rear. This door gave access to a narrow passage leading round to the courtyard. From the passage it was also apparently possible to reach some of the smaller rooms of the palace (*Odyssey* 22, 126 ff.). The side-door and passage are described in considerable detail, but their function in relation to the action is not made clear. It looks as though they might be traditional features that Homer felt bound to mention, but did not fully understand because they were not included in the houses with which he was familiar. In the Mycenaean palaces so far excavated the main hall has only one doorway. Wace suggested a possible parallel in the so-called House of Columns, which Tsountas uncovered in the eastern sector of the citadel of Mycenae in 1892. However, Mylonas has further explored the building and claims that Wace's restoration of the ground plan is untenable.[3]

More clearly perhaps than any other element in the epics, the picture of palace life reflects the Mycenaean world in the time of its greatest prosperity. Nestor and Menelaos lord it over their households and dispense hospitality with an easy grace and assurance. Nobles in their chariots travel swiftly over well-made roads. Storerooms are crammed with treasure from foreign parts, and gifts of gold and silver objects pass freely from hand to hand. Guests are entertained with vintage wine, and can count on the comforts of a good bath and a soft bed. The picture may be idealized, but the archaeological remains assure us that it is solidly based in history. Nor can it have originated at any later period. Neither post-Mycenaean Greece nor Homer's Ionia knew palaces of the complexity and refinement of those described by Homer. The Greeks of the early Iron Age had neither the wealth nor the skill to build them. The great Bronze Age mansions impressed their magnificence on the poetic tradition, and were never forgotten.

The world of the sea-rovers

The world of the palaces is a peaceful world but in the Homeric poems it is overlapped and overshadowed by a more virile and violent world – the world of warfare and wandering, of plunder and piracy. Menelaos has a foot in both worlds. When we meet him at Sparta in the *Odyssey* he is relaxing in the comfort of his royal home. But in the *Iliad* he shares all the hardships of the Achaean warlords in the long siege. After the fall of Troy he quarrels with Agamemnon, and sets off for home with his own squadron. But seven more years of suffering and wandering lie ahead of him, in the course of which he visits Cyprus, Phoenicia, Libya, and Egypt (*Odyssey* 4, 83–5). Homer elaborates on his contacts with Egypt, describing the gifts he received from a nobleman of Thebes, and also his adventures when marooned on the island of Pharos off the Delta (*Odyssey* 4, 128 and 351 ff.). These traditions must derive from the Bronze Age. In the Dark Age the Greeks lost all touch with Egypt, and contact was not resumed until *c.* 650, appreciably after the period when the Homeric poems took their present shape. Furthermore, *peaceful* contact between Greeks and Egyptians in the Late Bronze Age occurred before rather than after *c.* 1300. When Ramesses II restored Egyptian military power early in the thirteenth century, peaceful relations between Egypt and the Aegean came to an end. Therefore, if Menelaos's *floruit* is to be put about 1200, his relations with Egypt cannot have been as peaceful as Homer represents them. The tradition of a Laconian monarch deriving wealth from friendly intercourse with a native of Egyptian Thebes must go back to an earlier epoch, and has been wrongly attached to an Achaean who fought at Troy.

We get a very different picture of the Achaeans and Egypt, and one much closer to the historical realities of the closing years of the thirteenth century, in the tale told to Eumaios by Odysseus. His story includes a vivid account of a piratical raid by Achaeans on the Egyptian Delta, which appears to embody an authentic memory of a very disturbed period in Levantine history:

> My heart prompted me to take my faithful companies and sail against Egypt, after properly refitting the ships. So I commissioned nine vessels. Crews for them rallied quickly to me and to my feast which was sustained for six whole days by the many divine sacrifices I provided to furnish the tables. On the seventh

day we launched out from the coast of Crete and sailed with so fair and filling a north wind that it made the sea run like a stream in our favour. We just sat there in careless ease; nor did any ship meet harm with that wind and the helmsmen to steady us. On the fifth day we made the smoothly-flowing river which is Egypt and into its stream I brought our imposing fleet, anchoring it there and ordering my trusty fellows to stand by on ship-guard while I put out watchers into picket posts about. But the men gave themselves up to their baser instincts and the promptings of their ungovernable passions. In a trice they were ravaging the rich Egyptian countryside, killing the men and carrying off women and children. An instant alarm was given in the town: and the war-cry roused the townspeople to pour out against us at the first show of dawn. The entire valley filled with footmen and horsemen and the glint of bronze. Thunder-loving Zeus crumbled my men into shameful flight, leaving no single one of them the courage to stand firm and face it out. Disaster seemed to beset us on every side.

Odyssey 14, 246 ff.
(translation by T. E. Shaw)

Egyptian inscriptions and reliefs from the reigns of Merneptah and Ramesses III confirm that Egypt came under hostile pressure from adventurers from overseas.[4] Merneptah records a large-scale invasion of the western Delta in the fifth year of his reign (*c.* 1225).[5] The principal invaders were Libyans, but they were supported by various contingents of 'Sea Peoples' from the north (*i.e.*, from across the eastern Mediterranean). It has been suggested that the Libyan leader Meryui may have hired these 'northerners' as mercenaries. The 'Sea Peoples' included Akaiwasha, a name identified by a number of authorities with the *Achaiwoi* (Achaeans) of the Homeric poems.[6] Also in the host were Lukka (placed by Hittite and Ugaritic records in south-west Asia Minor, in or near later Lycia or Caria),[7] and Sherden (a people who had fought as mercenaries on the Egyptian side in the battle of Kadesh earlier in the century). The invaders were repulsed with losses running into thousands killed and captured. The dead of the Akaiwasha alone are listed at 1213 men.

An even greater threat had to be faced by Ramesses III in the eighth year of his reign (*c.* 1190). The Egyptian records speak of the northern isles as restless and disturbed, and tell how a large confederate host of marauders, some in ships and the rest on land with their wives and children in ox-carts, moved down the coast of Canaan from Cilicia. 'No land stood before them,' and 'they were fighting to fill their bellies daily' are two of the graphic phrases used of the invaders in the Ramesseid inscriptions on the temple at Medinet Habu in upper Egypt. A decisive battle was fought not far from the eastern Delta, and the Egyptian fleet managed to surround and destroy most of the ships of the 'Sea Peoples'. The raiders, who included Danuna (Danaans?), and Pulesati (Philistines),[8] were repulsed with very heavy casualties.

The 'Sea Peoples' were not racially homogeneous. They certainly included adventurers and pirates from the south-western and south-eastern coasts of Asia Minor, and probably also Greek-speaking marauders from the shores and islands of the Aegean. Crete would have been a likely base for Achaeans allied to Libyans, and the Hittites were troubled by Achaeans perhaps based in Rhodes.[9] The 'Sea Peoples' were in part the product and in part the cause of the turmoil and instability of the declining years of the Bronze Age in the eastern Mediterranean.

The Achaean expedition to Troy was in some respects not unlike a large plunder raid by 'Sea Peoples'. Nestor sums it up in these terms, representing it not as a glorious victory, but rather as a protracted series of raids and skirmishes in which Achaean losses far outweighed their gains:

> 'Ah, my friend,' exclaimed Nestor, the Gerenian charioteer, 'what memories the name of Troy brings back! The miseries we fierce Achaeans put up with there – raid after raid across the misty seas in search of plunder at Achilles' beck and call, fight after fight around the very walls of royal Priam's town! And

there our best men fell. There warlike Aias lies. There lies Achilles. There Patroclus, wise as the gods in counsel. There too, Antilochus, my own dear son, as good as he was brave, the fastest runner of them all, and what a fighter too! Nor is *that* the full tale of what the Achaean chivalry endured at Troy. There is no man on earth who could unfold to you the whole disastrous tale, not though you sat and questioned him for half a dozen years . . .'

Odyssey 3, 102–16
(translation by E. V. Rieu)

Odysseus was a master of stratagems, but there was a destructive side to his restless energy recgonized in the epithet 'sacker of cities'. With a brilliant insight Homer makes him voice the outlook of the typical corsair:

Labour I could never abide, nor the husbandry which breeds healthy children. My fancies were set upon galleys and wars, pikes and burnished javelins, the deadly toys that bring shivers to men of ordinary mould . . . Before the prime of Achaea went up to battle against Troy I had nine times commanded men and warships on foreign expeditions, at great profit to myself, with the leader's first choice of the booty to increase my individual share.

Odyssey 14, 222–32
(translation by T. E. Shaw)

Such was the ethos of the 'vikings' of the Aegean *c.* 1200. Their raiding generated pressures that disrupted old political patterns, broke empires, and caused widespread folk movements. Greek legends preserved a memory of heroes and tribes on the move before, as well as after, the Trojan War. Homer alludes to the exploits of Bellerophon who crossed the Aegean to campaign for the king of Lycia (*Iliad* 6, 171 ff.). In the Catalogue we have a summary account of the Heraclid Tlepolemos, son of a Thesprotian princess, who led a migration from Epirus to the Dodecanese (*Iliad* 2, 653–70). Pindar preserves a tradition that the sons of the Trojan Antenor migrated to Libya after the sack of Troy, and were well received because of their prowess in chariotry (*Pythians* v, 82 ff.). Egyptian records of the thirteenth and twelfth centuries BC lend some support to this tradition in so far as they represent the Libyan tribes of Retenu and Tehenu in ever closer association with the 'Sea Peoples'. The legend of Aeneas may well be based on a similar migration from the Troad to Italy, and it is not unlikely that the Sherden occupied and gave their name to the island of Sardinia.

The conquerors of Troy did not fare much better. We find the same pattern of enforced wanderings in the reported careers of the Achaean leaders and their sons. Diomedes returned to Argos only to find a usurper in power, and was compelled to migrate to Libya and southern Italy. Orestes became a fugitive after avenging his father's murder. Achilles's son Neoptolemos went across from Thessaly to Epirus, and founded the Molossian dynasty.

The wanderings of Menelaos mentioned by Homer, and those of Odysseus too, have a pattern which suits the epoch of the 'Sea Peoples'. The picture of mobile squadrons of raiders under the command of Achaean chieftains is consistent with what can be independently known about Mediterranean peoples in the disordered century that brought the Bronze Age to a close. The tradition of raids on Egypt cannot have been formed later than *c.* 1100. It is part of the complex legacy that Homer inherited from the Mycenaean period. While the picture of prosperous and tranquil palace life derives from the more stable era before the Trojan War, the sagas of the seafarers reflect a world in increasing turmoil, and it is more plausible to refer them to the twelfth century rather than to the thirteenth.

The onset of the Dark Age reduced Greek activity to a sub-heroic level. Trade and travel on the former scale were no longer attempted. Powerful kingdoms no longer pursued aggressive policies. Instead, fragmented communities sought survival in isolation and retrenchment. The great exploits of the Mycenaean period receded into the past and became the theme of commemorative song. There was no glorious present to engage the attention of the bards; their main activity must have been devoted to conserving the memory of what life had been like in the time of the heroes. As G. S. Kirk has argued, the early Dark Age must have been a very important formative period in the history of Greek epic.[10] Although the bards were drawing the materials for their songs from the past, they were not immune from the influences of the present. Certain conventions for depicting life in the Bronze Age were established, but the culture and customs of the post-Mycenaean world also began to make a mark on the tradition. This is particularly clear in respect of the use of metals.

Bronze Age and Iron Age in fact and in Homer[11]

Bronze was the working metal in the Mycenaean world, but objects of iron were not altogether unknown. Some of the earlier *tholos* tombs yielded iron rings, and an iron pendant overlaid with gold was found in a thirteenth-century chamber tomb at Dendra. From the twelfth century there are two iron daggers from the Perati cemetery, and one from Lefkandi. It is virtually certain that all these objects entered Greece from the east. The use of iron for personal adornment indicates that it was regarded as a precious metal, and possibly also that it was credited with magical properties. Hittite and Egyptian documents of the Late Bronze Age often feature iron as a valuable material. Iron technology was only beginning to develop at this time in eastern Anatolia and Syria, and had not yet been introduced into the Aegean. The Mycenaeans were skilled bronze workers, but there is no evidence that they ever experimented with the manufacture of iron.

Greece entered the Iron Age appreciably after the final collapse of Mycenaean civilization. The change-over from bronze to iron began to gather momentum about the middle of the eleventh century, and is closely linked in time and place with the rise of Protogeometric pottery. But the Iron Age cannot be said to have become established in any region until, as Snodgrass puts it, 'iron examples begin to preponderate over bronze in the same class of object'. A numerical balance in favour of iron usually indicates that a local iron industry has been established.

If we may base generalizations on the rather scanty evidence, iron was first utilized for knives and daggers, following the pattern in the Levant, where iron weapons precede iron tools. But for a number of reasons the change to iron was neither rapid nor sweeping. A well-hammered bronze blade can be as hard as mild steel, and it is difficult to surpass this degree of hardness in iron without rendering the metal extremely brittle. Also, in the absence of any technique for casting iron (a skill not to be mastered for many centuries), objects that could easily be cast in bronze, for example, spear-points and arrow-heads, were so made as long as bronze was available. But Greece has little copper and no tin, and with the virtual collapse in overseas trade after 1100, supplies must soon have become inadequate to meet the demands for new weapons and tools. To some extent the problem could be solved by melting down old bronze implements and remaking them. But necessity in the end drove the Greeks to exploit their own resources in iron ores, and to develop the required skills in iron-working. In Attica and the Argolid the trend towards iron becomes very marked between *c.* 1050 and 950. A grave from the Kerameikos, for example, dated close to 1050, yielded an iron dagger, an iron knife, and two bronze spear-heads. A century later iron greatly preponderates over bronze in the grave goods of the same cemetery. The Iron Age may then be regarded as fully established, with iron as the main working metal in everyday use by farmer and craftsman. Bronze, however, never became obsolete; it continued in use for objects like pins, brooches, basins and tripods, and later, in the hoplite period, it was the normal material for shields, breastplates, and greaves.

In the Homeric poems, bronze is the standard metal for offensive weapons. No spearhead or sword is ever said to be of any other metal but bronze. Helmets, shields, and cuirasses are often described as of bronze, and never of iron.

General references to bronze panoplies abound. By contrast, there is only one clear instance where iron is specified as the material of a particular weapon – the iron club of Ereuthalion, which was odd enough to earn its bearer the special nickname 'Mace-bearer' (*Iliad* 7, 136–41). The rule is certainly an old part of the epic tradition, and the exception may be. The convention that bronze is the normal metal for spear-points, swords, arrow-heads, helmets and body-armour reflects Mycenaean usage. But the Mycenaean world could have had room for at least one eccentric warrior who had fashioned a lump of unwrought iron (perhaps of meteoric origin) into a weapon. An object that may have been a mace-head fashioned from 'a crude mineral ore containing a high percentage of iron' was found at Troy in 1890.[12]

The convention about bronze persisted despite the fact that by the eighth century iron had long been the favoured material for offensive weapons. This fact is betrayed in the Homeric usage whereby *sideros* (iron) can mean 'a weapon', much as we use 'cold steel' for a sword or dagger. This usage occurs three times in the *Iliad* (once of an arrow-head and twice of a knife: *Iliad* 4, 123; 18, 34; 23, 30), and twice in the *Odyssey* in the proverbial phrase 'a weapon attracts a man' (*Odyssey* 16, 294; 19, 13). Though knives are among the earliest iron imports into the Aegean, these passages should not be used as evidence that in this respect the 'Homeric' world reflects the real world at the epoch of transition from bronze to iron. The passages are too few to support such a contention. They should rather be classed as instances of 'Homer nodding' – sporadic anachronisms breaking the general convention about bronze weapons.

If we turn from weapons to tools we find a closer balance between bronze and iron. Odysseus uses a *bronze* axe to build his raft, but the axes used as targets in the shooting contest in his palace are of *iron* (*Odyssey* 5, 244 and 21, 3). So are the ten double-axes and ten single axes of *Iliad* 23, 850–1. There are in all some eight references in the poems to the hewing of timber 'with bronze'. In the *Iliad* (13,

180) a fallen warrior is compared to an ash tree 'cut by the bronze'; but in the same type of simile another warrior lies like a poplar which a chariot-maker has 'cut out with the flashing iron' (*Iliad* 4, 485). In the *Odyssey* we find a simile drawn from the blacksmith's forge in which the technique of hardening iron by quenching it in water is clearly described (9, 391–3):

> As when a smith dips a great axe or adze hissing into cold water,
> doctoring it, for this makes the strength of iron . . .

When Hephaistos 'strikes out fetters' on a 'mighty anvil' (*Odyssey* 8, 274–5), he is using the technique of the iron worker, and there is a reference elsewhere to 'iron fetters' (*Odyssey* 1, 204). On the other hand, miscellaneous objects like a fish-hook, a cheese-grater, and a key, are of bronze (*Iliad* 16, 408; 11, 640; *Odyssey* 21, 7). In the funeral games Achilles puts up a lump of iron to serve both as a weight to be thrown by the contestants, and as a prize for the winner (*Iliad* 23, 826 ff.). He comments that it will furnish implements for shepherd or ploughman for five years.

The mixture of iron and bronze in these references has been taken to reflect a transitional period in which both metals were used for making tools. But a more likely explanation is that the poet, thoroughly familiar with iron and its processing, has no inhibitions about introducing it in craft contexts, whereas in battle scenes he feels much more bound by the convention that the heroes fight with bronze.

Iron objects in Homer are strictly utilitarian; no product of fine craftsmanship is ever said to be of iron. There are only a few passages which appear to envisage iron as a form of wealth, and even as a medium of exchange. The treasure chest in Odysseus's palace is said to contain 'much iron and bronze' (*Odyssey* 21, 61–2). When wine ships come from Lemnos to provision the army at Troy, the Achaeans acquire the wine in exchange for bronze, *iron*, leather, cows, and slaves (*Iliad* 7, 472–5). There is a formulaic line (five times repeated) in which iron may represent a climax in value: 'bronze, gold, and iron wrought with much toil'. If the order really implies that iron is more valuable than gold, the line would be a good example of a fact of Bronze Age life preserved by a formula. Miss Lorimer, however, thinks that the epithet, 'wrought with much toil', implies the Iron Age technique of producing mild steel by day-long hammering. In the *Odyssey* (1, 184) the relative value of metals in the poet's own age is much more faithfully represented by the reference to Mentes's ship with its cargo of iron, which is to be exchanged for bronze.

Familiarity with iron is further reflected in the fact that it is more common than bronze in metaphors. 'Iron-hearted' is a common phrase, and the poet once refers to the 'iron din' of battle. But one should not jump to the conclusion that iron weapons are intended without pondering the fact that the sound is said to rise up to the 'brazen heaven'. The heaven is also twice described as 'of iron', and poetically there cannot be much difference in meaning between the two epithets.

Turning from iron to gold, we find that gold is the metal most often used to express and measure wealth. Mycenae is 'rich in gold' and Agamemnon expects much gold as loot from Troy (*Iliad* 9, 137; *cf.* 22, 50; *Odyssey* 5, 39). Achilles would not accept Hector's weight in gold in return for the surrender of his corpse (*Iliad* 22, 351). Odysseus is given gold by the Phaeacians (*Odyssey* 8, 440). Prizes of gold in talents and half-talents are offered by Achilles at the funeral games (*Iliad* 23, 269, 614, 751, and 796). Golden utensils, especially cups, are ubiquitous, and gold is used to decorate chariots (*Iliad* 10, 438; 23, 503), furniture (*Odyssey* 23, 200), and as material for pins, beads, studs and rivets.

Gold is mentioned much more often than silver, and it is of interest to note that the proportion of gold found on Mycenaean sites is much higher than that of silver. On the Linear B tablets gold is mentioned several times, but silver only once.[13] In the *Odyssey* silver mixing-bowls and basins appear in the palace scenes, and Helen has a silver work-basket with gold overlay on the rim (*Odyssey* 4, 131–2). This, like the two silver baths in the same passage, came from Egypt. Menelaos proposes to give Telemachos a silver mixing-bowl with a gold rim which he had received as a present from the king of the Sidonians (*Odyssey* 4, 615–19). Ventris and Chadwick note an interesting parallel in the 'cup of silver with edges covered in gold' recorded on a tablet from Nuzi in Assyria.[14] There are also parallels from Mycenaean sites. Silver vessels with gold linings or with strips of gold riveted to rim and handle have been found at Mycenae, Dendra and Berbati. Remains of a silver cup with gold and niello inlay were found near the outer porch of the palace at Pylos, and these, together with fragments of silver vessels from some of the rooms, tend to confirm the historical basis of the Homeric formula:

> A maid came with water in a beautiful golden ewer and poured it out over a silver basin so that they could rinse their hands.
>
> *Odyssey* 4, 52–4
> (translation by E. V. Rieu)

The 'silver-studded sword' of a much-repeated formula (nine times in the *Iliad*, twice in the *Odyssey*) has also been shown to date from early Mycenaean times (see p. 114).

In general, excavation has confirmed that the poems are correct in attributing a wealth of precious metals to the palace centres. When Nestor proposes to make a sacrifice to Athena he produces gold for the gilding of the victim's horns (*Odyssey* 3, 437–8), and the fact that offerings of gold were made to the Pylian deities is corroborated by the Pylos tablets. But one must, of course, make a generous allowance for poetic exaggeration in the Homeric references to gold. In the epic tradition, gold functions as a symbol for excellence, and is therefore very freely attributed to kings and gods. The possessions of the immortals are even more golden than those of the heroes. Only the gods wear golden sandals and girdles, and sit on golden seats. Only their horses have frontlets, reins, hobbles, and goads of gold. The attribution of gold armour to some of the major heroes is to be understood as symbolizing their pre-eminence. Nestor, for example, has a famous gold shield, and there was a layer of gold in the shield of Achilles (*Iliad* 8, 193; 20, 268 ff.). There is a gleam of gold on the Trojan side too, for Hector has a gold ring on his spear, Pandaros has a gold tip to his bow, and Glaukos was clad in golden armour which he was foolish enough to exchange for the bronze armour of Diomedes (*Iliad* 6, 320; 4, 111; 6, 235–6).

Nestor summons a goldsmith (*chrysochoos*) to do the gilding (*Odyssey* 3, 425), and the profession of 'gold-worker' is attested by the tablets. Skilled workers in precious metals must have formed part of the ménage of Mycenaean palaces. The technique of 'painting in metal' was one of the high arts of the Mycenaean Age. It is represented for us by a few precious survivals like the inlaid daggers from the Shaft Graves and a silver bowl from Enkomi. The daggers show scenes picked out in yellow, white, and black against the background of the bronze blades. Plates of gold and silver were inlaid to give the yellow and white, and the black was formed with niello, an alloy of powdered sulphur with lead, copper, or silver. It can hardly be doubted that the technique lapsed with the fall of Mycenaean civilization; no examples are known from Greek lands from any later period. Yet a definite and detailed account of the appearance of such objects is clearly preserved in one passage in the *Iliad*. In the description of the Shield of Achilles (18, 478–608) there are some seven references to 'golden' figures or objects. The gold is sometimes combined with silver or tin to suggest a colour contrast — golden daggers on silver baldricks, for instance, and a 'golden' field that turns black as it is ploughed. The most elaborate contrasts are found in the vineyard scene (561 ff.), where the grapes show black against a gold background, and there are silver poles, a *kyanos* ditch, and a tin fence. No examples are known of tin or *kyanos* inlays in this genre, so the Homeric description goes beyond extant objects in this respect, but the poet clearly implies a mixture of metals to give a colour contrast, and this is the effect achieved by the Mycenaean technique. How was it remembered? It seems highly unlikely that specimens were to be seen in eighth-century Ionia, whether handed down as heirlooms or recovered from graves, though the possibility cannot be ruled out. The alternative is to regard the passage as yet another example of a Mycenaean memory handed down in the tradition of heroic song.

There is very little archaeological evidence for precious metals in Greek lands in the Dark Age. A Protogeometric warrior grave on Skyros yielded gold-leaf rosettes and blue glass beads – Mycenaean heirlooms, according to Snodgrass. The rosettes and other small objects of gold from tombs at Lakkithra in Kephallinia are also survivals from the IIIC Mycenaean world. In the Kerameikos cemetery three of the earlier Protogeometric graves included gold hair-rings, but these are the only evidence of precious materials at Athens before the Geometric period. Later, in the ninth century, gold fibulae, rings, and earrings began to reappear, matching some silver and ivory ornaments in contemporary Argive graves.

In the eighth century the trend towards increased wealth is confirmed by gold bands with animal friezes from the Kerameikos, and gold and silver in some quantity from Eretria. The gold was almost certainly imported, but the silver could have been Greek, for there is evidence that silver was smelted from lead at Argos and Thorikos as early as the Protogeometric period.[15]

We have already noted the reference to the quench-hardening of iron in a simile in the *Odyssey* as an indication that the working of iron was familiar to Homer and his contemporaries (see p. 67). Another simile in the *Odyssey* may indicate that the art of the goldsmith was less well known. The skill by which Athena enhances the charm of Odysseus's appearance is compared with the skill by which a man blends gold with silver to produce attractive works of art (*Odyssey* 6, 232–5). The poet does not make clear precisely what technique he has in mind. J. L. Myres suggested the Mycenaean technique of inlaying silver with gold. W. B. Stanford preferred to think of gilding, but there is said to be no certain example of gilding in the strict sense (*i.e.*, an amalgam produced with the aid of quicksilver) from the Greek world before the seventh century. Miss Gray may be right in thinking that no more is intended than the simple covering or plating of a silver vessel with a gold rim or band.[16] At all events the poet emphasizes the amazing skill of the craftsman, and says that he has been taught by Hephaistos and Athena. This perhaps suggests that such techniques were unfamiliar in eighth-century Ionia, and it is certainly likely that any fine work in gold and silver at this date would have to be imported from the Levant or Anatolia.

In the light of all the evidence about metal and metal-working, we must conclude that Homer's picture is composite, and not the reflection of any one era. It does not represent a world in transition from the Bronze to the Iron Age, for, as Miss Gray points out, 'bronze weapons, knowledge of iron-working and iron tools, and great wealth in gold never coexisted historically'. A valid picture of the Bronze Age is built up, largely with the aid of traditional formulae – a picture of bronze-clad warriors duelling with bronze-tipped spears and silver-studded swords, of palaces gleaming with treasures of gold and silver, of advanced techniques of inlaying bronze with precious metals. But underlying this world of splendid opulence is a humbler world where farmers and wood-cutters work with iron tools, where the blacksmith's forge is a familiar sight, and where works of art are the products of the gods or the gift of strangers. This is the world of the Early Iron Age, and the facts of this world appear in simile and metaphor, and occasionally invade the action. So the picture is an amalgam of what Homer and his hearers knew about the present and believed about the past. These beliefs were not mere fancies; they were grounded in past realities, but the underlying facts had been schematized and idealized by generations of bards, and items from different epochs had been generously but arbitrarily compounded. The resultant blend of imagination and reality is well symbolized by Hera's chariot (*Iliad* 5, 722 ff.), whose wheels had golden felloes, silver knaves, tyres of bronze (bronze-bound chariot wheels are attested by tablets from Knossos and Pylos), and turned on an iron axle.

Homer's own world: the Phoenicians[17]

Many of the details in the life and culture depicted in the poems cannot be dated with any precision. For example, the cult of Zeus and many of the other Olympian gods is now attested for Mycenaean times by the Pylos tablets, and the same gods must have continued to receive worship all through the Dark Age down to Homer's own day. Allusions to farming and seafaring tend to have a timeless quality about them; the types of stock reared and crops cultivated did not alter between the Late Bronze Age and the eighth century, nor, apparently, did the types of shipping. But one aspect of trade in the Aegean that receives fairly frequent mention throughout does appear to relate to the Geometric period and not to any earlier epoch. I refer to trading in Greek waters by Phoenicians (*Phoinikes*), and the importation into the Aegean of works of art from Sidonia.

A realistic and unflattering picture of Phoenician traders is given in the reminiscences of Eumaios (*Odyssey* 15, 403 ff.). He calls them 'greedy knaves', and recalls how they kidnapped him as a boy from his father's kingdom in the island of Syrie 'above Ortygie'. The identification of these places has been much discussed, but the balance of probability appears to favour Syros and Delos in the Cyclades.[18] The Phoenicians had come thither on a trading venture with 'countless trinkets in their black ship'. The king happened to have a Phoenician slave-woman in his household, and she was seduced by one of the crew. In return for the promise of a passage home to Sidon, she undertook to lure the young prince on board the ship so that he could be sold in part payment for her fare. The plan took a year to mature, during which time the traders were filling up their ship with cargo. Then, at the decisive moment, one of the merchants distracted the attention of the womenfolk at the palace by displaying a gold and amber necklace, and while they were admiring it the slave-woman stole off with the boy and three golden goblets. But her villainy brought her no profit for she died at sea, and Eumaios was sold to Laertes in Ithaca.

Odysseus also claims to have had a good deal to do with Phoenicians, who, as always in Homer, are represented as sailors and traders. In one of his 'lying tales' (which are always designed to be as plausible as possible) he tells how he paid for a passage in a Phoenician ship travelling from Crete to the western Peloponnese. He wanted to be put on shore at Pylos or in Elis, but a storm diverted the ship to Ithaca, and there the Phoenicians abandoned him and sailed back to 'populous Sidonia' (*Odyssey* 13, 256–86). In another fictitious narrative he tells of being taken from Egypt to 'Phoinike' by a deceitful and wicked Phoenician merchant. After spending a year there he was forced to take ship with the merchant, and to sail west past Crete for Libya, but the ship was sunk by a storm in the open sea, and he drifted for nine days clinging to the mast until cast ashore in Thesprotia (*Odyssey* 14, 285–315).

In the *Iliad* there is only one mention of the Phoenicians: they are said to have shipped a silver mixing-bowl made by Sidonians, and given it to Thoas, the king of Lemnos (*Iliad* 23, 743–5). Earlier in the poem, veneration is expressed for Sidonian craftsmanship in metal and fabrics (*Iliad* 6, 290–1), and this attitude is a feature of the *Odyssey* too (4, 615–19; 15, 115–19).[19]

The above references fit together to give a picture consistent with the facts of Phoenician expansion in the eighth century. It seems that there could not have been any awareness of Phoenician merchandising in the Aegean before *c.* 900, and their trading activities are not likely to have attracted the attention indicated by the Homeric references before *c.* 800. J. N. Coldstream has given an authoritative summary of the archaeological evidence for the stages of their westwards expansion. The Tyrian colony at Kition in Cyprus was founded perhaps as early as *c.* 925, and there was a considerable export of unguents to the Dodecanese in Phoenician-type vases between 850 and 800. Phoenician trade in ivories to Crete may also be dated to this period when 'the isolation of the Greek world was at last coming to an end'. Coldstream believes that Crete was frequently visited by Phoenician traders between 800 and 750, and that these voyages were a prelude to the decisive movement of Phoenician expansion which took them westwards to found Carthage *c.* 730 and Motya in western Sicily a decade or so later. There would have been two main sailing routes westwards from Crete, one leaving the port on the south coast, later known as Phoinikous, and striking across the Libyan Sea, and the other heading north-west to pass Cythera (where there was another Phoinikous) and the western Greek islands *en route* for south Italy and Sicily. Odysseus, in his two 'lying tales', shows a knowledge of both these routes. Coldstream therefore concurs with the previous assessment of M. Nilsson that 'Homeric passages referring to the Phoenicians fit in best with the eighth century'. The eighth century was also a time of great expansion of Greek trade by sea to the Levant and westwards to Sicily. Greek merchants would have been in keen competition with the Phoenicians in many markets, and the repeated characterization of them in the *Odyssey* as 'skinflints' is perhaps a reflection of the kind of tension between the two peoples that would have been prevalent in the eighth century but not earlier.

The Greeks owed their alphabet to the Phoenicians. The date and place of the first borrowing cannot be precisely determined, but a good case has been made out for the Greek trading post at Al Mina on the Syrian coast as the point of transmission. The date can hardly be later than *c.* 750, and may be a decade or so earlier. The Greeks at once realized the value of the innovation, and literacy spread rapidly. Hexameters appear scratched on an Attic vase dated *c.* 730, and there are examples of similar inscriptions on pottery from Ithaca and Ischia before the end of the eighth century (see p. 132). There is no reason why longer poems could not have been inscribed on papyrus or vellum at the same period. The existence of a manuscript of the Homeric poems by *c.* 700 is by no means out of the question. We may well owe the preservation of the text to an eighth-century copyist.

However that may be, it seems clear that no events after the close of the eighth century made any widespread or significant impression on the tradition that culminates in the *Iliad* and *Odyssey*. In our text there may be one or two short interpolations dating from the seventh century or even later. Passages that seem organic to the narrative, like the brooch of Odysseus or the lamp of Athena (*Odyssey* 19, 226–31; 19, 34), have been judged by some critics to be descriptions of seventh-century objects, but this is by no means certain. The conclusion suggested by the materials analyzed in this chapter is, I think, quite tenable. According to this view, the epic tradition reaches back to the Late Bronze Age, and remained quite fluid and receptive of new elements down to the eighth century, but not later. The fluidity lasted as long as oral transmission was the only means by which the tradition could be handed on. The fixing of the tradition was the direct result of the advent of literacy. Homer stands on the borderline between the preliterate and literate stages of Greek culture. His comprehensive grasp of the oral tradition gave him an historian's insight into the past, while his feeling for the deeper realities of human experience saved him from any tendency to pedantic antiquarianism. He felt free to include significant elements from his own world in his poetic evocation of the Heroic Age. Hence the depth and richness of the presentation, which this chapter has attempted to explore under the concept of 'overlapping worlds'.

4 The picture and the record: some problems of Homeric interpretation

Homer's picture of Achaean society

In the *Iliad* the Achaeans are encamped in hostile territory, and conduct their affairs against a background of battle and crisis. Heroic values are highlighted in passionate conflicts, but the texture of political and social life remains obscure. From proceedings in assembly and council we learn something about the relationship between Agamemnon and his peers, and between the high command and the rank and file. But on the whole we have to depend on incidental allusions for reconstructing the pattern of Achaean society as Homer envisaged it. When we turn to the *Odyssey* we find a picture with much more depth and detail. Homer there shows us the peacetime life of kings and commoners, and takes us into their homes and palaces for conversation and entertainment. Three typical scenes, summarized from three different books, will serve to illustrate different aspects of life in the world of Odysseus.

The first scene depicts the hospitality offered by Nestor to Telemachos (*Odyssey* 3, *passim*). Telemachos had decided to seek news of his absent father. He has provisioned a ship, manned it with twenty volunteers, and set sail at nightfall for Pylos. The following day he reaches his destination and finds the Pylians assembled on the beach in nine companies for the sacrifice of a hecatomb of bulls in honour of Poseidon. He is welcomed with friendly courtesy by one of Nestor's sons, and invited to share in the feast. After a time Nestor speaks:

> 'Now that our visitors have regaled themselves, it will be no breach of manners to put some questions to them and enquire

who they may be.' And turning to his guests, 'Who are you, sirs? From what port have you sailed over the highways of the sea? Is yours a trading venture; or are you cruising the main on chance like roving pirates, who risk their lives to ruin other people?'

Odyssey 3, 69–74
(translation by E. V. Rieu)

After Telemachos has explained his business, Nestor recalls his friendly association with Odysseus at Troy, and launches into a long account of the fortunes of the returning heroes, making it clear that he has not seen or heard of Odysseus since that time. By now it is sunset, and Telemachos is invited to spend the night at the palace. He shares a bowl of vintage wine (ten years old) with the royal family, and then retires to rest in the 'echoing portico'. The following morning Nestor gives orders for a heifer to be sacrificed to Athena. A goldsmith is summoned to cover the horns of the victim with gold provided from the royal treasury. Meanwhile Telemachos has been bathed and anointed with oil by the princess Polycaste, and takes his place by Nestor at the banquet 'with men of gentle birth to wait on them and fill their gold cups with wine'. Finally the king puts a chariot and pair at his disposal to carry him on his way to Sparta.

My next scene is set in the hut of Eumaios the swineherd (*Odyssey* 14, *passim*). Odysseus in disguise as a beggarman has made his way thither, and finds Eumaios sitting in his well-fenced yard making himself a pair of sandals. Three of his mates have taken the swine out to pasture, and the fourth has gone to town with a hog for the suitors in the palace. The dogs run barking at the beggar, but Eumaios drives them off and invites the old man in to share a meal with him. He seats his guest on a goatskin flung over a pile of brushwood, and prepares a meal of tender pork roasted on skewers and washed down with wine from an olive-wood bowl. While Odysseus eats, he talks about the inroads the suitors are making into the royal flocks and herds, and mentions their plot to ambush Telemachos on his way home from Pylos. Only then does he enquire about his visitor's name and family. Odysseus spins him a colourful yarn about his upbringing as the bastard son of a Cretan nobleman and his buccaneering exploits around the Aegean, ending with the mischance that has brought him in rags to Ithaca. Meanwhile the other hands return, and all together enjoy a meal of wine and roast pork. Odysseus is honoured with the best portion, and regales the company with a lively anecdote about the Trojan War. He is rewarded with a bed by the fire and a thick cloak to keep him warm, while the faithful Eumaios prepares to spend the night out of doors, guarding the swine.

My third scene is the Ithacan assembly called by Telemachos to discuss the situation in the palace (*Odyssey* 2, *passim*). We are told that there has been no such gathering since Odysseus left for Troy twenty years before. A senior noble and landowner, Aigyptios, begins the proceedings by asking who has called the meeting and on what business. Telemachos then explains that he wishes to discuss a matter which is personal rather than public, the evil which has fallen on his household in the continued absence of the king his father and in the importunate presence of the suitors for Penelope. He insists that their reckless consumption of food and wine is an intolerable burden which will destroy the resources of his house, and appeals for relief from their depredations. In reply Antinoos puts the blame on Penelope for her delaying tactics, and says bluntly that the suitors will continue to eat Telemachos out of house and home until the question of her remarriage is settled. He wants Telemachos to send her back to her father Ikarios so that a new match can be arranged with his help. Telemachos rejects his proposal: he cannot evict his mother against her wishes, especially when it is not certain that Odysseus is really dead; besides, he would have to repay a large dowry to Ikarios. He again appeals to the suitors to leave, and concludes with a prayer for their destruction if they continue to batten so rapaciously on his estate. Mentor then tries a different approach; he had been appointed guardian of the estate by Odysseus, and he attempts to involve the people in the issue. He reminds them that Odysseus had been a just and benevolent ruler, comments on the risks the suitors are running in case the king should return, and criticizes the people for failing to protest against the depredations. This draws a sharp protest from Leokritos. He denies that the people will have any interest in intervening in what is essentially a private quarrel. The suitors are numerically superior to the household of Odysseus and will remain perforce until their demands are met. Telemachos, if he wishes, may make arrangements for his journey to Pylos, but otherwise the situation will remain as it was. At this point the assembly is dismissed, the people return to their homes, and the suitors go back to the palace.

The three scenes differ markedly in background and tone. The first is dominated by the dignified and courteous figure of Nestor entertaining regally in a luxurious palace. Such palaces existed in Greece in the Mycenaean Age, but not after it. Homer is looking back nostalgically to a grandeur that vanished centuries before his day. In the second scene the worthy swineherd dispenses good-humoured hospitality in his humble cottage. We see the timeless world of the Greek countryside with its goatskin rugs and *souvlakia*, and its ready welcome for the stranger. In the third scene we witness an acrimonious clash between the scions of noble families. The time reference here is much more disputable, and the social scene in Ithaca needs more analysis before we can attempt to assign it to any one epoch.

All the speakers in the Ithacan debate are members of the land-owning aristocracy. They dominate the proceedings, debating their grievances in front of a silent and passive people who do not indicate their opinion, and apparently do not wish to become involved in the quarrel. The king is absent and there is serious doubt if he will ever return. The right of succession is not clear-cut. In an earlier passage Antinoos concedes that the kingship has been hereditary in the family of Odysseus, but prays that Telemachos may not succeed his father. Telemachos replies that he would like to do so: 'It is no bad thing to be a king; his house at once becomes rich and he himself is more honoured.' But he concedes that there are many other 'kings' in Ithaca, and that any one of them might succeed to the throne. ('King' must here mean 'head of household.') At all events he intends to continue as lord of the household which he will inherit once Odysseus's death is confirmed (*Odyssey* 1, 386 ff.).

We can see here the outline of a power struggle with kingship as the prize for the most powerful noble. But the situation is further complicated by the role of Penelope. It is clear (though never stated in so many words) that the successful suitor could hope to become king. Penelope's choice of husband would legitimize the succession, and Telemachos could then be left to enjoy his goods in peace. Why Penelope should enjoy such a prerogative in a partriarchal society is never made clear. It is possible, as some scholars have suggested, that older versions and ancient motifs are colouring the story, and that these may ultimately derive from matriarchal times.

In the absence of the king, the sole arbiters of power in Ithaca are the landowning nobles. The concept of the aristocratic household is central in the debate initiated by Telemachos. Power resided with the nobleman in his hall, but only so long as he could command the allegiance of his retainers and servants, and draw sustenance from his estate. The occupation of the palace by the suitors is striking at the root of Telemachos's social position and economic security.

Does the picture fit what can be known or inferred about society in the Mycenaean Age? Or must it be referred to a later century or centuries? M. I. Finley thinks that Ithaca appears as 'more household and kinship bound, less integrally a civic community than many a civilised centre of earlier centuries'.[1] Nor, in his view, is the Ithacan situation untypical; it is representative of 'Homeric society' in general. He thinks that Homer deploys his narrative against the background of the world of the tenth and ninth centuries, and is opposed to the view that the epic tradition embodies much memory of the Mycenaean world. That world, he believes, had a much more complicated social and economic structure, and the evidence for this is to be found in the Linear B tablets.

The relation between the tablets and the Homeric tradition is examined in greater detail below. The discussion here will be confined to the question whether they invalidate the historicity of Homer's picture of Achaean society.

It is clear that the tablets provide good evidence for a system of tight control over the economy exercised from the palaces with the aid of written records. In what Page has aptly called an 'annual amassing of infinite detail', note was taken of the acreage of tenants' holdings and the quantities of raw materials issued to craftsmen. Returns of produce were checked against assessments, and deficits recorded. Itemized lists of stores and personnel were drawn up. All this activity presupposes a literate bureaucracy and a hierarchy of officialdom of which little or no trace appears in the Homeric poems. (Some possible vestiges of a tradition of palace control of the economy are noted on pp. 93–94.)

In contrast with the tablet system, the organization of Odysseus's estate seems very unsophisticated. For example, Eumaios keeps the tally of his master's stock in his head, and there is no mention of scribes or memoranda in Ithaca. But the epic tradition does not completely exclude writing from the world of the palaces. It remembered that Bellerophon was sent to the king of Lycia with a 'folded tablet' on which were scratched 'baneful signs' (*Iliad* 6, 168–9). Kirk apparently overlooks this passage when he asks rhetorically: 'Would it [*sc.* a poetic tradition originating in the historical palaces] have omitted all reference to scribes and writing?'[2] The Bellerophon story depends on the transmission of a *written* message of whose content Bellerophon is unaware. As told by Homer, it appears to embody a significant memory of the way in which diplomatic exchanges were conducted in the Late Bronze Age. Such a description cannot have originated in any subsequent practice between then and Homer's day.

Apart from this passage, it is true that heroic society is depicted without the dimension of literacy, but it does not follow that the general picture is derived from conditions between *c.* 1100 and 750 and cannot reflect the world before 1100. There is reason to think that literacy must have been very restricted in the Mycenaean world. Apart from a few pot-marks, no inscriptions other than the tablets have been found. The sudden and complete loss of the art of writing in the Dark Age suggests that it was more or less confined to a scribal class attached to the palaces. There may be no anachronism in showing Achaean heroes unable to read and write, as in the scene where the noblest Greeks 'make their mark' on lot-tokens (*Iliad* 7, 175 ff.).

In this, as in other respects, the tablets may give a very one-sided impression. Page considers that they present the 'world of Mycenaean Greece'.[3] But they may give as incomplete and misleading a picture of the totality of the Mycenaean world as Homer has been accused of giving. The Knossos tablets document Minoan Crete two centuries before the Trojan War. The Pylos tablets date from approximately the same period as the war, but they come from a region that was much influenced by Minoan culture. The kingdom of Pylos may not have been typical of all regions of Achaean power. Unfortunately there is not yet enough tablet evidence from Mycenae or Thebes to show in detail how their kingdoms were organized. Since they used the same script and accounting procedures, there is a presumption that the administration conformed to the Pylian pattern, but we do not know for certain that this was so. As one moved west from the Argolid or north from Boeotia, one probably came to regions of the Mycenaean world where the palace bureaucracy was much less in evidence. Indeed, it seems very unlikely that outlying areas like Thessaly, Aetolia, or Ithaca were ever organized in the Knossian or Pylian way.

The tablets, as has often been pointed out, find their

closest parallel in documents like the temple accounts from Sumerian Lagash, or the palace archives from Nuzi or Ugarit. The concept of a kingdom as a 'palace estate' run under centralized control was not native to Greece. Like some other features of high Mycenaean civilization, such as fresco painting and ivory carving, palace bureaucracy was an exotic import derived via Crete from the east. I suspect that the scribal system was only lightly grafted on the stock of a more 'European' world in which society was more loosely organized under local chieftains.

Finley speaks of the world of Odysseus as one in which a man's life was defined by three distinct but overlapping groups, class, kin, and household. He sees this world as emerging in the Dark Age to replace the more civilized communities of the Late Bronze Age. But the contrast may not have been as sharp as he suggests. The world of which he speaks may have already existed in Mycenaean Greece under the veneer of the palace culture. Consciousness of class, kin, and household has always been the mark of the aristocrat. The Achaean nobles in Homer show this consciousness to a marked degree. They are proud of their lineage and connections, jealous for their property, and always ready to assert their superiority over common folk. In the opulent conditions of the Palace Age the line between aristocrat and commoner is likely to have been drawn even more firmly than in later and more unsettled times. If so, the Homeric picture of the class structure could in essentials reflect the Bronze Age as well as the Early Iron Age.

The great kings of the Greek world between 1400 and 1200 are likely to have risen to eminence on the shoulders of a landowning aristocracy. Their champion warriors, equipped with superior armour and chariots, will have been recruited, like medieval knights, from noble families; but such overlordship tends to be precarious. If the ruler lacked personal prowess, or if he became estranged from his nobles, he would have found it very hard to maintain his authority over a wide territory.[4] The power of the nobles over their retainers and estates was more circumscribed but also more durable. An aristocrat with a loyal following could maintain his position even in times of revolution and migration. This, I suggest, was what happened as the Mycenaean Age faded out. The major kings and the palaces disappeared together, but the lesser 'kings' maintained their authority in an impoverished world. The trappings of fine art and literacy were lost, but the class system was not radically altered.

If one compares Homeric society with the outline of society revealed by the tablets, one finds a broadly similar structure. The monarch (*wanax*) is at the top of the pyramid and the slaves are at the bottom. The intervening layers tend to polarize towards the extremes, leaving a marked gap between nobles and commoners. There are quite a number of officials mentioned on the tablets whose titles find no analogue in Homer, but the proliferation of such titles need not imply a large number of social classes. On the contrary, it is perhaps more likely that the officials all came from much the same social class.

Long before the tablets were deciphered, the bardic tradition had been shown to run back into the Late Bronze Age and to preserve valid memories of what life was then like. The tradition is worthy of credence in its own right, and does not need to be confirmed by the tablets. If the Homeric poems give a different picture from the tablets, that does not mean that their witness has to be rejected. The Mycenaean world was complex, and scribe and bard may simply be reflecting different aspects of it. To take a modern analogy: the cost of the Crimean War could be ascertained from British Parliamentary papers, but financial statements would be a very poor guide to the spirit in which the campaign was fought. For this, Tennyson's *Charge of the Light Brigade* would be a much more revealing source, and one that no historian would neglect.

It does not seem possible to prove that the structure of Homeric society reflects the period 1000 to 800 rather than 1300 to 1100. Finley, for instance, regards the customs of gift-exchange and guest-friendship as characteristic of the rougher and poorer world of the tenth and ninth centuries. But I can see no reason to doubt that such customs flourished also in the world of the Mycenaean kingdoms. They would be facilitated by the background of wealth and good communications. If Hittite monarchs and Pharaohs could exchange gifts, so could Achaean rulers. A guest-friendship between the houses of Diomedes of Argos and Glaukos of Lycia prevents the two champions from fighting each other at Troy (*Iliad* 6, 212–36). In view of the latest archaeological evidence for Mycenaean penetration into south-west Asia Minor, the possibility of such a relationship in the Late Bronze Age cannot be excluded.[5]

Homer and the Linear B Tablets[6]

It is accepted that there are important linguistic parallels between the tablets and the Homeric poems, but the nature and extent of material parallels is much more controversial. For some scholars the tablets provide abundant confirmation of the accuracy of many Homeric traditions about the Bronze Age. Others are more sceptical about the relationship. For them the Homeric world is completely post-Mycenaean, differing not merely in scale but also in fundamental structure from the world revealed by the tablets. The problem is complicated by the fragmentary nature of the tablets, and by continuing controversy about the reading and interpretation of much of the material. Despite these difficulties, it has seemed worthwhile to try to assemble and comment on some of the more significant evidence.

Given that the tablets are administrative records, one would not be surprised to find little or no overlap between their subject-matter and the themes of Homeric poetry. The world of the scribe is a humdrum world, and his listing and counting lack poetic appeal. As an example of the prosaic and unheroic quality of the tablets I quote from a Pylian set dealing with the issue of metal from the palace (*Documents*, No. 253):

Smiths at Akerewa having an allocation:
Thisbaios: 1.5 kg. bronze; Q^u hestawon: 1.5 kg. bronze . . .
[*six names follow, each with the same allocation*]
And so many smiths without an allocation:
[*four names follow*]
And so many slaves: [*those*] of Keweto . . . etc.

The words for 'smith' and 'slave' recur in Homer, but such parallels only confirm the continuity of the Greek language from the Mycenaean Age onwards. It is of much more significance to note that the centralized control of metal-working here attested is not a feature of the Homeric world. For parallels to the system one goes instead to Sumeria:

> beaten copper, from the office located at the chariot shed, delivered to the smiths at 16⅓ manehs 2 shekels [=8.25 kg.] per head.
>
> (Tablet No. 354 from Ur, *c.* 2100 BC)

or to Syria:

> 4 half-talents [=60 kg.) of copper for the smiths of the town Berašena, 4000 shekels [=33.5 kg.] of copper for arrowheads, and 600 shekels a4W=5 kg.] of copper for doors.
>
> (Tablet No. 402 from Alalakh, Late Bronze Age)

Some of the Pylos tablets refer to troop musters and movements of naval personnel, and this would seem to be a more likely field in which to look for epic parallels. In fact, some quite striking similarities of phrasing, and even of rhythm, have been noted.[7]

The tablets dealing with land forces conform to a general pattern.[8] First comes a proper name in the genitive followed by the word *o-ka*. A widely accepted translation is: 'Command (*orcha*) of X'. If this is correct, the Mycenaean word for 'command' is preserved in the early epic word *orchamos*, 'leader', which occurs only in the set phrases 'leader of men' and 'leader of the people'. Next follows a list of names in the nominative, presumably the subordinate officers of the detachment. The names range between a minimum of three and a maximum of seven. Then come totals of troops, all in multiples of ten, with place-names or ethnics. It is interesting to compare the placing of the pickets in *Iliad* 9, 80–8, where seven captains are listed, each leading a company of 100 men. Finally there is the phrase: 'And with them the Follower (*e-qe-ta*) X'. The title 'Follower' is taken to refer to members of an élite corps specially associated with the king. It seems probable that the Followers constituted a corps of charioteers, since other tablets credit them with an allocation of slaves, distinctive garb, and chariot-wheels. On the *o-ka* tablets the Follower's name is usually dignified by a patronymic, indicating that he is a person of noble rank. Homer has no noun corresponding exactly to Follower – the epic tradition seems to have substituted the term 'Companion' (*hetairos*) – but he often uses the verb 'follow' when eminent warriors parade with their men, even in contexts where no movement is implied. For example, the Myrmidons are *standing* round the bier of Patroklos, and the poet adds: 'and with them *followed* swift-footed Achilles' (*Iliad* 18, 233–4). In the light of the tablets this may be paraphrased: 'and with them stood their leader Achilles'. The *o-ka* tablets therefore tend to suggest that some vestiges of Mycenaean military terminology were preserved in the epic tradition.

An analysis of the words for royalty points to a similar conclusion. Homer has two words for 'king', *wanax* and *basileus*, and in most contexts they are indistinguishable in meaning.[9] The same words occur on the tablets, but there is a wide difference in status between the persons denoted by each term. *Wanax*, though not of frequent occurrence, is rightly taken to be the title of the sovereign ruler. In one important document (*Documents*, No. 152) the 'private estate' (*temenos*) of the *wanax* is listed first, and is three times larger than the *temenos* of the *lawegetas* who comes next in the list. Elsewhere there are references to the potter of the *wanax*, the fuller of the *wanax*, and to the appointment by the *wanax* of an official who inspects and lists ewers belonging to the *wanassa* (presumably the Queen). *Basileus* on the tablets denotes a less exalted but not unimportant official, perhaps in some cases the governor of a provincial town (as in *Documents*, No. 38). In Homer, then, the word *basileus* has gained in prestige; though it sometimes means no more than 'noble', it can denote the king of a community not subject to any other authority. As such it is synonymous with *wanax*. But *wanax* retains some overtones of grandeur that *basileus* cannot quite match, partly from its attribution to Agamemnon in the formula '*wanax* of men', and also from the fact that it is sometimes used as a title for gods,[10] while *basileus* applies only to mortals. These semantic shifts can be explained by historical changes. *Wanax* in the epic retains a certain aura of majesty because it was used as the title of great kings in Mycenaean times. The *basileus* administered districts or towns under their overlordship. Then, with the collapse of the large centralized kingdoms, the local governors asserted their independence, and gained in status to the point where they became 'kings' in their own right.[11]

The tablets acquaint us with the title of a number of other functionaries, presumably including senior palace officials as well as local mayors or village headmen, but yield no firm information about their status or powers. Correlates like *ko-re-te* and *po-ro-ko-re-te, du-ma, po-ro-du-ma* and *me-ri-du-ma*, suggest a hierarchy of officialdom but remain etymologically opaque. These and other titles find no place in epic language or society. Here the discontinuity of the tradition must be significant. Presumably the officials who held the titles ceased to have any function when the palace bureaucracies were dissolved.

One important personage on the tablets, the *lawegetas*, has a good Greek name meaning 'leader of the *lawos*'. This title does not appear in Homer, but *lawos* is common, often used generally for 'folk' or 'people', but not infrequently found in contexts that suggest the more specialized meaning of 'troops' or 'fighting men'. This lends some support to the view that the *lawegetas* was a military leader, though nothing in the tablets certifies him as such. He apparently ranks next below the *wanax*, and like him is the possessor of a 'private estate' (*temenos*). Traces of an analogous relationship between sovereign and army chief have been noted in Homer. The *wanax* of Lycia recognizes the prowess of the hero Bellerophon by the gift of his daughter in marriage and the proverbial half of his kingdom, including 'a fine *temenos* of orchard and arable land' (*Iliad* 6, 192–5). In this case there was no previous kinship between the two; but in the story of Meleager it is the king's son who is offered a *temenos* to induce him to defend the people of Kalydon against the forces besieging their city (*Iliad* 9, 573 ff.). The heir-apparent would always be a natural choice for *lawegetas*. In the relationship between Hector and Priam we seem to have a duplicate of the Oineus-Meleager situation, with a prince of the blood royal acting as war leader under an elderly *wanax*.[12]

Land tenure is a singularly unheroic topic, so it is hardly surprising that the epic, unlike the tablets, offers very little detail on this aspect of social life. The bureaucrat is interested in tenants and leases, the bard is not. But the bard *is* concerned with the king and his prerogatives, and it is precisely at this point that we find a significant parallel between the tablets and Homer. Both allude to the 'royal estate' or 'preserve of the king', and both use the same word *temenos*, a term which in later Greek is applied only to a 'temple precinct'.[13] Alkinoös is credited with a '*temenos* and flourishing orchard' (*Odyssey* 6, 293), and Odysseus with a 'big *temenos*' (*Odyssey* 17, 299). The mixed character of a *temenos*, part arable and part orchard, is explicitly stated in the case of the *temenos* assigned to Bellerophon and the *temenos* offered to Meleager and Aeneas (*Iliad* 6, 195; 9, 579–80; 20, 185). The estate of Tydeus, though not called a *temenos*, is said to comprise ample wheatland and orchards (*Iliad* 14, 121–3). At Pylos there was an important person called Ekhelawon, who may even have been the king himself, as

Ventris and Chadwick suggested, and a tablet can be interpreted as a census of his private estate, specifying the acreage under wheat, and the number of trees (*Documents*, No. 153).

There appears to be a fair measure of agreement between the tablets and the Homeric poems in regard to royal or princely estates. I would also venture to say that what Homer implies about land tenure in general is not inconsistent with some important indications of the E series of Pylos tablets. To make even this cautious assertion is to venture on hotly disputed territory.[14] Homer is far from informative about the ownership of land, and it is possible to interpret his scattered hints in different ways. So far as Pylos is concerned, it is Chadwick's considered view that 'the terms upon which land was held and cultivated are entirely unknown, despite ingenious speculation.'[15] He does, however, concede that in the area covered by the Pylos E series (which is certainly not a very extensive area and may be exceptional) there were two kinds of land: that in private ownership, and that belonging to the *damos*. Land belonging to the *damos* must in some sense be 'communal' land. Now there is good reason to suppose that, in the *Iliad* at least, there are memories of an ancient 'common field' system.[16] The phrase 'common arable land' is found (*Iliad* 12, 422), and one of the scenes on Achilles's shield may represent a Mycenaean 'Plough Monday' with the villagers all at work in their great common field (*Iliad* 18, 541–9).

The Ithacan background of the *Odyssey* makes it somewhat more informative about land tenure. The epithets *poluklēros* ('rich') and *aklēros* ('poor') – neither of which occurs in the *Iliad* – mean literally 'with many allotments' and 'with no allotment', and strongly imply private possession of land. It is also implied that nobles like Aigyptios and Noemon have their own estates (*Odyssey* 2, 22; 4, 634–7). Homer does not make clear whether he envisaged the ordinary folk of Ithaca as serfs or tenants or peasant proprietors. He does, however, make Eumaios hope for the reward of a house and a plot of land 'such as a kindly *wanax* is wont to give to his retainer' (*Odyssey* 14, 62–4). This implies that kings like Odysseus had the power to give land to their supporters. Odysseus also appears to have extensive grazing rights, for his servants are herding goats and swine for him in the rough land at the southern extremity of the island furthest away from the palace. From there Eumaios is required to send animals to the palace at the request of the suitors. His stock of hogs (360 in all) is considerably less than his sows (600) because of these requisitions. From Knossos and Pylos there are livestock tablets for sheep on which the figures probably represent animals arriving as tribute at the palaces. On them we find a situation complementary to that on Eumaios's farm, with rams greatly outnumbering ewes. As Ventris and Chadwick say (*Documents*, p. 198): 'The high number of rams . . . would naturally occur if the owners were obliged to supply so many sheep annually. They would of course pick out the least useful members for the regeneration of the flock.' Eumaios seems to have followed the same management principles.

Mycenaean noble landowners may have been bound by a system of obligations of the type that we would call 'feudal'. Something of this sort has been inferred from the tablets by Ventris and Chadwick, and also by F. H. Stubbings, who writes: 'We shall not be far wrong in reading into the tablets a feudal system of administration in which members of the ruling class govern and enjoy allotments of territory in return for contributions of produce in kind and of service in war.'[17] There appear to be vestiges of such a system in the Homeric poems. The wealthy Echepolos of Sikyon gave the mare Aithê as a 'gift' to Agamemnon 'so that he might not have to follow him to Troy' (*Iliad* 23, 296–9). According to the Catalogue, Sikyon was in the realm of Agamemnon, so it looks as though Echepolos was contracting out of a feudal obligation, a conclusion that will be strengthened if 'follow' bears the technical sense noted above (p. 88). Euchenor of Corinth may have been under a similar obligation. He is said to have 'avoided the grievous penalty of the Achaeans [*i.e.*, a heavy fine]' by coming to Troy (*Iliad* 13, 669).

When Agamemnon promises seven cities to Achilles, he remarks that the inhabitants will

> honour him with *gifts* [*dotine*, a word which recurs in a third-century BC inscription in the sense of 'rent in kind'] like a god, and under his sceptre will accomplish their shining *dues* [*themistas*].
>
> *Iliad* 9, 155–6

The last clause has been plausibly interpreted as meaning that they will fulfil their assessment quotas. The use of *themis* in this sense appears to be Mycenaean.[18]

Contributions in kind from the people (perhaps in return for rights in the common land) are implied by the statement that the Achaean leaders 'drink public wine' (*Iliad* 17, 250). Such contributions are explicitly envisaged in Phaeacia, where Alkinoös promises his peers that they can recoup their gifts to Odysseus by a levy on the people (*Odyssey* 13, 14–15; *cf.* 7, 150). At the palace of Menelaos, 'guests' (apparently a euphemism for 'vassals') are seen arriving with contributions of sheep, wine, and corn (*Odyssey* 4, 621–3). In Ithaca, Telemachos undertakes to send clothing and corn from the palace to support the new arrival at Eumaios's farm (*Odyssey* 16, 82–4).

The effect of these isolated examples is cumulative. They seem to imply that the palace-centred economy, documented so abundantly in the Linear B tablets, left an imprint on the bardic tradition that was never completely erased.

It has often been claimed, on the evidence of the tablets, that labour in the Mycenaean world was specialized to a degree unknown in the later epic. The versatility of Odysseus as carpenter, boat-builder, ploughman, navigator and hunter is contrasted with the division of labour that seems to have been practised in Knossos or Pylos. But Odysseus is an exceptionally gifted person, and it does not seem right to use his heroic adaptability as a basis for a general comparison. A fairer approach would be to review all the occupations of slave, peasant, and craftsman mentioned in Homeric narrative and simile, and then to compare the resulting list with the occupational terms definitely identified on the tablets. If this is done, the structure of trades in the two sources will be found not to differ greatly in complexity. On my reckoning, of 26 trades definitely identified in the tablets,[19] 23 were known to Homer. That leaves only three trades with no Homeric equivalent named or implied: fulling, tailoring, and unguent-boiling (for the perfume trade). I would not deny that the specialization of labour was somewhat more pronounced in Mycenaean times, especially among the staffs of the palaces. There were bakers (male), for example, whereas in Homer's world baking was just one of a number of tasks performed by housewife or slave-woman. Also, some of the doubtful terms on the tablets, such as *pi-ri-je-te* (cutler?) and *a-pu-ko-wo-ko* (headband-maker?), probably denote specialized workers with no Homeric equivalent. The Mycenae tablets mention *kyanos*-workers, a luxury trade that was not practised in Iron Age Greece. But on the whole, the difference between the two worlds in respect of trades has been, in my opinion, unjustifiably exaggerated.

A more marked difference is detectable in the scale on which industry was organized. For example, Homer must have known great houses where slave-women worked at the corn-mill or the loom. He projects this feature back to the palace of Alkinoös, grandly assigning fifty females to these tasks (*Odyssey* 7, 103 ff.). The reality, as we can now deduce it from the tablets, was on a far larger scale. On a series of ration tablets from Pylos (the Aa Ab group), about 750 women and 750 children are listed. Over 1100 of them are located at Pylos itself, and many are described as spinners, weavers, and carders. As Chadwick says: 'This indicates that the production of textiles was a major concern of royal establishments and that the work force was fed from the palace stores.'[20] A similar picture emerges from an enumeration of the bronzesmiths in Nestor's realm. There were some 400 in all, and they were grouped in bands of up to 20 or more. We are not then concerned with village smithies, but with something like a factory system, no doubt geared to an export trade.

Even before the decipherment, a good case had been established for the Mycenaean or Minoan ancestry of many of the Olympian gods and goddesses. It was therefore gratifying, if not surprising, to find many of their names listed together with prescribed offerings. Taking the Knossos and Pylos texts together, we find probable mention of the following: Zeus, Hera, Poseidon, Athena, Artemis, and (possibly) Hermes. Special veneration seems to have been paid to Poseidon at Pylos, and it is interesting to find that Homer describes a public sacrifice of 81 bulls offered to Poseidon by the Pylians (*Odyssey* 3, 4–9). But there are significant differences also. The tablets record a number of deities who do not figure in the cult of later times. They also give the impression that the cycle of offerings was closely regulated month by month, and of this there is no hint in Homer.

One titbit of cult information in Homer is confirmed. We learn from the *Odyssey* (19, 188) that Eileithyia was worshipped in a cave at Amnisos, the port of Knossos. It is therefore satisfying to find a Knossos tablet beginning: 'Amnisos: one jar of honey to Eleuthia . . .' (*Documents*, No. 206).

Another stray piece of information in Homer concerns chariots. When a chariot is being made ready for Hera, we are told that 'Hebe quickly fastened the curved wheels to the car' (*Iliad* 5, 722). When Zeus had completed a journey, Poseidon unyoked the horses for him and 'put the chariot on a stand, covering it with a cloth' (*Iliad* 8, 441). From tablets found in the armoury at Knossos we can deduce that it was the practice to store chariot bodies and wheels separately. There is an ideogram for a wheel-less chariot, and some of the tablets list wheels by themselves (*Documents*, p. 361).

Finally, something must be said about personal names.[21]

Ventris and Chadwick listed 58 names from the tablets that can be exactly paralleled in Homer. The list includes an Achilles (*a-ki-re-u*) from Knossos and Pylos, an Ajax (*ai-wa*) from Knossos, a Hector (*e-ko-to*) who is a 'slave of the god' (lessee of temple land?) at Pylos, a Theseus (*te-se-u*), an Orestes (*o-re-ta*), and many more familiar names. It is remarkable that, in addition to Hector, names borne by nineteen other Trojans or Trojan allies figure in the list. In Homer, some of these Trojans are of minor importance (*e.g.*, Pedaios, Pedasos), but Antenor (*a-ta-no*) and Pandaros (*pa_2-da-ro*) are major figures. According to Webster, there are only two possible explanations for this high percentage of Mycenaean names among the Trojans: either Troy was a Greek-speaking kingdom (as others have suggested for different reasons), or else these names were introduced into the Troy saga from a traditional Mycenaean siege poem.

It is an odd coincidence that in Homer Antenor has a son called Laodokos, and that these names are also associated at Pylos, where a Laodokos holds land in the district where an Antenor is an official.[22] Homer also records a *Greek* called Laodokos, who is a Pylian. In view of the considerable duplication of names between Knossos and Pylos, Ventris and Chadwick suggested that 'there was a comparatively limited range of names in use in Mycenaean times.' This hypothesis *might* account for some of the facts. But where minor Homeric characters are concerned, poetic manipulation of an inherited stock of names is likely to have occurred. For example, two other Greeks and Trojans (besides Laodokos) share the same name now known to be Mycenaean.[23]

Obviously, we cannot infer that any given Homeric hero is historical simply because he bears a Mycenaean name. But, as Miss Gray has shown, Homeric proper names now authenticated as Mycenaean tend to cluster in the genealogies of the Neleids and the Atreidae, and some other major families that must undoubtedly have been prominent in the

Late Bronze Age. To this extent the reliability of the Homeric tradition again receives some support from the tablets.

The Greek and Trojan Catalogues[24]

An elaborate list of the Greek forces in 29 contingents prefaces the first battle in the *Iliad* (2, 494–759). Generally known as the Catalogue, it parades before us a bewilderingly large number of place-names, 164 in all, from which the troops were drawn, interspersed with the names of 46 commanders (nearly half of them with patronymics and other biographical details) and 16 tribes or peoples (Boeotians, Phocians, Locrians, etc.). The number of ships brought by each contingent is also given, making a grand total of 1186. Answering to the Catalogue of the Greeks is a much shorter Catalogue of the Trojans and their allies (*Iliad* 2, 816–77). In it we meet Dardanians from the Troad and 11 other 'nations' (Thracians, Lycians, etc.), and learn the names of 26 commanders (with family details of all but ten of them). The number of locations mentioned is 33. It can be seen that the geographical detail and saga material in the two lists is formidably complex.

Exhaustive studies have been made of the two Catalogues, and there is a respectable body of scholarly opinion in favour of the view that the lists took shape before the end of the Mycenaean era, and that they reflect without excessive distortions the political geography of the period before *c.* 1150. The Dorians are not mentioned, nor are places, later to become important, like Megara, Corinth, Smyrna and Ephesus. It is hard for us to believe that such detailed lists could have been transmitted orally for several hundred years, but parallel feats of memory are known from other oral cultures.[25] If the case for the antiquity and authenticity of the Catalogues can be made out, it carries with it important implications for the general reliability of the tradition that culminates in the Homeric poems.

If the details of the Greek Catalogue derive from the Mycenaean era, we should expect a close correlation between its place-names and sites certified as Mycenaean by archaeological investigation. And this, in fact, is what we find. T. W. Allen was the first to make systematic use of this line of argument in his *Homeric Catalogue of Ships* (1921). V. Burr, reviewing the evidence in 1944, claimed that 60 of the identifiable places (roughly 60 per cent) had been shown to have been occupied in Mycenaean times. The percentage has been considerably improved since then. On the basis of post-war excavations and their own thorough field surveys, R. Hope Simpson and J. F. Lazenby claim in their *Catalogue of the Ships in Homer's Iliad* (1970) that 75 per cent of the identifiable places are now known to have been occupied in the Late Mycenaean period. They further add that none can be shown not to have been inhabited then.

It has been pointed out that many of these places were continuously inhabited from Mycenaean times on, and so would have been known to later poets as ancient settlement sites. This is true. But there is a special category of identifiable places that were inhabited during the Mycenaean Age, and were then deserted, and not reoccupied (if at all) until after Homer's time. Examples are Eutresis in Boeotia, and Englianos (Pylos) and Dorion in Messenia. The category is not large, but it is significant as proof that authentic memories of a vanished world were embodied in the Catalogue.

The Catalogue was intensively studied by ancient geographers, but despite all their efforts they failed to identify about forty places. Typical of these 'lost' sites were the Arcadian towns of Rhipe, Stratie and Enispe (*Iliad* 2, 606), of which Strabo despairingly remarks: 'It is difficult to find these, and you would be no better off if you did find them because nobody lives there.' The most plausible explanation is that these places really were Mycenaean towns and villages destroyed and abandoned in the disasters that brought down Mycenaean civilization. As Page has written: 'It is inconceivable that such a list should have been first compiled during or after the Dark Ages; for there was never again a time in the history of Greece when so many places might disappear from the memory of man.' The conclusion stands that the Catalogue preserves well-founded memories of the map of Mycenaean Greece, including not only famous sites like Argos and Athens that were continuously inhabited, but also a considerable number of minor places that faded entirely from the scene in the Dark Age.

If the list of names is not then the product of later poetic imaginings, there is a presumption that the distribution of towns in kingdoms and principalities reflects the political divisions of the Mycenaean world. But at what stage in its history? The absence of Thebes from the list provides a rough *terminus post quem*, for the final destruction of Thebes seems to have occurred within a decade or so of the middle of the thirteenth century. Opinion then divides, with some scholars arguing that the power structure is that of the late IIIB period before the disasters of *c.* 1200, while others hold that the Catalogue reflects the more fragmented world of the twelfth century (IIIC). There are difficulties on either view. The importance attached to Nestor's kingdom appears to favour a pre-1200 dating. But against this, the prominence of the Boeotian contingent argues for a date perhaps not earlier than *c.* 1150 when, according to Thucydides (1, 12), Boeotians occupied the territory that was previously called the land of Kadmeia. The debate remains inconclusive, but both sides agree that the political geography of the Catalogue is not fictional. It is certainly hard to credit that a Dark Age poet would have invented features as implausible as the partition of the Argolid between Agamemnon and Diomedes, the three separate kingdoms in the Dodecanese, and the comparatively small area assigned to Achilles. The quirks of history rather than the vagaries of poetic imagination must in some way account for these oddities.

It has been suggested that the Catalogue originated as a muster-list compiled officially at the time of the Trojan campaign, and subsequently versified. But it seems very improbable that bards would utilize scribal documents as sources for their songs. Lists have always been a feature of oral poetry, and it seems much more likely that the Catalogue *originated* as a poetic composition to preserve the memory of a great enterprise. In the torn and troubled Mycenaean world after the fall of Troy there would have been both the knowledge and the incentive to compile a detailed memorial of the campaign on the scale of the Catalogue. Such a compilation would acquire the prestige of a canonical list, and would tend to be memorized and transmitted verbatim, for a series of names offers little scope for imaginative development. Something of this sort seems to have happened: the Catalogue became fixed and frozen at an early date, while the wider tale of Troy expanded in the telling.

A number of details combine to prove that the Catalogue was composed independently of the rest of the *Iliad*. With its emphasis on *ship* numbers, the Catalogue is more appropriate to the mustering of the Greek forces at Aulis than to a battle taking place in the tenth year of the siege. When the poet of the *Iliad* decided to introduce the Catalogue early in his poem, presumably to lend dignity to his first battle scene by recalling the great scale of the conflict, he was obliged to bring it up to date by some minor additions. Thus, after the passage in which Protesilaos is named as leader of the men from Phylace and five other towns, he adds: 'While he was alive, but by then the black earth held him.' He further explains that Protesilaos was the first Achaean casualty, struck down as he leaped ashore from his ship (*Iliad* 2, 695–702). There could be no clearer proof that the Catalogue was originally independent of the *Iliad* in composition and time reference. There is a similar gloss in the entry relating to Achilles's contingent to explain that they were *not* mustering for battle because of their leader's quarrel with Agamemnon (*Iliad* 2, 686–94).

The independence of the Catalogue is also apparent in relation to some of the other contingents. It gives pride of place to Boeotia with 6,000 troops gathered from 29 towns.[26] Next come the men of Orchomenos, Phocis, Locris, and Euboea. These five entries include more than one-third of all the place-names, yet neither the troops nor their commanders figure at all prominently in the rest of the *Iliad*. The Arcadians are credited with sixty ships filled with seasoned warriors (*Iliad* 2, 603–14), but they are never mentioned again. Of the 46 commanders named in the Catalogue, nine never reappear in the narrative. On the other hand, we later meet quite a number of minor officers who are not named in the Catalogue. We might even feel that independence is carried to the point of incompatibility when we notice that three heroes who figure prominently in the rest of the *Iliad*, namely Patroklos, Teukros, and Antilochos, have no place in the Catalogue.

It is clear that the Catalogue was not originally designed to fit our *Iliad*. It is a poem within a poem. Yet one can overemphasize the divergences. All the really major heroes do appear in the Catalogue, and most of them are described in the style so familiar from the rest of the poem. Agamemnon is 'king of men', Nestor is the 'Gerenian horseman', Diomedes is 'good at the war cry', and Achilles is 'swift-footed'. If the Catalogue is indeed several centuries older than the *Iliad*, here is proof of the high antiquity of these stock epithets. In the treatment of some very minor persons the *Iliad* also follows the tradition represented by the Catalogue. For instance, whenever Sthenelos is mentioned in the *Iliad* he is linked with Diomedes as in the Catalogue (*Iliad* 2, 563–4, with *e.g.*, *Iliad* 5, 835–7). Leïtos is twice paired with his fellow Boeotian Peneleos, and in one of these later passages we learn his father's name (*Iliad* 2, 494 with 17, 597–602). Ialmenos makes his sole subsequent appearance with his brother-officer Askalaphos (*Iliad* 2, 512 with 9, 82).

A reasonable explanation of the divergences and the agreements is that the one tradition is represented at different points in its transmission. The tradition derived ultimately from certain facts in the history and geography of the Late Mycenaean period. The Catalogue, we may suppose, first took shape when the facts lay in the quite recent past. The rest of the *Iliad* is the result of a much later and freer handling of the traditional tale of Troy.

Comparisons can be made between certain Bronze Age documents and parts of the Catalogue to test its reliability. From the Hittite archives we get glimpses of Achaean freebooters operating in south-west Asia Minor in the latter part of the thirteenth century. The island of Rhodes must have been an important base for such activity – close to the coast, yet protected by the sea from Hittite reprisals.[27] If we turn to the Catalogue entry for Rhodes, we find it dominated by the turbulent Tlepolemos (*Iliad* 2, 653–70). We are told that after killing his great-uncle he fled from his home and took ship with a band of followers to seek his fortune overseas. Fate brought him to Rhodes, where he settled before joining the Trojan expedition with nine ships. At Troy, as we learn from a later passage, he was killed by Sarpedon (*Iliad* 5, 627 ff.). Now Sarpedon was king of Lycia on the mainland east of Rhodes. Thus the epic tradition of an Achaean sea-rover operating for a time from Rhodes and extinguished by a Lycian monarch *c.* 1200 is in rather striking agreement with conditions in that area as revealed by contemporary Hittite records.

A second source of comparison is the Pylos tablets, and the Pylian entry in the Catalogue has naturally been closely scrutinized in relation to them. The tablets twice record a group of *nine* places which seem to stand in a special administrative relation to the palace, and it has been noted that the number *nine* figures prominently in Homeric mentions of Pylos. When Telemachos arrives by ship from Ithaca, he finds Nestor with his people assembled in nine companies on the beach for a sacrifice to Poseidon (*Odyssey* 3, 4–8). Again, in the Catalogue, Nestor is said to be in command of contingents from nine cities. At first sight the accuracy of the Homeric tradition seems to be confirmed, but closer scrutiny reveals a problem. The Catalogue list and the group of places on the tablets have at most only one name in common (Aipu), and even that identification has been challenged by Chadwick.[28] There are, however, many other place-names recorded on the tablets, and from them it is possible to pick out a number which answer reasonably well to some of the Catalogue names. The following table sets out the identifications that have been suggested:

Catalogue names	*Suggested identifications from the tablets*	*Remarks*
Pulos	pu-ro	Generally accepted.
Arene	none	
Thruon	?	tu-ru-we-u was first taken to be a place, but is now thought to be a man's name, possibly Thrueus. But this might be 'man from Thruon'.
Aipu	a-pu$_2$	Generally accepted, but rejected by Chadwick.
Kuparisseeis	ku-pa-ri-so	Generally accepted.
Amphigeneia	a-pi-ke-ne-a	From a broken tablet. Not certainly a place-name; it might be a woman's name.
Pteleon	none	
Helos	e-re-i	Generally accepted.
Dorion	none	

Three of the nine names in the Pylian entry (Pulos, Kuparisseeis, Helos) thus correspond to place-names documented for the kingdom of Pylos *c.* 1200. Two more (Aipu, Amphigeneia) may do so. Three have no equivalent in the documents (Arene, Pteleon, Dorion). In the case of Thruon there is no direct equivalent, but a man's name may reflect the place-name.[29]

The evidence is distinctly equivocal, and tends to be interpreted in accordance with preconceived notions about Homer's historicity. Partisans of Homer the historian might credit him with up to six 'hits'. Opponents would admit only three, and would stress the absence of overlap between the 'nine' of the tablets and the 'nine' of the Catalogue. Granted the common assumption that the tablet 'nine' were major centres of administration in one of the two 'provinces' of the Pylian kingdom,[30] their absence from the Catalogue (with the possible exception of a-pu_2 = Aipu) is disturbing and calls for explanation. The other province[31] had seven (possibly eight) major towns, of which one, e-re-i, appears in the Catalogue. So, if we list the major towns of the two provinces and include pu-ro as the capital, we have a total of 17 (possibly 18) names, of which only three at most can be found in the Catalogue. On this basis, the Pylian entry must be regarded as a poor guide to the political geography of the Pylian kingdom *as it existed immediately prior to the destruction of the palace.*

This does not necessarily mean that the Pylian entry is devoid of any Mycenaean foundation.[32] It could reflect a greatly changed situation in the western Peloponnese towards the close of the IIIC period, with Dorians now on the scene in sufficient strength to imprint their names on an ancient habitation site. Many of the towns named on the tablets may have been destroyed at the time the palace fell. Villages and minor towns that survived may have gained in importance. Refugees could have organized a new Pylian kingdom in Triphylia closer to the Alpheios and including towns that had not been within the borders of the previous kingdom. We know that the pattern of Mycenaean settlement in the area altered greatly between the thirteenth and twelfth centuries, and this seems to provide a possible explanation of the discrepancies between the tablets and the Catalogue.

The Trojan Catalogue (*Iliad* 2, 816–77) has not attracted as much attention as the Greek, but its historical significance is potentially as great. If the date of its composition can be assigned to Mycenaean or Submycenaean times, it will go far towards confirming that the Trojan War really took place. At that early period there would have been no incentive for any bard to compose a versified list of Trojans and their allies, unless there had actually been hostilities between them and the Greeks.

The list of geographical locations is quite varied, and includes 15 towns or districts, five mountains, five rivers, one lake, and the Hellespont.[33] Most of these places can be identified, but very few have been systematically excavated. In the absence of archaological data about the sites, it is not possible to argue, as in the case of the Greek Catalogue, that the place-names reflect the spread of settlement in Mycenaean times. But in respect of its personal names, it agrees with the Greek in showing marked discrepancies with the rest of the *Iliad.* Eight of its 26 commanders do not reappear at all, and only five, namely, Hector, Aeneas, Sarpedon, Pandaros, and Asios, play a large part in the action. Conversely, notable heroes like Paris, Polydamas, Helenos, and Deiphobos are not named in it. Page perhaps exaggerates the discrepancies when he writes that 'the greater part of the scanty information given by the Trojan Catalogue is either flatly ignored or briskly contradicted by the Iliad'. For instance, there need not be any contradiction in the references to Amphios *son of Merops* (*Iliad* 2, 830–1) and Amphios *son of Selagos* (*Iliad* 5, 612); they may well be two different people since the latter is associated with Paisos, a place not mentioned in the Trojan Catalogue. It is hard to deny, however, that the poet of the *Iliad* was not much concerned to see that his narrative harmonized with the Catalogue. For example, the Catalogue informs us that Ennomos and Amphimachos were slain by Achilles 'in the river', but when we come to the account of the river battle in *Iliad* book 21 we find no mention of their names. Again, the *Iliad* mentions commanders of the Mysians, Kikones, and Paeonians who are not named in the Catalogue.

As in the case of the Greek Catalogue, the most likely explanation of the inconsistencies is that the Trojan Catalogue took shape at an early period, and was treated by later poets as an heirloom worthy of preservation as it stood. The later poets were Ionians, and it is hardly credible that they could have been the authors of a Catalogue that makes no mention of any coastal town or island south of the Troad except for Miletus, and that they should have represented Miletus as under the control of 'Carians of foreign tongue'. It has been suggested that they may have deliberately aimed at an archaic effect by excluding references to their Ionia. But this suggestion fails before the presence of the name Mount Phthiron in the Carian entry (*Iliad* 2, 868). The other place-names in this entry (Miletus, River Maeander, Mount Mykale) raised no problems of identification in the ancient world, but not so Mount Phthiron. No one knew for certain where it was. If Ionian bards had introduced it, its whereabouts would not have been forgotten by the classical period. Yet early in the fifth century the Ionian geographer Hekataios, himself a native of Miletus, was puzzled by it. The same argument can be used about Alybe, the 'birthplace of silver' (*Iliad* 2, 857). This was a standing puzzle for Greek geographers, showing that there was no valid Ionian tradition about its location. There seems to be only one adequate explanation for these uncertainties. Mount Phthiron and Alybe, we must suppose, were survivals from a time before the Ionian migration. They ceased to be current names before *c.* 1000, but were preserved like unidentified fossils in an antique fragment of oral poetry.

In general, then, the Trojan Catalogue probably represents a summary of what the last Mycenaeans and their immediate successors knew about the Troad, Thrace, and some regions of Asia Minor. Most of the town names are clustered in the Troad, and the districts there are listed in a coherent order. For the rest, large regions like Thrace, Phrygia, and Lycia, receive only very sketchy treatment. This suggests that the information derived mainly from a Trojan War saga supplemented by reports of traders and colonists. It may be significant that detailed geographical information about Asia Minor south of the Troad is confined to the neighbourhood of Miletus, which was a Mycenaean colony, and Sardis, where Mycenaean pottery has recently been found.

Burial rites[34]

Burial rites are described in considerable detail in a number of passages. In one case Nestor makes a proposal for a mass cremation of Greek casualties, and the ritual is carried out as he suggests (*Iliad* 7, 331–7 and 430 ff.);[35] elsewhere the funerals are always those of individuals. Cremation and the raising of a tumulus and grave-marker (*stēlē*) over the remains figure prominently in most of the descriptions.[36]

The most elaborate and impressive description is of the funeral of Patroklos (*Iliad* 18, 343–55 and 23, 12–14, 128 ff.). First the corpse is washed and anointed, and the wounds filled with 'stored-up unguents'.[37] Then it is clothed and laid on a bier, draped with a white shroud, and the Achaeans keep a night-long mourning vigil. After Achilles has killed Hector, the ritual is resumed with the Myrmidons driving their chariots three times round the bier. The bier is then carried in procession to the spot chosen for the pyre, and the mourners cut off locks of their hair and strew them on the corpse. A great pyre is erected and the body, wrapped in the fat of slaughtered sheep and cattle, is placed on top – a device to speed the reduction of the body to ashes.

Then he set beside him two-handled jars of oil and honey leaning them against the bier, and drove four horses with strong necks swiftly aloft the pyre with loud lamentation. And there were nine dogs of the table that had belonged to the lord Patroklos. Of these he cut the throats of two, and set them on the pyre; and so also killed twelve noble sons of the great-hearted Trojans with the stroke of bronze, and evil were the thoughts in his heart against them, and let loose the iron fury of the fire to feed on them.

Iliad 23, 170–7
(translation by R. Lattimore)

The pyre would not kindle properly until strong winds came at Achilles's invocation. Then, as the fire flamed through the darkness, Achilles poured libations of wine and called on the soul of his dead companion. When the fire had burnt itself out the burnt bones of the dead man were collected in a golden bowl, enfolded in two layers of fat, covered with a light cloth, and placed in a hut shelter, ultimately to be mingled with the ashes of Achilles himself under a lofty tumulus (*Odyssey* 24, 77). In the meantime a smaller mound was raised to mark the site of the pyre.

Cremation was not entirely unknown in Greece in the Mycenaean period. About two dozen instances have been noted from *c.* 1550 to 1125, with the largest concentration in the IIIC cemetery at Perati.[38] But inhumation was the almost universal practice, and remained so in many regions through Submycenaean and Protogeometric times. Athens was exceptional in that cremation became fashionable there as early as the mid-eleventh century. In the Kerameikos cemetery from the Protogeometric period, fifty-one cremations and six inhumations are known. In the Early Geometric period all the burials are cremations, but then a swing back to inhumation started, and in Late Geometric times inhumations outnumber cremations by four to one.

The old view that cremation was introduced by the Dorians is not supported by the archaeological evidence now available. The main impetus towards the fashion appears to have come from Anatolia in the late thirteenth and twelfth centuries. Cremation was practised by the Hittites as early as *c.* 1600, and appears to have been the universal practice at Troy VI at the time of its devastation by earthquaker *c.* 1300. The cemetery of Troy VIIa has not yet been found, but we may agree with Miss Lorimer that the inhabitants probably kept up the practice of cremation. Cremation is attributed to the Trojans by Homer for a mass burial (*Iliad* 7, 428–9), and for the obsequies of Hector (*Iliad* 24, 782 ff.). It is possible, as Miss Lorimer suggests, that the Achaean besiegers of Troy VIIa adopted the Trojan custom as 'particularly suited to the conditions of warfare on foreign soil'. If so, the epic tradition of cremation as the appropriate rite for a warrior's funeral will have an historical basis. But one must emphasize that no Mycenaean burials of any kind have been found in the Troad.

Mylonas holds that 'the similarities of burial custom existing between the Mycenaean and the Homeric world are many and weighty'. They include the placing of drinking cups, weapons, tools, and storage jars with the deceased, the marking of the tomb with a *stēlē*, the heaping of earth over the top, libations, and a funeral feast. Andronikos, on the other hand, insists that cremation marks off the Homeric ritual as quite different from the Mycenaean. Since all the features of Homeric ritual can be paralleled from excavations or vase paintings later than 900, he concludes that the Homeric picture owes nothing to the customs of the Mycenaean era, and is based on much more recent usage.

Both these rather extreme views tend to oversimplify a very complex situation. The criterion of cremation must be used with caution. For example, the cremation burials of the Kerameikos are unlike those described in Homer in that they do not exhibit the standard Homeric features of conspicuous tumulus and grave-marker. To find archaeological parallels for cremation-cum-tumulus in Greek lands one has to come down to the eighth century. Burials of this type were found at Colophon, and also at Halos near the territory traditionally associated with Achilles. The Colophon graves are, at present, unparalleled in Ionia, but the data from this area are very patchy. They are at least close in date and place to Homer himself, and a scene like the funeral of Patroklos could have been studied from life. But there is a difficulty in the supposition that the Homeric picture of funeral ritual originated in the Late Geometric period. Such a view seems to allow insufficient time for the development of the system of funeral formulae implying cremation. The simple verb 'bury' (*thaptein*) is several times glossed with 'burn'. Expressions like 'grant the right of fire' and 'mount the funeral pyre' are closely woven into the descriptive language.

There is a strong presumption in the epic tradition that

the dead will be cremated. Antikleia puts this clearly to Odysseus at their meeting in the Land of the Dead:

> But this is what always happens to mortals whenever one dies. The sinews no longer hold flesh and bones together, but the strong might of blazing fire subdues the bodily parts when once the warm breath leaves the white bones, and the soul flits off like a dream.
>
> *Odyssey* 11, 218–22

Yet this statement must be viewed against the fact that cremation was never the preferred rite in all parts of Greece at the same time. At all periods the majority of interments seem to have been by inhumation.[39] There is, therefore, an element of artificiality in the Homeric picture. It does not fully reflect the customs of the Late Bronze Age or the Early Iron Age. The poets who moulded the epic tradition seem to have selected cremation for special, indeed exclusive, emphasis. There could well be a saga memory at the base of the tradition, an ultimate recollection of a custom adopted by the Achaean army in the Troad. Yet other factors must have operated to reinforce and perpetuate the convention. The noble families may have favoured cremation as a more impressive (and expensive) way of disposing of the dead. There is something lordly, indeed heroic, about the great pyre flaming to the heavens. The legendary self-immolation of Herakles on a pyre on Mount Oeta shows how much this image was part of the heroic tradition. Those who die in battle normally receive special funeral honours, and cremation may have come to seem particularly appropriate for war heroes. Such a convergence between aristocratic preference and patriotic sentiment would be sufficient to explain the dominant place held by cremation in the epic tradition.

There is one unusual aspect of Homeric ritual which calls for comment. This is the custom, occasionally mentioned, of erecting a memorial mound, in effect a cenotaph, to commemorate a dead hero. Athena advises Telemachos to do this for Odysseus if his death away from home is confirmed (*Odyssey* 1, 289–92). Menelaos raised a mound for Agamemnon in Egypt on hearing of his death (*Odyssey* 4, 584). If we look to archaeology for a parallel we find at least one Mycenaean tomb generally thought to be a cenotaph.[40] This is tomb 2 at Dendra, a chamber tomb of LH IIIB date. A pit near the entrance was full of bronze vessels. Two other pits were in the inner part of the chamber, one empty and the second full of animal bones. There was a hearth or altar by the wall at the back, and extensive traces of ash, but no signs of any human bones or any evidence that the tomb had been used for an interment. The excavator, A. W. Persson, interpreted the tomb as a cenotaph, and this has been generally accepted.[41] No other certain example of a cenotaph is at present known from the succeeding centuries down to Homer's day, so there is a distinct possibility that his tradition here displays a memory of a Mycenaean custom.

Perhaps the closest archaeological parallel to Homeric ritual is provided by recent excavations in the necropolis of Salamis in Cyprus.[42] The large size of many of the tombs makes them conspicuous monuments, and their chambers had usually been plundered long before the recent campaign of excavation was undertaken. By making a thorough search of the approaches to the tombs Dr Dikaios and Dr Karageorghis discovered many remarkable objects that had been overlooked by the tomb robbers, and were able to reconstruct in detail the ritual of the interments. Burial customs previously unknown in Cyprus were thus documented, and shown to go back to about 750 BC.

The normal pattern was as follows. The corpse was conveyed to the tomb on a chariot drawn by horses. The animals were slaughtered while still yoked to the vehicle, and left lying as they fell in the sloping approach passage (*dromos*) that led down to the stone-built, rectangular tomb chamber. Sheep and cattle were also sacrificed, and in one case (tomb 2) human skeletons were found in the earth fill of the *dromos*. The excavators believe them to be the remains of slaves killed and buried with their master. They compare them with the twelve Trojans killed by Achilles at the funeral of Patroklos. The corpse was cremated on a pyre in the *dromos*, and the remains were then collected, deposited in an urn or amphora, and interred in the tomb chamber. Finally, the *dromos* was filled in with earth, and a tumulus was raised over the whole grave. In some cases large amphorae were found stacked against the sides of the *dromos*. They were probably containers for olive-oil and honey, and one amphora actually carried the inscription 'of olive-oil'. Again, the parallel with the obsequies of Patroklos is close and striking. The combination of details in the ritual indicates, as J. N. Coldstream remarks, that 'the tombs were built for Greek Cypriot princes, whose burials were conducted with strict attention to Mycenaean precedent as described by Homer'.[43]

Was this a survival, or a revival, of ancient custom? In the classical period Cyprus was noted for the survival of customs and cultural features that had disappeared from the rest of the Greek world. Among these archaic aspects of Cypriot life were the use of chariots in warfare and the recording of inscriptions in syllabic script. Could Cypriot conservatism have preserved through the Dark Age a funeral ritual brought to the island by Mycenaean refugees in the twelfth century? It is not out of the question, but at present the only archaeological evidence for such continuity is one eleventh-century cremation in the Royal Tomb at Kaloriziki, and that leaves a long gap to be bridged down to the earliest horse burials at Salamis in *c.* 750.

The lay-out of the Salamis tombs, with stone-built burial chamber approached by revetted *dromos*, is reminiscent of the Mycenaean *tholos* tomb. One tomb (tomb 3), dated *c.* 600, had a beehive-type dome in mud-brick, which Karageorghis suggested might be a remnant of a Mycenaean tradition in tomb architecture; but the burial chambers of the earlier tombs are roofed with flat slabs. There is also the difference that *tholos* burials were by inhumation, whereas cremation is the rule in the Salamis interments. On balance,

Top: A file of soldiers on the Warrior Vase found by Schliemann at Mycenae, and dated c. 1200 BC. It gives a useful glimpse of the arms and armour of Achaean soldiers roughly contemporary with the Trojan War. Bottom: A fragmentary silver rhyton (with gold rim) from Shaft Grave IV, Mycenae, sixteenth century BC. The repoussé reliefs show a battle by a walled city. Note the olive trees above, the excited women on the terrace, and the helmeted figure below, apparently poling a boat towards land.

Sophie Schliemann wearing a diadem and other jewellery from the great treasure hoard found by Schliemann at Hisarlik.

One of Schliemann's own photographs of the 'Treasure of Priam', as he called it. In fact, it is a hoard of precious objects from Troy II in the third millennium BC.

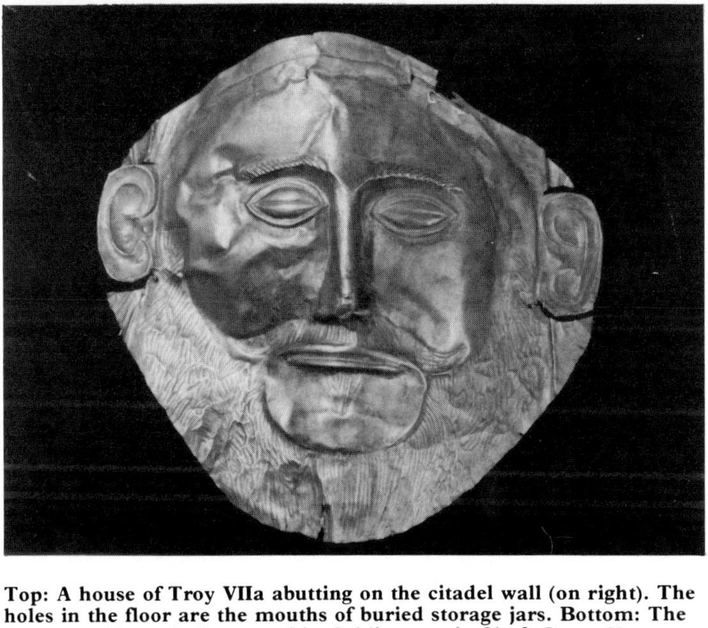

Top: A house of Troy VIIa abutting on the citadel wall (on right). The holes in the floor are the mouths of buried storage jars. Bottom: The famous gold mask discovered by Schliemann in Shaft Grave V at Mycenae, and 'recognized' by him as the face of Agamemnon.

Top: An aerial view of the citadel of Mycenae. The Lion Gate is to the left, with Grave Circle A inside the wall, and the palace on the summit. Bottom: The 'Throne Room' at Knossos as reconstructed in the final phase of the palace in the fifteenth century BC. The 'throne' is original, the griffin frieze a copy of that found on the walls in 1900.

A party of visitors at the Lion Gate after it had been cleared by Schliemann. Right: The dromos and entrance of the 'Treasury of Atreus'. The door was flanked by engaged columns of green marble, large portions of which are now in the British Museum. The 'relieving triangle' over was probably faced with a carved slab of limestone.

Top: Part of a battle scene from an eighth-century Attic vase. An oared galley is manoeuvring close in to shore while warriors engage in fighting with spear, sword and bow. Bottom: The bathroom adjoining the Queen's megaron at Pylos. Water and oil containers stood on the stand in the far corner.

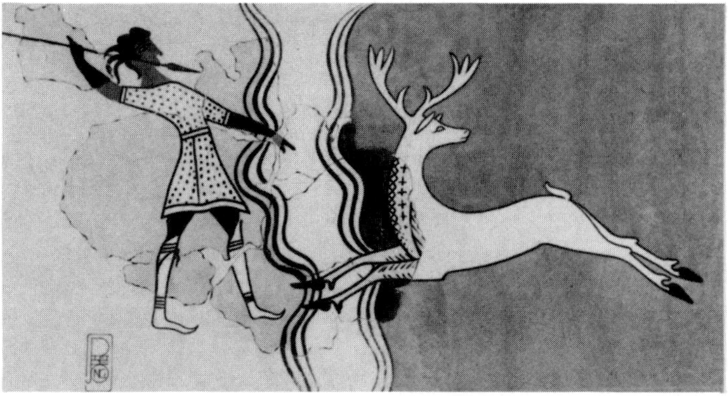

Top: A hunting fresco from the palace at Pylos. The hunter appears to be wearing white greaves laced at knee and ankle. Bottom: A scene from the temple of Ramesses III at Medinet Habu commemmorating his defeat of the invading Sea Peoples. Warriors with feathered head-coverings tumble from their galley before the Egyptian onslaught.

Top: Silver cup from Mycenae decorated with inlaid heads in gold and niello. A similar head detached from its setting was found at Pylos, indicating a thirteenth-century BC date for this piece. Below: The first Linear B tablet found at Pylos. It is a muster-list of rowers to be sent to Pleuron in Aetolia. Lines 2 to 5 give (left) the place of origin of each group, and (right) the numbers (one stroke per man).

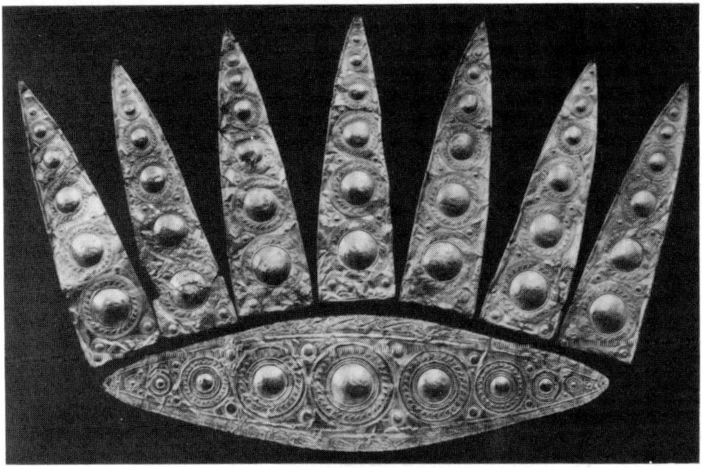

Top: A gold diadem from Shaft Grave III, Mycenae. The pieces will have been mounted on a backing of leather or fabric. Bottom: A bronze statuette of a hoplite from Dodona, c. 500 BC. He is brandishing a spear (lost), and wears a 'Corinthian' helmet, bell-shaped cuirasss, and greaves.

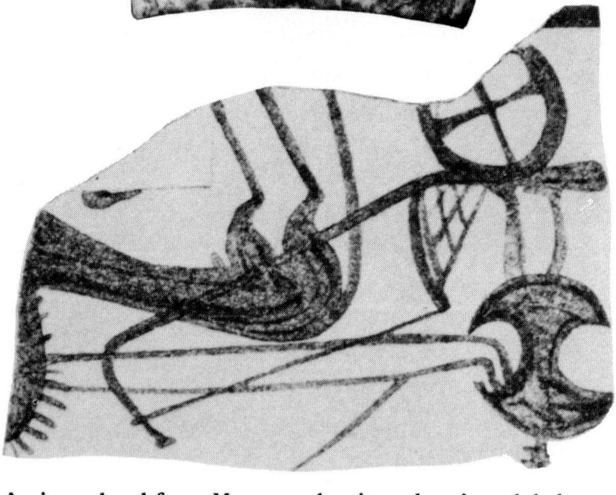

Top: An ivory head from Mycenae showing a boar's tusk helmet with back-piece and chin-strap. Bottom: A Late Geometric chariot. The warrior is helmeted and carries a Dipylon shield.

Top: A Late Geometric Boeotian statuette of a chariot with shield-bearing warrior and charioteer. Bottom: Mycenaean chariot from a Pylos fresco.

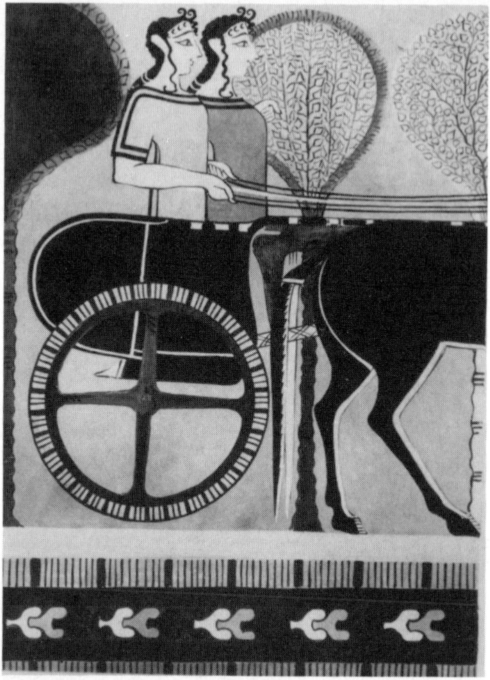

Top: Ladies driving out into the country in a gaily painted two-horse chariot. From a Tiryns palace fresco. Bottom: A remarkable scene embossed in relief on the neck of a seventh-century pithos from Mykonos. The Greek warriors appear to be lowering weapons from the inside of the Wooden Horse. It is not clear whether the warriors outside are Greeks who have emerged, or Trojans escorting the Horse into the city.

Top: The South Gate of Troy VI, probably the 'Dardanian Gate' of Homer. The masonry on the left is the flanking tower. Much of the masonry on the right dates from Roman Ilium. Bottom: An Assyrian siege engine of the eighth century. A battering ram mounted on wheels is breaching a city wall under covering fire from archers.

A view of Ithaca looking north from the summit of Mount Aetos. Right: The entrance to the main shrine of the Oracle of the Dead at Mesopotamos, Epirus. The fine Hellenistic masonry is remarkably well preserved.

Top: A bronze cauldron stand on wheels, from Cyprus. The group of musicians are playing instruments typical of the Levant. Bottom: Eighth-century nobles in a four-horse chariot: a figure scene from a Late Geometric Athenian neck-amphora.

Menelaos (on left) duelling with Hector over the corpse of Euphorbos. They are shown as typical Greek hoplites with blazoned shields. One of the earliest vase scenes to give the names of the contestants, c. 625 BC. Right: Chariot-crater from Enkomi in Cyprus. The central scene shows a god (Zeus?) standing before the departing warrior holding in his hands the scales of destiny which will decide the warrior's fate (compare *Iliad* 22, 209-13).

it seems more likely that the ritual of the Salamis interments was not an indigenous survival from the heroic past, but was developed under the influence of new arrivals from Greece. Pottery found in the *dromos* and chamber of the earliest tomb is thought to be of Euboean origin and to date from the mid-eighth century. At about the same date, Euboean colonists on Ischia were cremating their dead and covering the remains of the pyre with a cairn of stones. It rather looks as if the Euboeans on their overseas ventures were propagating a type of burial ritual analogous to that described in Homer. This is not necessarily to suggest that our *Iliad* and *Odyssey* were known in Cyprus as early as 750. We have seen reason to think that the cremation-cum-tumulus ritual featured in the epic tradition from a much earlier period, and earlier epic poetry must have circulated in Cyprus, perhaps prompting a Cypriot princeling to emulate the heroes in his burial rites. Then, with the fashion established, later and grander royal interments may have been ever more closely modelled on a canonical description like that of the funeral of Patroklos in the *Iliad*.

5 Weapons and warfare[1]

The elaborate battle scenes of the *Iliad* furnish us with a wealth of detail on the equipment of the heroes. Descriptions of weaponry must always have been a major preoccupation of the oral poet; the stock of traditional formulae is exceptionally rich and includes some very ancient phrases. For example, the epithet *arguroelos*, 'with silver rivets' or 'silver-studded', is commonly used to describe a sword. The archaeological evidence indicates that this formula almost certainly originated in the early Mycenaean period. A number of swords and daggers with *silver-headed* copper rivets for fastening the blade to the hilt were found in the Shaft Graves at Mycenae. Rivets with gold-plated heads are more common, both in the Shaft Graves and in later Mycenaean contexts, but some weapons continued to be made with the silver-headed type of rivet, for example, a dagger with an inlaid blade from Prosymna (*c.* 1450–1400). Recent metallurgical research on a dagger from Gournia (perhaps to be dated *c.* 1450), has revealed that the silver heads were bonded under pressure to the copper rivets by a sophisticated process involving temperatures of *c.* 800C°. The process is basically that used in the making of Sheffield plate, an invention usually credited to Bolsover in 1743, but now known to have been in use in Minoan Crete.[2] Such an advanced technique would tend to have been reserved for prestige weapons, and these in turn would have attracted the attention of bards, leading to the coinage of the formula *phasganon* (or *xiphos*) *arguroelon*.[3] It has been observed that *chrysoelon*, 'gold-plated', will not scan in a hexameter, but the memory of gold-headed rivets was not unknown to the Homeric poems for Agamemnon once arms himself with a sword in which 'gold rivets glittered' (*Iliad* 11, 29–30), though elsewhere (e.g., *Iliad* 2, 45) he wears the standard silver-studded sword. After the end of the Mycenaean age there are no examples of swords with hilt studs of precious metal until the seventh century when silver-studded swords reappear in royal graves in Cyprus. At this date it is quite possible that Cypriot custom was being influenced *by* the Homeric poems (as was suggested for the burial ritual, above). At all events the formula cannot have originated as late as this, and, on present evidence, must be referred back to a time well before the Trojan War.

Another familiar formula that is probably ancient is 'well-greaved Achaeans'. Bowra has reviewed the evidence for greaves in the Mycenaean period.[4] He notes that they are not shown in representations of warriors from the Shaft Grave period, but become common in the thirteenth century, especially on vases from Mycenae. Their introduction is plausibly associated with the change from an earlier large body-shield to a smaller and less cumbersome type of round shield. The body-shield reached from head to foot and protected the shins; the introduction of the smaller shield made some form of leggings very desirable. The epithet 'well-greaved' would have lacked point unless the wearing of greaves served to distinguish the Mycenaean warrior from his contemporaries. In fact, Late Bronze Age soldiers from Egypt or Syria are never depicted with greaves, whereas no Late Mycenaean representation of warriors shows them without greaves.

In the era of hoplite fighting after 700 bronze greaves became standard equipment.[5] It has been suggested that the phrase 'Achaeans with *bronze* greaves', which occurs only once (*Iliad* 7, 41), may be a late importation, influenced by hoplite conditions. But recent finds have rendered such a supposition unnecessary. Specimens of Mycenaean greaves in bronze are now known, notably from the Dendra warrior tomb *c.* 1400, and from Enkomi in Cyprus. The finds encourage the belief that the Achaean champions wore metal greaves, and these would have been a good and distinctive addition to their body armour. The rank and file may have had to make do with less durable materials, and the close-fitting black leggings shown on the Warrior Vase are commonly supposed to be of leather. But, as Bowra notes, the spear-points are painted the same colour, so black may represent bronze in both cases. A fresco from the megaron at Mycenae shows a falling warrior attired in white greaves. Here the colour perhaps indicates padded linen, but tin, or bronze plated with tin, is another possibility.[6] It is odd that the Linear B tablets contain no ideogram, and apparently no word, for greaves, but the same is true for shields.

A striking proof of the antiquity of the weapons tradition is afforded by the description of a special type of helmet in the *Iliad*, Book 10. Odysseus is about to go on a night patrol with Diomedes to gain information about the dispositions and plans of the Trojan forces:

> He set on his head a helmet made of ox-hide; inside, it was made of thongs tightly strained and on the outside the tusks of a white-toothed boar, thick-set, ran in contrary directions, well and skilfully set, and in between a cap of felt was fitted.
>
> *Iliad* 10, 261–5
> (translation by H. L. Lorimer)

The function of the felt, as Miss Lorimer says, was to provide 'a soft, smooth, and pliant backing' to which the slivers of tusk could be attached with less fear of their splitting. Reichel was the first to connect this description with the perforated plates of boar's tusk that have been found on many Greek mainland sites in contexts dating mainly from the LH I and LH II periods.[7] It is generally accepted that such plates are the remains of helmets of the type described in Homer. The arrangement 'in contrary directions' may be seen on representations like the boar's tusk helmet vase from Katsamba, or the two ivory heads from Mycenae, or the ivory plaque from Delos. Each plate retained the curve of the tusk from which it was cut, and the plates were set in rows with the crescent facing alternately right and left. It is estimated that between forty and eighty pairs of tusks would have been needed for one helmet. They must therefore have been prized possessions of men of eminence. An elaborate 'pedigree' is supplied for the piece worn by Odysseus. His maternal grandfather Autolykos is said to have acquired it by rifling the 'compact house' of the Boeotian Amyntor (did he rob a *tholos* tomb?), and from him it went through various hands to the Cretan Meriones who lent it to Odysseus (*Iliad* 10, 266–70). Specimens have been found dating back to the Middle Helladic period. It used to be thought that the boar's tusk helmet went out of fashion after 1400, but several warriors are depicted wearing it on the Pylos frescoes (*c.* 1200), and a specimen is now known from the twelfth century.[8]

Apart from the tusks, the materials of such helmets were perishable. It is very unlikely that any Greek in the Dark Age would have had the materials or the incentive to construct one, and no specimen can have survived intact down to Homer's day. The *Iliad* can only have received the picture from the oral tradition, a picture transmitted with remarkable fidelity for upwards of 400 years.[9]

An interesting parallel may be found in the oral traditions of the Congo. There the Kuba people still remember a tradition of invading white men wearing garments of 'soft iron'. This memory derives from the coats of mail worn by Portuguese invaders, and must go back 400 years at least, for the Portuguese ceased to wear such coats early in the sixteenth century. The unusual detail caught the imagination of the tribesmen, and was preserved in a paradoxical formula that must now be unintelligible to them.[10]

Similar considerations apply in the case of an archaic type of shield well illustrated on the Lion Hunt dagger from the Shaft Graves, and familiar as a decorative motif in Minoan art. This was a shield of ox-hide large enough to shelter a man from head to foot. It sometimes took a rectangular shape with a curved upper rim, the so-called 'tower' shield; more often it resembled a 'figure-of-eight' in outline. The hide was stretched over a simple frame of wooden batons. The shield was slung from the left shoulder by a leather strap (*telamon*) and it must have been awkward to manipulate, but it did obviate the need for a corslet or greaves. A warrior armed with a long thrusting spear could manoeuvre close to an opponent behind its shelter. Most of the representations of the body-shield in use come from the objects found in the Shaft Graves. It seems that, like the silver-studded sword, the body-shield was a piece of equipment that became obsolete by about 1400. It was superseded by a much smaller shield with a central hand-grip, which gained in mobility what it lost in overall protection. This type of shield was usually round in shape, and was also slung by a strap from the shoulder so that it could be dropped to leave both hands free to brandish spears. Made of overlapping circles of leather, and sometimes reinforced with a bronze boss or bosses, it remained in use for centuries until the change-over to the hoplite panoply after *c.* 700. In this panoply the shield was the most distinctive feature. Made of wood or hide with a bronze facing or blazon, it was fitted with an interior band through which the left forearm was passed and the hand-grip was *on the rim*.

Most of what Homer says about shields can be related to the simple targe which remained in use from the Late Mycenaean period through the Dark Age and down to the end of the Geometric period. Standard epithets like 'bossed' and 'well-rounded' fit it well, and its material is emphasized in the soldiers' slang that dubbed it 'leather' and 'ox'. But there is one description that is quite inappropriate, namely, the epithet 'reaching to the feet', which is uniquely applied to the shield of a certain Periphetes (*Iliad* 15, 646). Obviously this epithet is appropriate only to the man-covering body-shield of early Mycenaean times, and the context requires that such a shield be envisaged. Periphetes, significantly a native of Mycenae, became a victim of

Hector by an unfortunate accident.[11] He tripped over the rim of his shield and fell on his back inside the shield. Lying thus, like a beetle with legs in the air, he was quite defenceless against Hector's spear. Presumably Periphetes was shifting his body-shield to cover his back prior to a retreat when the accident happened. In an earlier passage (*Iliad* 6, 116–18) Hector has successfully completed such a manoeuvre, for as he moves away from the battlefield 'the dark skin [*i.e.*, the rim of his leather body-shield] struck against his ankles and his neck'.

Reminiscences of the ancient body-shield are probably to be detected in some other isolated passages and phrases. In a clash between Deiphobus and Idomeneus, the poet emphasizes that the latter was *completely concealed* behind his shield (*Iliad* 13, 405–8). Again, Ajax, believed on other grounds to be a very ancient saga figure, is three times described as 'bearing a shield like a tower' (*Iliad* 7, 219; 11, 485; 17, 128), a formula that may well have been devised originally for the body-shield.

Metal body-armour

Before World War II there was virtually no archaeological evidence for body-armour of metal in the Mycenaean age. The only exception, a fragmentary bronze greave from Enkomi in Cyprus, dated *c.* 1200, did not seem to provide a basis for inference about mainland Greek practice. But the picture has been materially altered by a series of important discoveries in the post-war period. In 1951 a bronze helmet dating from *c.* 1400 was found in a tomb near Knossos, and in 1957 a Submycenaean bronze helmet was found at Tiryns. In 1953 a pair of bronze greaves, closely similar in design to the Enkomi fragment, was recovered from a LH III grave in Achaea (near Kallithea). Yet these discoveries were outshone in importance by a remarkable find in the necropolis at Dendra in the Argolid in 1960. The Graeco-Swedish expedition excavated a LH II grave (tomb 12) which yielded a suit of bronze armour consisting of the following parts:[12]

Two 'shells' that could be laced together to form a solid metal corslet covering the body of the warrior (the Homeric *guala*).[13]
Two shoulder guards, attachable to the 'shells' by small semicircular metal hoops.
Two arm shields attached to the under part of the shoulder guards.
Two triangular sheets of metal fastened on the shell to provide extra protection for the breast.
One neck guard.
Six 'girdles', three for the front and three for the back (perhaps the Homeric *zosteres* and/or *mitra*).

This discovery threw light on previous finds from other places: two decorated 'breast plates' from Shaft Grave 5 at Mycenae, and bronze plates from a tomb at Phaistos, were now seen to come from similar suits of armour. A few years later two shoulder pieces, two breast pieces, and two arm pieces turned up in a context dated somewhat later than the Dendra find. These finds, taken together with the evidence of the Knossos and Pylos tablets, confirm that metal body-armour was in common use in the Mycenaean world over a period of several centuries.[14]

The new evidence has completely transformed our understanding of the equipment available to a Mycenaean warrior, and has rendered obsolete much previous discussion of Homeric passages, particularly on the problem of the corslet. Where *metal* corslets are explicit, or implicit, in the Homeric account, it is no longer necessary to suspect the presence of late interpolations.[15] On the contrary, it can now be seen that the tradition of the bronze-clad hero is ancient and authentic, with its roots going right back to the Mycenaean world.[16]

The skirt-like attachments of the Dendra corslet could be the original of the epic *mitra* several times mentioned as part of the body-armour of Menelaos, and explicitly said to have been made by bronzesmiths (*Iliad* 4, 137, 187, and 216).[17] The expression 'double-corslet' (*Iliad* 4, 133 *et al.*)

may also have originated from the reinforcements on the breast-plate of the Dendra-type corslet.

The full panoply of the Homeric warrior is set out in a stock passage which is repeated (with variations) four times when major heroes arm for battle.[18] The equipment is always donned in the same order: greaves, corslet, sword, shield, helmet; finally, the warrior picks up his spear(s), and is ready for combat. Greaves are put on first while the warrior can still bend down to fasten them unencumbered by other items. Sword and shield are suspended by belts over the shoulders, and so are put on before the helmet. Practical considerations determine the order, but history has helped to mould the details. The sword is 'silver-studded', recalling early Mycenaean weaponry (above, p. 114). But the variation whereby two spears are taken instead of one reflects a change in methods of fighting dating from the Early Iron Age. The single *thrusting* spear was the offensive weapon *par excellence* in the Mycenaean period. In the Geometric period the preferred equipment was a pair of *throwing* spears. This latter mode of combat tends to dominate the fighting throughout the *Iliad*. In one of the arming passages it is instructively conflated with the older method, as Kirk has pointed out.[19] Patroklos is putting on Achilles's armour, but he refrains from taking the spear 'heavy, large, sturdy', which only Achilles could wield. This massive weapon is the old Mycenaean thrusting spear here remembered in a significant context. Instead, Patroklos takes 'two stout spears that fitted the palm of his hand' (*Iliad* 16, 139–41). This formula was originally devised for the single spear. We find it in its original form in the arming of Paris: 'he took his stout spear that fitted the palm of his hand' (*Iliad* 3, 338). It is adapted with the minimum of change to the preparations of Patroklos, but one can see that it is less appropriate to say that two spears fit the palm of the hand. This is an instructive example of how the tradition clung to the old facts and resisted change of formula, allowing only the minimum alterations to take account of new conditions.

In the *Frogs* of Aristophanes (1034–6), Aeschylus is made to praise Homer for his worthy instruction in martial skills including troop placing (*taxis*) and arming for battle (*hoplisis*). This is special pleading; Homer may be good for morale, but he is a poor teacher of the art of war. His battle scenes are full of threatenings and slaughterings, and convey with impressive vigour the stress and horror of hand-to-hand conflict, but they give no clear picture of how troops were marshalled and weapons handled. Chariots rush in to battle, masses of infantry are deployed, champions advance brandishing spears, arrows fly, sword clashes on helmet, but most engagements lack discipline, clarity, and ordered purpose. Perhaps Homer meant to show war in this way, but it is also clear that he is working within a tradition that was conventional, selective, and conservative. Stock epithets tend to generality: spears are 'sturdy', swords 'sharp', shields 'tough' and 'well-rounded', helmets 'fitted with bronze'. Patterns of conflict are stylized and arbitrary: for instance, a Greek hero on foot often kills two Trojans in a chariot, but only once is this feat attributed to a Trojan. Nothing of historical value can be gleaned from such data as these. Occasionally, as we have seen, an epithet or description is distinctive enough for it to be related to objects revealed by archaeology. Inconsistencies can sometimes be explained as due to the welding of earlier and later customs into an artificial amalgam. There is also another formative factor of considerable importance – the aristocratic bias of epic poetry which tends to select situations in which the qualities of the individual hero can be displayed to best advantage. Homer does not give us a simple picture of warfare as waged at any one epoch. The complexities of his presentation will be apparent from a consideration of two distinct aspects of warfare, archery and chariot fighting.

Archery and the bow in the Homeric poems

Archery plays only a minor part in the fighting in the *Iliad*. The rank and file on both sides use bows (*e.g.*, *Iliad* 15, 313–14; 16, 773), and the shooting of arrows by anonymous bowmen is an incidental detail in a number of battle scenes, but it is never suggested that the fusillades have any effect on the course of the fighting. The major heroes scorn the use of the bow. Diomedes voices the approved attitude when Paris wounds him in the foot with an arrow:

You archer, foul fighter, lovely in your locks, eyer of young girls!
If you were to make trial of me in strong combat with weapons
your bow would do you no good at all, nor your close-showered arrows . . .
this is the blank weapon of a useless man, no fighter.

Iliad 11, 385 ff.
(translation by R. Lattimore)

The ideal warrior is the spearman fighting at close quarters and standing his ground in the *mêlée*. In keeping with this attitude, the poet depicts only lesser heroes as bowmen. Though Paris favours the bow, he does fight with a spear in his duel with Menelaos (*Iliad* 3, 340 ff.) Helenos pits his bow and arrows against Menelaos's spear and comes off the worse (*Iliad* 13, 581 ff.). The notorious Pandaros fights only with the bow; it is he who treacherously wounds Menelaos in contravention of the agreed truce (*Iliad* 4, 104 ff.). Teukros is the leading archer on the Greek side, but even he arms himself with helmet, shield, and spear after his bowstring breaks (*Iliad* 8, 266 ff.; 15, 442 ff.). In the archery contest at the funeral games of Patroklos (*Iliad* 23, 859 ff.) he is unexpectedly defeated by Meriones who, with one exception (*Iliad* 13, 650–2), always figures as a spearman. However, the bow must have been traditionally associated with him for he lends one to Odysseus for his night mission in the Doloneia (*Iliad* 10, 260). Perhaps, as Miss Lorimer suggests, his defeat of Teukros is 'a tribute to the acknowledged superiority of Cretan bowmanship'.

Archaeological evidence suggests that Cretan expertise in archery has a long history stretching well back into the Bronze Age. The so-called 'composite' bow is featured occasionally in Minoan art from MM III onwards, but is never depicted in the art of mainland Greece. The composite bow was much more powerful than the 'simple' (or 'self') bow represented in the Shaft Grave finds (but not thereafter in Mycenaean art). The simple bow was made entirely of wood, either from a single stave, or from two or more jointed pieces. It was easily strained or cracked by excessive bending. The composite bow was much more complicated in construction, its wooden staves being reinforced with horn and sinew.

Over two dozen specimens of composite bows survive from ancient Egypt, and one of these, now in the Brooklyn Museum, has been published in illuminating detail.[20] The central core consists of a piece of reddish brown wood extending unbroken through its length from tip to tip (1.372 m.), and reinforced at the centre by a much shorter piece of wood (.34 m.) with a marked double taper. Bevelled wooden side strips, slightly greater in width than the core, run on each side of it, producing by their overlap a shallow channel or groove on the front and back of the bow. In the inner groove a layer of yellowish horn about 3 mm. thick is still in position. Its outer face has been carefully planed down, the marks of the file still being visible. The filling of the outer groove is not so well preserved; it may have consisted partly of horn and partly of another strip of wood giving a laminated construction. There are traces of animal sinew as a binding to reinforce the hand-grip. In its unstrung state the bow has a marked 'elbow' in the centre, giving it a typical 'reflex' profile.

The composite bow was an Asiatic invention, and was doubtless introduced into Bronze Age Crete as a result of her contacts with Syria and Egypt.[21] The addition of the horn gave great flexibility and 'weight' to the weapon, but made it much less easy to string.

The only detailed description of a bow in Homer is of the bow of Pandaros (*Iliad* 4, 105–11), and it is not very informative or balanced. Four lines are devoted to the hunting of the goat whose great horns 'sixteen palms long' provided the raw material, and only two lines to the actual fashioning:

> and them [*i.e.*, the horns] a craftsman skilled in horn polishing prepared and fitted, and having smoothed all well added a golden tip.

Did Homer understand what he was talking about? An uncharitable interpretation would be that the poet thought of the bow as simply consisting of the two horns joined by a 'bridge'. Such a construction would be totally impractical – no man could bend it. On the other hand, the quoted lines do suggest some knowledge of the most distinctive and difficult aspect of the manufacture of a composite bow, namely, the cutting, shaping, fitting, and planing of the strip of horn (keratin).

An incidental detail shows that the famous bow of Odysseus is also to be thought of as a composite bow. When the suitors have tried and failed to string the 'bent-back' (*i.e.*, reflex) bow, it is passed to Odysseus who inspects and tests it carefully in case 'the horn might be worm-eaten' (*Odyssey* 21, 395). After satisfying himself that all is in sound condition, he then strings it 'without exertion', as easily as a musician strings his lyre. Did Homer know the trick, or is he glossing over his ignorance with an attractive smile? A composite bow cannot be strung by the pull of the arms alone. The archer must *squat* with the bow braced over one thigh and under the other knee. Some of those who tried and failed, for example Telemachos and Leodes, are explicitly said to have *stood up* for their attempt (124 and 149). Odysseus, on the other hand, is seated when he receives the bow, and is seated when he shoots the arrow through the axes (420). The implication is that he strung the bow without getting to his feet, knowing the knack of handling a weapon unfamiliar to the suitors. The scene required that the bow should be unusual and that Odysseus should be an exceptionally skilful archer, and we have been prepared for both these points. At the court of Alkinoös, Odysseus boasts that he was the best archer of those who went to Troy with the exception of Philoktetes (*Odyssey* 8, 215ff.). He admits, however, that men of former times like Herakles and Eurytos were superior performers. Later (21, 11 ff.) we learn that the great bow had once belonged to Eurytos, and that his son gifted it to Odysseus.

The picture of Odysseus as a skilled archer is confined to the *Odyssey*, and may be part of the legacy of Cretan influence that has coloured the poem at various points.[22] In the *Iliad* Odysseus always fights as a spearman, and never gives any indication of prowess with the bow. For the night patrol he borrows a bow from the Cretan Meriones, and uses it to whip horses (*Iliad* 10, 260 and 513–14)! This is in conformity with the general tendency of the tradition to associate archery either with heroes older than those of the Trojan War or with foreigners. Such a perspective is not inconsistent with the archaeological data. The Mycenaeans must have known about the composite Asiatic bow, either from their contacts with Asia Minor and the Levant or through Crete, and yet this more efficient type of bow never became naturalized on the Greek mainland. It is never represented in Mycenaean art, and even the simple bow does not appear after the Shaft Grave period. The importance of the bow may really have declined by the time of the Trojan War.[23]

The subsequent history of archery in Greek lands is not easy to determine. Arrowheads are almost completely absent from the Greek mainland during the Protogeometric and Early Geometric periods. In Crete, on the other hand, they continue to occur in some quantity, and a Bronze Age type persists. To judge from scenes on Late

Geometric vases, archery increased in importance in Greek warfare during the course of the eighth century, and Crete may have been the source from which it was reintroduced as an effective mode of combat.[24] But this eighth-century development will have come too late to have much effect on the epic tradition. Eighth-century practice may have contributed some colour to Homer's general picture of archery in battle scenes, but the association of the bow with heroes like Herakles, Paris, and Odysseus, must go back to a much earlier date.

The use of chariots

The tablets reveal something of the realities of chariot power in the Mycenaean world. The ruler of Knossos had at his disposal more than 400 chariots, though some may have been for ceremonial use only. The king of Pylos too had his chariots.[25] Wheels, bodies, and harness were manufactured in workshops adjacent to the palace, and stored in arsenals. At Knossos a series of 140 tablets was found in a small archive room in the west wing of the palace, and has been identified by Chadwick as the 'muster roll of a chariot brigade: each tablet records a man's name, a chariot complete with wheels, a cuirass, and a pair of horses'.[26] Some of the ideograms used by the scribes to depict these cuirasses are strikingly similar to the Dendra corslet (above, p. 119). On some tablets an ingot ideogram has been substituted for a corslet idoegram, probably indicating, as Sir Arthur Evans supposed, that an issue of bronze was made in lieu of the corslet itself. It seems that the king of a well-organized Mycenaean kingdom was able to put into the field a mobile striking force of chariotry. The well-armoured fighting men mounted in their chariots and squired by their drivers would tend to constitute a warrior élite. It is reasonable to equate them with the Followers who appear to have a privileged position in the Pylian armed forces (above, p. 87), and who are known to have possessed chariots.

This type of organization seems to have been developed

before 1500 in Syria and Asia Minor, notably by the Mitanni and the Hittites, and was copied by the Egyptians. At the battle of Megiddo (1479) the Pharaoh Tuthmosis III captured 924 chariots from the kings of Megiddo and Kadesh.[27] The function of the chariots was to break the enemy line by massed charges, and to pursue and cut down fugitives. The Hittite chariot fighters used thrusting spears, while the Egyptians developed the chariot as a mobile platform for archers. Reliefs of the battle of Kadesh (1288) at Abu Simbel show Hittite chariots with spearmen charging the Egyptian lines and then succumbing to a barrage of arrows.

The first representations of the chariot in Greece come from the Shaft Graves, and the rise of Mycenae has been attributed to the introduction of this new military arm from Asia Minor. A well-known document from the Hittite archives, the Tawagalavas letter, indicates that Achaean princes learnt their driving drill from the Hittites.[28] Possession of a chariot must have served to mark off noble from commoner. The chariot was used for hunting, for travel on the Mycenaean road system, and gave its owner a privileged position in the fighting forces. Chariot murals adorned the palaces at Mycenae, Tiryns and Pylos. As Emily Vermeule says: 'the use of the horse and the expensive chariot squadron is particularly associated with aristocratic militarism in the Bronze Age.'[29]

After the breakdown of the palace-centred system, chariot brigades presumably ceased to be maintained on the scale attested by the tablets, but chariots must have continued in use at least until the end of the Mycenaean world. LH IIIC sherds from Mycenae and Tiryns show warriors in chariots.[30] After that, representational evidence for chariots in Greece ceases until the Late Geometric period.

Did the chariot continue in use on the Greek mainland during the Dark Age, and did it accompany the colonists to Ionia? Miss Lorimer believes that the chariot persisted without essential change from the Mycenaean period onwards. She points out that when it emerges to view again in Geometric art it still shows three typical features of the Mycenaean vehicle: the four-spoked wheel, the central position of the axle, and a pole support (wooden bar or thong) running from the front rail to the yoke end of the pole. Snodgrass thinks it more likely that the earlier eighth-century pictures of chariots were not drawn from life, but represent the 'heroic chariot' as imagined by the artists. The typical features just mentioned could, he thinks, have been derived either from surviving representations of Mycenaean chariots, or from contemporary four-wheeled wagons. Only in the late eighth century was the chariot reintroduced to Greece, and then for racing and processions, not warfare.[31]

In general, we may note that the technique of shipbuilding survived the Mycenaean collapse, and so may the art of chariot making. Chariot racing became a recognized event in the Olympic Games early in the seventh century, indicating that the possession and use of chariots must have been widespread in Greece for at least a generation or two beforehand. Indeed, familiarity with chariots in the eighth century is strongly suggested by the references to them in Homeric similes (*Iliad* 22, 22–3; 23, 517–21; *Odyssey* 13, 81–3). The hypothesis that the aristocracy maintained the use of chariots in unbroken succession from Mycenaean times seems more likely than the hypothesis of discontinuity and reintroduction.

The evidence of the *Iliad* on the chariot must be interpreted against this background. No major battle scene lacks a reference to the massing of chariot squadrons,[32] although there is virtually no account of any concerted action by these squadrons. No chariot charge is ever made by the Greeks, and only one mass attack by the Trojan chariots is described, and that briefly (*Iliad* 15, 352–5). References to individual chariots fall into the same general pattern. With two notable exceptions,[33] all the major heroes on both sides ride to battle in chariots, but clashes between chariots are very rare. Miss Lorimer went so far as to assert that 'no clash of chariots is described in Homer', but this is incorrect. There is an elaborate incident in Book 8 of the *Iliad* (78 ff.) in which Nestor gets into difficulties when one of his horses is killed by an arrow. Hector in his chariot is bearing down on him, but Diomedes rescues him, takes him into his own chariot, and counterattacks Hector, killing his charioteer. Later in the same book (8, 256 ff.) Diomedes, from his chariot, kills a Trojan warrior who is also in a chariot.[34]

Normally the major heroes drive into the fray in their chariots and then dismount to fight on foot. It is the mark of a second-class fighter to remain in his chariot. Inferior Trojans often do so, and become the prey of a Greek hero on foot, who kills one or both of the occupants of an opposing chariot. This feat is performed three times in quick succession by Agamemnon (*Iliad* 11, 91–147). I have noted only two cases where the victim in this pattern of combat is a Greek.[35] While the warrior is out of his chariot, it is the duty of the driver to keep the vehicle close at hand, ready to convey him to safety if he sustains a wound or comes up against superior forces.

Some writers have doubted the feasibility of such tactics, and Rhys Carpenter went so far as to state that 'Homer did not know what battle-chariots were for.'[36] But proof that chariots could be, and were, used in the way described is provided by Caesar's account of Celtic chariot tactics as encountered by his forces in the invasion of Britain. He says:

> Their manner of fighting from chariots is as follows: first they drive all over the battlefield hurling their weapons, and frequently throw the enemy ranks into confusion by the terrifying sight of their horses and the noise of the chariot wheels. Then, when they have infiltrated into the cavalry squadrons, they leap down from their chariots and fight on foot. Meanwhile their charioteers withdraw a little from the battle and station the chariots so that the warriors may have a convenient retreat to their own forces if many of the enemy

bear down on them. In this way they combine in battle the mobility of cavalry and the stability of infantry.

Gallic War IV, 33

Diodorus compares this Celtic mode of warfare to that used by 'the ancient Greek heroes in the Trojan War'.[37] The parallel is indeed close, and justifies J. K. Anderson's verdict that 'Homeric chariot tactics are not purely fantastic and imaginary'.[38] On Mycenaean vases close in date to the Trojan War, warriors armed with shields and spears are shown riding in chariots. Now the newly published Battle Fresco from Pylos includes a chariot from which a warrior armed with spear and boar's tusk helmet has just dismounted.[39]

Homer's descriptions are mostly confined to the forays of individual chariots, but one or two passages indicate that his tradition goes back to the palace period when chariot squadrons were in use. In the Catalogue the Athenian leader Menestheus is described as outstanding at marshalling chariots (*Iliad* 2, 554). Again, when Nestor is marshalling his forces (*Iliad* 4, 293 ff.), he puts his charioteers in front of his infantry,[40] and orders them to keep strictly in line and to make a concerted advance until they come close enough to the opposing chariots to use their spears. 'With such tactics,' he concludes, 'the men of former days used to sack walled cities.' It is not made clear how the chariots could hope to sack Troy. Perhaps Nestor means that the squadron will be able to cut off the routed host from their city (as Patroklos does in *Iliad* 16, 394 ff.), and might hope even to rush the gates if opened to admit stragglers. At all events Nestor the 'Gerenian horseman' clearly prides himself on his expertise in chariot handling.[41] However, his approach is represented as old-fashioned, and his advice is not in fact followed, for the Greeks never perform any manœuvre of the kind he recommends.

Mention of Nestor prompts me to digress briefly from warfare to consider the remarkable drinking vessel which he brought with him to Troy. This vessel is almost certainly to be classed with the boar's tusk helmet as a Mycenaean object whose description was preserved in the epic tradition. It was

a beautifully wrought cup which the old man brought with him
from home. It was set with golden nails, the eared handles upon it
were four, and on either side there were fashioned two doves
of gold feeding, and there were double bases beneath it.
Another man with great effort could lift it full from the table
but Nestor, aged as he was, lifted it without strain.

Iliad 11, 632–7
(translation by R. Lattimore)

Pairs of doves appear on the rims of ritual vessels from Cyprus (*c.* 2600–2100),[42] but, with one exception, no cup or vessel found in Mycenaean or Early Iron Age Greece is so adorned. This exception is the celebrated Dove Cup found by Schliemann in Shaft Grave IV. Made of gold, and standing about 5 inches high, it has an unusual shape, well explained by Miss Lorimer as due to 'the mounting of the [*sc.* typical] flat-bottomed Minoan mug on a stem'. The doves may lend it some religious significance as a ceremonial chalice or loving-cup. Some authorities have been reluctant to identify it with Nestor's Cup: it is small, whereas Nestor's Cup is envisaged as very massive, and it has only two handles as against four in the Homeric description. But against these discrepancies must be set the remarkable coincidences of the doves and the 'double bases'. Whether the latter are to be equated with the side supports, or with the cup bottom and stem base, of the Shaft Grave specimen, may be disputed, but either feature is unusual, and in combination with the dove ornament make it probable that the Dove Cup is the type of vessel from which the Homeric description is ultimately derived. No other drinking vessel is described in such detail in the poems, and 'Nestor's Cup' clearly impressed itself on the Greek imagination, for a very early inscription from Ischia alludes to it. The inscription is incised on the body of a capacious clay cup of East Greek style found in a tomb, and is dated before 700.[43] The reading is somewhat disputed, but one possible restoration gives the following sense: 'Nestor had a fine drinking cup; but whoever drinks from this man's cup, at once desire for fair-crowned Aphrodite will seize him.' So this inscription, perhaps the second oldest Greek alphabetic inscription yet known, may also contain the first literary allusion to Homer's Iliad, and to a passage which recalls the gold plate of a Mycenaean palace. Thus interpreted, the Ischia cup is graphic testimony to the continuity of Greek tradition about the heroic age.

To return to the subject of chariots: in general, Trojan chariots are more prominent than Greek. The chariot squadrons are emphasized in the scene where the Trojan army bivouacs on the plain outside Troy (*Iliad* 8, 542 ff.), and the major Trojan heroes all use chariots. In contrast, two major Greek heroes, Ajax and Odysseus, never use them. There are also some anomalies in the presentation of Achilles and his chariot. Much is made of his immortal horses Xanthos and Balios, and he mourns Patroklos as his beloved charioteer (*Iliad* 16, 145–51; 23, 280); but in all the fighting that he does, from Book 20 on, there is only one allusion to his chariot (*Iliad* 20, 498–500). History may have coloured the tradition here. One would have expected the Trojans, with their wide plains and horse-breeding traditions, to have deployed strong chariot squadrons in defence of their city. The Greeks would have found it difficult, though not impossible, to transport their chariots and horses overseas. One must also take into account the Homeric preference for the duel on foot as the heroic encounter *par excellence*. In none of the major duels (Menelaos and Paris, Hector and Ajax, Achilles and Hector) are chariots even mentioned.

It seems reasonable to suppose that chariots were in use in Greek warfare in Homer's own time. On a number of Late Geometric vases, wheeled vehicles are depicted with two occupants, a warrior and a driver. The vehicles are rarely shown in actual conflict – there appear to be only two scenes of fighting from a chariot in Geometric art – but this is probably because the vase scenes are mainly concerned with funeral ritual. It is hard to believe that the chariot-owning Knights of Athens (who commissioned the vases) used their chariots only for races and processions.[44] There is a record (in a late source) of the forces of Eretria at the close of the eighth century as consisting of 3000 hoplites, 1500 cavalry, *and 60 chariots.*[45] The leading cities of Ionia at this time could also presumably muster some chariot forces as well as their cavalry. Aristotle defines the dominant Knights (*Hippeis*) of the pre-hoplite period as 'those who used horses in their wars against their neighbours', a definition that could cover chariotry as well as cavalry (*Politics* 1289, b38). With the rise of the hoplite phalanx, chariots became generally obsolete, but in Cyprus they remained in use for warfare in the classical period, and Cyrene was still using them, for military transport at least, in the Hellenistic age.

We may conclude that chariots were familiar to poets and their audiences at all stages in the formation and transmission of heroic poetry. Homer's perspective reaches back to the Mycenaean palace period with its chariot brigades, and also to the century after 1200 when Mycenaean warriors still used chariots, but not, we may suppose, in the older and more disciplined formation fighting. In the Dark Age, warfare can have amounted to little more than desultory skirmishing between isolated communities. In the ninth century, and still more in the eighth, the various cities in Greece and Asia Minor must have become organized and armed for wars on a more prolonged and serious scale. All through these centuries, the possession of a chariot would have marked off the chief or noble from the common foot-soldier. Heroic poetry that preserved the memory of Achaean chariotry in phrases like 'swift-mounted Danaans', or 'old Peleus the Knight', or 'with spear and horsemanship', would not have seemed irrelevant or obsolete. By Homer's time the well-armed infantryman was probably the decisive factor in armed conflict; he recognizes this in his preference for conflict on foot as the ultimate test of heroic valour. However, the adjuncts of chariotry are still much in evidence in battle scenes, partly as a legacy from the past, but still meaningful in terms of contemporary practice. What Homer says about chariots in warfare makes sense, and is not impractical or imaginary.[46]

In material details Homer's descriptions conform well to the Mycenaean realities. Although he knows about four-horse racing chariots (*Iliad* 11, 699 and *Odyssey* 13, 81), he admits only two-horse chariots (occasionally with a trace-horse, *e.g.*, *Iliad* 16, 466–75; cf. *Odyssey* 4, 590) to the fighting scenes and the chariot race at Patroklos's funeral. This is correct by Mycenaean practice as evidenced by the representations and the tablets. The Mycenaean chariot body was very light, consisting of a frame of bentwood covered with ox-hide or wicker-work. The floor of the car was probably made of plaited leather thongs. Some chariots were very gay in appearance, painted crimson, and inlaid with ivory. On the Pylos tablets some chariot wheels are listed as bronze-bound, and one pair as silver-bound.

All these features appear in Homer, sometimes in rather garbled form. Diomedes proposes to pick up and carry off the chariot of Rhesos (*Iliad* 10, 504–5). A stock epithet for chariots is 'well-plaited' (*Iliad* 23, 335 and 436). Hera's chariot has 'stretched thongs' though miraculously they are of gold and silver (*Iliad* 5, 727–8). Chariots generally are 'picked out with bronze' (*Iliad* 4, 226; 10, 322 and 393). The chariot of Diomedes is stiffened with gold and tin (*Iliad* 23, 503) and that of Rhesos adorned with gold and silver (*Iliad* 10, 438). Once, absurdly, reins are described as 'white with ivory' (*Iliad* 5, 583).

The battle scenes in the *Iliad* are largely constructed out of individual encounters, and are mainly designed to enhance the glory of individual warriors. In turn, various heroes dominate long stretches of the fighting, with all the emphasis on their personal prowess and success. Thus

Diomedes takes the lead in Book 5, Agamemnon in Book 11, Patroklos in Book 16, Menelaos in Book 17, and Achilles in the fighting from Book 20 on. The hero is the fighter who is brave enough to advance ahead of the ruck, and to stand his ground as a 'front-fighter'. As the two hosts approach each other for the opening encounter of the *Iliad*, Paris makes a spectacular appearance, leopard skin on shoulder, and, brandishing two spears, challenges all the best men of the Argives to battle it out with him. But is courage is short-lived, for on seeing Menelaos leap down from his chariot he retreats into the throng of his comrades (*Iliad* 3, 15–32). Even the stoutest warriors retreat from time to time when pressed by superior numbers, or if they feel that the gods are working against them, but it is not long before they are straining towards the front again. The obligations of 'front-fighting' derive from high rank in society. This is very clearly stated by Sarpedon in a fine speech to Glaukos as he prepares to attack the wall round the Greek camp. After recalling their privileges of honour and property he continues:

> *Therefore it is our duty in the fore-front of the Lykians*
> *to take our stand, and bear our part of the blazing of battle*
> *Iliad* 12, 315–16
> (translation by R. Lattimore)

We have here the code of aristocratic militarism made explicit. The war leader with his *temenos* (see pp. 90–91) is to be located in the society of the Late Bronze Age before its decline and dissolution, rather than in the Dark Age of migrations and the early colonial era. This is not to deny that the Early Iron Age had its heroic leaders and champions; their exploits would have been recited according to the pattern set in earlier centuries when weapons were of bronze and chariots a regular arm of the fighting forces.

Homer's perspective on warfare has a depth of many centuries. He looks back past the spear-throwing of the ninth and eighth centuries to the spear-thrusting of the thirteenth and twelfth centuries. The Achaean warrior by the end of the Bronze Age, with bronze helmet, bronze corslet, bronze greaves, and long thrusting spear had come close in equipment and technique to the classical hoplite. He fought as an individual, not as a member of a phalanx, and his isolation heightened his heroic aura. Behind him we can catch a glimpse of a still earlier type of fighter, the warrior of the Shaft Grave period, with far simpler equipment, armed merely with bow and body-shield, or spear and body-shield, and wearing a boar's tusk helmet. The great shield obviated the need for corslet and greaves, and the tradition of Ajax with his 'shield like a tower' must go back to this early Mycenaean period. It is remarkable that he alone of all the major Achaean heroes is never described as wearing a corslet. Appropriately his brother Teukros is an archer, and together they figure in a unique and obviously very early type of battle manœuvre, in which Teukros shoots his arrows from under cover of the great shield of Ajax (*Iliad* 8, 266–72). Nowhere else in the *Iliad* does this type of joint operation occur.

Personal combat most engages the poet's attention. The broader movements of battle receive much more summary treatment, in largely stock lines and similes. Such are the marshalling of the troops under their leaders, the flash of bronze as the ranks advance, the breaking of the phalanxes, the sudden flight 'like deer', the rallying under the exhortation of a leader, the counterattack. Such passages may be conventional, but they are not unrealistic. Military men have always responded to the ring of truth in the Homeric battle scenes.[47] This is the higher truth of poetry which expresses for us what *always* happens rather than what *has* happened. But, as this chapter has tried to show, the epic tradition about weapons and warfare is a vehicle for historical truth also.

6 Troy and the Trojan War

At the beginning of *Iliad* Book 13, Poseidon is watching the progress of the fighting from the lofty summit of wooded Samothrace:

> for from thence all Ida was visible, and visible too was the city of Priam and the ships of the Achaeans.

Samothrace lies between 40 and 50 miles from the mouth of the Hellespont, with the mountainous island of Imbros in a direct line between it and the Plain of Troy. To all appearances Poseidon's view was a physical impossibility. So it seemed to William Kinglake as he studied the map before his visit to the Troad. But after the visit he knew better, as a memorable passage in *Eothen* (1844) relates:

> Well, now I had come: there to the south was Tenedos, and here at my side was Imbros, all right, and according to the map; but aloft over Imbros – aloft in a far-away heaven – was Samothrace, the watch-tower of Neptune!

Mount Fengari, the central peak of Samothrace, rises to over 5000 feet, high enough to overtop Imbros even at a distance of over 40 miles. In the course of a number of visits to Troy, I was once lucky enough to hit a day when the air was clear enough for Samothrace to be visible. The sight of the towering pyramid, faintly blue on the horizon behind the spreading flanks of Imbros, was indeed most impressive. I found it hard to resist Kinglake's conclusion that Homer himself had visited the area, so telling was this 'congruity betwixt the *Iliad* and the material world'.

It would have been a simple matter for Homer to take

ship from Chios or Smyrna and sail up the coast past Lesbos to the Troad. That he did so is perhaps indicated by another passage in which sailors are described passing the Troad in their ship and recalling the heroes from the sight of a grave mound. Tumuli are conspicuous on the low line of hills to the south of Cape Sigeum. In an otherwise featureless shoreline they catch the eye as one enters the Hellespont:

> And some day one of the men to come will say, as he sees it, one who in his benched ship sails on the wine-blue water: 'This is the mound of a man who died long ago in battle, who was one of the bravest, and glorious Hector killed him'.
>
> *Iliad* 7, 86 ff.
> (translation by R. Lattimore)

If Homer had landed and made his way across the plain to the hill of Hisarlik, he would almost certainly have seen only a shapeless pile of ruins overgrown with scrub and brambles. About three to four hundred years elapsed between the final destruction of Bronze Age Troy and the re-establishment of a town on the site by Greek colonists.[1]

The well-fortified citadel known as Troy VIIa was burnt in the second half of the thirteenth century. This destruction level is now generally associated with the main siege and sack of Greek tradition. After plundering the fallen city, the Greeks are said to have sailed for home, and in fact there is no evidence of Mycenaean occupation of the site. The place was reconstructed and reinhabited, presumably by the former occupants, since the pottery and other products of Troy VIIb show continuity with those of VIIa, at least for a time. In the second phase of Troy VIIb the sudden appearance of pottery of a completely different type, hand-made and crude in appearance, indicates the arrival of barbarian invaders from the Danube Basin. Under their occupation, Troy continued to eke out an impoverished existence for perhaps a generation or two, but after another disastrous fire the site was finally abandoned at a date not far from 1100. Aeolian Greek colonists revived the place *c.* 700. They called their city Ilion, the more common of the Homeric names, a clear indication that tradition associated the site with ancient Troy-Ilion.

This tradition was familiar to Homer and his hearers. In the *Iliad* the landscape is assumed rather than described. The main features are few and easily comprehended: a beach opening onto the Hellespont, a plain, two rivers (one larger, one smaller), and a 'beetling' citadel. This was the simple stage on which the Trojan War was enacted. As Leaf says, 'the plain of Troy is certainly not picturesque'.[2] It is a level expanse of alluvium averaging about 2 miles in width, and curving back for about 8 miles between low featureless ridges. Dotted with marshes and swampy hollows, and often inundated by winter floods, it is barely habitable.[3] Its cultivators live almost entirely in villages on the higher ground. The larger of the two rivers, now known as the Menderes, is one of the three main rivers of the Troad – a substantial stream flowing down in a course of some 40 miles from the Ida massif to the south-east. The smaller river, the Dumbrek, is little more than a local brook, and much of it dries out in summer. There can be no doubt that the Menderes is Homer's Skamander, but it is far from certain that it has always followed its present course along the western edge of the plain. The whole plain is full of disused watercourses and old flood channels, and the Skamander may once have flowed rather closer to the hill of Hisarlik. The Dumbrek is to be identified with the Simoeis. It has its own small alluvial plain running back along the northern flank of the ridge that ends at Hisarlik, and it finds its way to the sea at the eastern edge of the beach that lies between the ridges of Sigeum and Rhoeteum.[4] This beach was an obvious landing-point for a seaborne expedition coming to attack Troy, and is the generally accepted location for the Greek camp.[5] Three miles inland rose the great royal fortress of Priam, well placed to dominate the plains of the two rivers and command the entrance to the Hellespont.

If there ever was a Troy it must surely have stood at Hisarlik. The name means 'fortress', and was given by the Turks because of the ruined walls visible at the end of the ridge running west from the village of Chiplak. The bedrock of the bluff is only some 50 feet above the level of the plain, but the debris of centuries of occupation had raised the summit of the tell by a further 55 feet. Today most of the habitation level has been dug away, and the impressiveness of the site as a commanding citadel has been much reduced.

In the ancient world, as in modern times, the claims of the site to be that of Homeric Troy did not go altogether unchallenged. A native of the Troad, Demetrius of Scepsis (*floruit c.* 175 BC), wrote extensively on the problem, and favoured a place called the 'village of the Ilians' about 3 miles east of Hisarlik. His conjecture was accepted by Strabo (who never visited the Troad), but has little to commend it.[6]

Some interesting details about the history of the problem in the modern period have been assembled by T. J. B. Spencer in his *Fair Greece, Sad Relic.*[7] Travellers in the sixteenth century mistakenly identified the Roman ruins of Alexandreia Troas as Priam's Troy. This error was not finally refuted until the early eighteenth century, when better-informed visitors made their way to the promontory near Sigeum, and from there surveyed the 'plains of Ilium'. Among them was Lady Mary Wortley Montagu, who wrote about her visit in a letter: 'While I viewed these celebrated fields and rivers, I admired the exact geography of Homer, whom I had in my hand. Almost every epithet he gives to a mountain or plain is still just for it.' Her enthusiasm moved Pope to comment with graceful irony on 'the loss that Homer has sustained for want of my translating him in Asia'. In his important *Essay on the Original Genius of Homer* (1767), Robert Wood expressed his conviction that 'the Iliad has new beauties on the banks of the Skamander, and the Odyssey is most pleasing in the countries where Ulysses travelled and Homer sung'. Wood was mainly concerned to give a general account of the Troad, and made only a very tentative suggestion about the actual site of Troy, which he thought must have been 'lower down than the springs of the Skamander, though higher than the plain'.

The next generation of Hellenic travellers went much more thoroughly into the problem, with the result that by the last decade of the eighteenth century the topography of Troy had become the subject of bitter controversy. Two Frenchmen, Choiseul-Gouffier and Le Chevalier, favoured a site at Balli Dagh above the village of Bunarbashi. An argument considered important was the claim of Choiseul-Gouffier to have found near the village the hot and cold 'springs of the Skamander' which Homer sets close to the walls of Troy (*Iliad* 22, 147–56). The springs are tepid and copious, and are still used as washing pools by the local women; but no later traveller has ever detected any appreciable difference in the temperature of the various sources.[8] An Englishman, Jacob Bryant, published a rejoinder in which he argued that Troy never existed. The noted topographers of the early nineteenth century, Gell, Clarke, Dodwell, and Leake, all gave their views on the problem. Byron lashed out at the sceptics:

> We do care about 'the authenticity of the tale of Troy'. I have stood upon that plain *daily*, for more than a month in 1810; and if anything diminished my pleasure, it was that the blackguard Bryant impugned its veracity . . . I venerated the grand original as the truth of *history* . . . and of *place*; otherwise it would have given me no delight.

Balli Dagh, the 'false Troy', is a rocky acropolis on the left bank of the gorge by which the Menderes debouches on to its sea plain. The site is quite picturesque and impressive, but it bears no ancient remains of any consequence, and its strategic value is in fact small. Nor can it be reconciled with the Homeric indications, being too far from the sea and the plain, and not visible from Mount Ida.

The first modern writer to make a well-reasoned case for Hisarlik was Charles Maclaren. His *Dissertation on the topography of the plains of Troy* (Edinburgh, 1822) was based on a study of the Homeric text and the controversy, not on personal acquaintance with the Troad.[9] His view won the support of Frank Calvert, whose family had settled in the Troad many years before Schliemann's arrival. Calvert was interested in the antiquities of the area, and had acquired possession of part of the hill of Hisarlik. He made a small sounding there in 1865, finding Roman, Hellenistic and prehistoric pottery.[10] The help he gave to Schliemann has already been noted (above, pp. 24f.).

Schliemann was convinced that his excavations entirely vindicated the Homeric tradition, and by and large, this is true. Some Homeric landmarks such as Batieia (*Iliad* 2, 811–15), the tomb of Ilos (*Iliad* 10, 415; 11, 166 and 371–2; 24, 349), and the ford of the Skamander (*Iliad* 14, 433; 21, 1) cannot now be indentified. But this is of little consequence, for Batieia and the Ilos tomb were man-made barrows, and will have long ago been obliterated by floods, and a ford on a river like the Skamander is an impermanent feature. Schliemann pointed out that there is a slight rise in the plain between Hisarlik and the foreshore, and identified this with the 'swelling of the plain' often mentioned in the battle scenes (*e.g.*, *Iliad* 10, 160; 11, 56; 20, 3); Transient features like the 'oak' (*Iliad* 11, 170) and the 'fig-tree' (*Iliad* 22, 145) can readily be imagined in appropriate locations.

There is really only one distinctive detail in the landscape that stubbornly resists identification by the Homerists. Two springs, one hot, the other cold, are said to have gushed out near the city wall, supplying water for stone washing-troughs (*Iliad* 22, 147–56). No springs with a marked temperature difference have been found near the mound of Hisarlik. One could invoke some forgotten earthquake to account for the discrepancy since earthquakes often disrupt the flow of springs, but other explanations have been given. It has been noted that Homer calls the springs 'springs of the Skamander', and not far from the headwaters of the river a pair of springs has been found, one considerably warmer than the other.[11] These springs, however, lie on the slopes of Ida 30 miles from Troy. Leaf allows that this particular pair of springs may have influenced Homer's picture, but his preferred explanation seems to me more plausible. He points out that what Homer describes is 'very characteristic of the Troad at large, though not of the immediate surroundings of Troy. The hot springs of the Troad are as marked a feature as the cold which break out all over many-fountained Ida; the poet has done no more than bring them together into the very centre of his scene.'[12] It is a mark of the epic style that it distills generic features of a district into distinctive epithets, and Leaf is in effect suggesting that the poet has followed the same procedure to produce a distinctive description. Alternatively, we might suppose that the springs of Bunarbashi have inspired the description. It is also to be noted that the Homeric description *may* be partly supported by archaeological findings. Schliemann discovered the remains of an ancient washing-place about 150 yards south-west of the citadel of Hisarlik. A tunnel had been driven into the hillside, and conduits brought the water of three springs into stone basins.[13]

Some of the Homeric epithets for Troy, like 'lovely', 'holy', 'well-founded', are used also of many other cities and are in no sense distinctive. But there are five epithets and one short descriptive phrase that are used only of Troy. The phrase is 'mighty citadel', and the epithets are 'solidly-built', 'well-walled', 'well-towered', 'beetling', 'rich in horses'. All these descriptions are fully justified by the site and its remains, especially the fortifications of Troy VI and VIIa. The walls were so well built that considerable stretches of them still survive to an impressive height. The remains of at least four towers can still be made out. Horse bones are confined to the strata of Troy VI and VIIa, but are very common in them. The ridge is steep enough on its northern and north-western flanks, and the ring of walls and towers crowning it must have looked very formidable when viewed from the plain. As Bowra remarks, this group of epithets suggests 'actual observation and local knowledge' of Troy, and 'were surely chosen with an eye to its appearance and character'.[14] If this conclusion is accepted, it follows that these epithets became fixed in the bardic tradition before the end of the Bronze Age.

There is also a group of epithets appropriate to Troy but not confined to it. From them we learn that Troy was 'windy', and that it had 'lofty gates' and 'broad streets'. All visitors to the site have commented on the strong north wind that blows for most of the year. Excavation has revealed traces of at least seven gates, though not all of these were in use at the same time. 'Broad streets' are also attributed to Athens and Mycenae, and they, like Troy VIIa, had notably well engineered roads leading up to and through their citadels. The 'well-built streets' of Troy are mentioned in Hector's walk through the city from his house to the Skaian Gate (*Iliad* 6, 391).

The Skaian Gate is the most frequently named gate. The Trojan warriors use it for getting to the battlefield, and chariots could descend from it to the plain (*Iliad* 3, 263). It was flanked by a tower called the 'great tower of Ilios' (*Iliad* 6, 386; 21, 526). It should probably be identified with the West Gate of the archaeologists which faces towards the site of the Greek camp, though there is now no trace of a tower beside it. However, two of the existing gates, the North-East Gate and the South Gate, are flanked by towers. The Dardanian Gate is three times mentioned (*Iliad* 5, 789; 22, 194 and 413). Dörpfeld took it to be the gate through which the road from Dardania in the upper Skamander plain entered. It is best identified with the South Gate.

The summit of the citadel was called the Pergamos (*Iliad* 4, 508; 24, 700). Here stood the temple of Apollo (*Iliad* 5, 446) and Priam's palace. Unfortunately, the top of the mound was shaved off in the Roman reconstruction of Ilium, and there are no archaeological remains from the

Bronze Age there to compare with Homer's witness. Near the summit stood other great houses, including those of Hector and Paris (*Iliad* 6, 317). Paris's house had been built to his orders by the best craftsmen in Troy (*Iliad* 6, 314–17). Remains of fine free-standing houses, skilfully constructed of cut stone, are a feature of Troy VI.

One final detail of the fortifications as described by Homer calls for more extended comment. Andromache once ventures to give some military advice to Hector:

> Post the people by the fig-tree where the citadel can most easily be climbed and the wall scaled.
>
> *Iliad* 6, 433–4

She reminds him that three previous assaults had been made by the Achaeans at this spot. The fig tree (and lookout post) were near the Skaian Gate (*Iliad* 22, 137 and 145), and so Andromache almost certainly has in mind the western sector of the walls. Excavation has revealed a stretch of walling here about 38 yards long that is much less massive than the sections to the east. Built with a very marked batter, it dates from an earlier building phase, and was doubtless due to be replaced in the reconstruction plans for the whole circuit, plans which for some reason were never completed. Below it lay a small plateau which could conveniently be used as a mustering point for a concerted attack. As Leaf well says: 'The curious thing is that Andromache should say that this vulnerable part of the wall stands where the city is best approached; and that this, unlikely though it seems in itself, should be exactly confirmed by the existing remains.'[15]

Patroklos once pressed the attack on the walls to the point where he reached the 'angle' or 'elbow' of the wall (*Iliad* 16, 702). This term is explained by the distinctive construction. The lower face of the walls with its marked batter presented a steep but not unclimbable slope to the attacker, but the upper portion consisted of a *vertical* parapet of brick or stone superimposed on the broader base.

In these passages we seem to have a memory of actual fighting round a particular set of walls. There is nothing generalized about the incidents. Once Troy had been ruined and deserted, these features of its walls would have become hard to discern. Greek knowledge of them can best be explained as deriving ultimately from Achaeans who took part in the siege.

Even at their maximum extent, the walls of Troy enclosed an oval space of only about 200 yards from east to west and 175 yards from north to south. The enclosed area was a citadel, not a city. The walls protected the king's palace and the great houses of his nobles, and the bulk of the people must have lived outside the walls on the plateau to the east. The garrison, even with the increase noted in the VIIb phase (above, p. 26), can never have numbered more than a few thousand. But Troy, like Mycenae, was the main bulwark of a prosperous kingdom. It was the key to the Troad, commanding the main access by water up the Hellespont and the main access by land up the valley of the Skamander.

By conquering Troy, the Achaeans would win a prize rich in itself, and would also open a door to political and commercial expansion in north-west Asia Minor. Here is the most probable motive for the war. Redress for the abduction of Helen can hardly account for an expedition on this scale. The injured pride of an Achaean king may or may not have operated as a contributory cause; in the conditions of the time such a motive is not intrinsically improbable, but we have no means of checking its historicity. In the Hittite archives we have documents independent of the epic tradition, and with their aid, as Page has shown, the Achaean assault on Troy may plausibly be related to Anatolian history in the thirteenth century.[16]

In the first half of the century the Hittites dominated most of Asia Minor except the north-west sector, but their authority was progressively undermined from *c.* 1250.

The Hittite king Tuthalijas IV (*c.* 1250–1220) had to contend with a revolt led by the powerful kingdom of Assuwa. Assuwa is probably the same as the Greek *Asia*, a name which in Homer is associated with the valley of the river Cäyster (*Iliad* 2, 461). A document from the Annals of Tuthalijas informs us that the league of Assuwa included twenty-two places ranging from *Luqqā* (Lycia) in the south to *Truisa* in the north. Philology does not rule out the equation of *Truisa* with *Troia*, and we may accept with Page the likelihood that 'Troy did march with Assuwa against the Hittites'. Tuthalijas claims to have mastered the revolt, but Hittite supremacy was not destined to last long. In the reign of his successor Arnuwandas (*c.* 1220–1190), the Hittite Empire collapsed, creating a power vacuum in western Asia Minor.

This is the precise point at which Page finds the historical background to the Trojan War. As a result of the Hittite withdrawal, he suggests, the Achaeans were brought into direct confrontation with the league of Assuwa. His theory will retain general plausibility even though some of the details may have to be revised. From the Hittite records and the data of archaeology, we can deduce that the Achaeans had gained an important footing in the south-west corner of Asia Minor during the thirteenth century. Their commercial contacts with Troy in the north-west corner were also of long standing; but they seem to have been virtually excluded from the coastlands running north from Miletus to the Troad. The presence of the hostile power of Assuwa in this area would account for this exclusion. By attacking Troy, the Achaeans might hope to outflank Assuwa on the north, and weaken her by overcoming her northernmost ally. But the Trojans, backed up (as the Homeric Catalogue indicates) by allies from the western provinces of Asia as far south as Lycia, put up a very stubborn resistance. Though the Achaeans sacked Troy in the end, they were not able to achieve their strategic goal of gaining a permanent foothold in the area.

According to Mylonas, the Hittite evidence implies that

the Trojan War 'occurred after 1230 BC, and possibly even after *c.* 1220 BC'.[17] This will put the fall of Troy not far from 1200, a date that has commended itself to a number of modern authorities on other grounds.[18] Blegen, however, disagrees with this dating. He first put the fall of Troy VIIa at *c.* 1240, and later tended to revise the date upwards to 1270.[19] The controversy turns mainly on the classification and dating of the Mycenaean sherds found in the successive strata of Troy VI, Troy VIIa, Troy VIIb 1 and Troy VIIb 2. Whole or nearly whole Mycenaean pots are rare on the site, and it is sometimes not easy to date small fragments. Nor are Mycenaean sherds all that common, particularly in the layers later than Troy VI. Finally, there is always the possibility that some have been displaced by foundation-sinking in Hellenistic or Roman times. Despite these difficulties, there is a fair measure of agreement among the experts that the IIIB style had come into existence before Troy VI suffered its devastation by earthquake, and that the IIIC style is *not* found in Troy VIIa.[20] IIIC sherds appear first in Troy VIIb 1, but it cannot be determined whether they appear early or late in that phase. The problem is compounded by wider disagreement about the absolute dating of the transition between the IIIB and IIIC styles. Furumark's influential works on Mycenaean pottery (published in 1941) set this transition about 1230; if he is right, Blegen's view will be more plausible. Recent finds of IIIB pottery in Palestine have indicated that Furumark's dating needs to be revised downwards by thirty years or more, and this would bring the dating of Troy VIIa down by about the same amount.[21]

In the ancient world the first recorded date for Troy appears in Herodotus. From a study of the traditions and records available to him, he concluded that the Trojan War took place 'about 800 years before my day', *i.e.*, *c.* 1250–1230 (2, 45). The culminating point of ancient chronology is the work of Eratosthenes (*c.* 275–194 BC), who calculated the dates of the Trojan War at 1193–1183. It is interesting to note how closely these estimates agree with the range of modern estimates based mainly on archaeological data.

It should not be forgotten that Greek traditions about Troy and the Troad span a much wider period of time than the Trojan War.[22] Before the Troy of Priam they remembered the Troy of Laomedon. Laomedon engaged Poseidon and Apollo to build the great walls of the citadel for him. They were assisted in their work by a mortal, Aiakos of Salamis, who produced an inferior stretch of walling. According to Pindar, it was the weakness of this sector that led to the capture of the city (*Ol.* viii, 42; see p. 145 for the Homeric tradition on this point). When the walls were finished the gods claimed their wages, but Laomedon refused them their due, and thus incurred the lasting enmity of Poseidon.[23] Laomedon also treated Herakles shabbily in a deal over horses (*Iliad* 5, 650–1) – perhaps a memory of actual trade in bloodstock between Trojans and Mycenaeans – and Herakles revenged himself by sacking the city. Homer several times alludes to this earlier sack of Troy by Herakles, listing his force as 'six ships only, and a weaker band of men' (*Iliad* 5, 640–2; cf. 14, 250–1). Herakles was no stranger to the plains of Troy where he had an earthwork fort built for him by the Trojans as a place of refuge from a sea-monster (*Iliad* 20, 145–8). The monster had been sent by Poseidon to plague the Trojans in revenge for his unjust treatment by Laomedon, and Herakles was presumably called in as an expert in coping with such problems.

These legends imply that Greeks were at Troy before the great siege, trading and working with the Trojans, and this implication is entirely consistent with the archaeological findings from Troy VI.[24] In the fourteenth century many Mycenaean products found their way to Troy: arrowheads, bronze daggers, sword pommels of marble and alabaster, steatite and beads of carnelian, ivory objects, and fine pottery. There is no evidence for Trojan exports in return, but it is plausible to suppose that these included textiles and horses.[25] The splendid fortifications of the citadel would have impressed all Greeks who visited the place, and would naturally have been attributed to divine workmanship. Then this impregnable fortress was suddenly shattered by an earthquake. In the Aegean, earthquakes are often accompanied by seismic sea waves. If the plains of Troy were inundated by such waves, the event could easily have led to the legend of a monster sent by the angry Poseidon. Perhaps a squadron of Greek ships was in the Hellespont at the time, and its commander filched some plunder from the stricken city, thus creating the story of the sack by Herakles. Troy was firmly established in Greek legend before Agamemnon's generation. The city may well have been the subject of song in the fourteenth century, and many of the stock epithets that characterize it in the Homeric poems (for which see p. 144) may go back to this era of more peaceful contact.[26]

The earthquake devastation of Troy VI is dated *c.* 1300–1275. Subsequently, in the period of Troy VIIa, trade with the Mycenaean world declined. The evidence that the city made preparations to meet an attack, and that it was eventually sacked and burnt, has been given in an earlier chapter (see pp. 26f.). The pattern of Mycenaean aggression, from Knossos through Thebes to Troy, is all too familiar: first trade with your neighbour, then covet his wealth, and finally attack him. The Achaeans were no strangers to Troy as trade over the previous two hundred years shows, but they may have underestimated its strength. A quarrel between the royal houses over Helen could have been part cause and pretext for the expedition. (It was a quarrel between King Dermot McMurrough and his peers that brought the Normans to Ireland, and his beautiful daughter Eva played a big part in that saga.) The expedition became the focus of Greek traditions about Troy because it was an *overseas* expedition, perhaps the first to be attempted on a large scale, and because victory was so dearly bought. It was also remembered best because it was the last great military achievement of the Mycenaean world.

The story of Troy in the Bronze Age extends a little past the destruction of VIIa. After plundering the city of Priam, the Achaeans sailed home, and in fact there is no evidence for Mycenaean occupation of the site. People of the same cultural tradition reconstructed the houses, patched up the fortifications, and clung on to their ancestral home for a generation or so. This phase, Troy VIIb 1, also made some mark on Greek tradition. After Priam's Troy, they said, came the Troy of Aeneas. Homer records that, after the fall of Priam's dynasty, Aeneas and his descendants survived to rule over the Trojans (*Iliad* 20, 306–8). But, say the archaeologists, the survival of Trojans at Troy was short-lived. An abrupt culture break ushered in Troy VIIb 2, a poor place dominated by barbarian invaders who surged in from the Danubian basin bringing with them a crude black hand-made pottery. Did a Trojan remnant take ship and sail west to found a new home in Italy? So the Romans believed, but that is a story that cannot be followed out here. Suffice it to say that the possibility of some migration from the Troad to the central Mediterranean is by no means discounted by modern scholars.

Like so many of its predecessors, Troy VIIb 2 was burnt at a date not far from 1100. Now at last 'the corn grew where Troy had been'. The ancient site was abandoned and lay deserted for some four hundred years, until a small band of Aeolian Greeks restarted a modest settlement there near the close of the eighth century.

In general, the Greek tradition about Troy and its various rulers fits in well with the successive phases of the Bronze Age site as revealed by excavation. But excavation cannot do much more than apprise the historian of broad periods and major disasters. When we come down to the details of the Trojan War, archaeology can give very little help in corroborating the literary tradition. An instance like the weak segment of wall (see pp. 146f.) is quite exceptional. Details like the mustering of the expedition at Aulis and the siting and fortification of the Greek camp can only be assessed in terms of their inherent plausibility. There is no external control for such facts. It is likely that the campaign proved much longer and more costly than expected and also that the Achaeans supported themselves by plundering and sacking lesser centres in the Troad like Thebe and Lyrnessos.[27] It is not improbable that they imported wine from Lemnos (*Iliad* 7, 467–8). Further speculation is hardly profitable.

When we consider the final capture of Troy, our trust in, and understanding of, the epic tradition comes under considerable strain. Everyone knows that Troy was taken with the aid of a wooden horse, but many will be surprised to learn that there is no mention of this stratagem in the *Iliad*. The action of the *Iliad* is set in the last year of the siege, but the poem ends with the death of Hector. The fall of Troy is predicted, but not described. In the *Odyssey*, however, Homer shows that he is familiar with the traditional account of the capture of the city. He makes Odysseus ask the bard Demodokos for a song about the horse, and then summarizes the main points (*Odyssey* 8, 492–520; further details in *Odyssey* 4, 271–89; 11, 523–32). The Achaeans, he says, fired their camp and set sail, ostensibly for home, leaving a large wooden horse in the 'meeting-place' outside Troy. The horse had been built by Epeios, and a picked force of champions was concealed in its recesses under the command of Odysseus. The Trojans then dragged it into the citadel and debated what to do with it. Some thought it should be chopped to pieces or hurled over a cliff, but in the end it was decided to leave it as 'a great propitiatory offering to the gods'. Later the heroes emerged from their hiding-place and sacked the city.

Virgil amplifies this account (*Aeneid* 2, 13 ff.), chiefly by introducing the wily Sinon, who poses as a deserter and persuades the Trojans that it is in their interests to bring the horse into the city.[28] It is too big to fit through the gates, so they dismantle a stretch of wall to admit it. While the Trojans are carousing that night, Sinon opens the fastenings on the horse's belly and releases the hidden

Greeks. Virgil gives more details, and a plausible motivation for the Trojan actions, but the framework of his account is Homeric.

In the standard rationalization of the story, current alike in ancient and modern times, the horse is interpreted as a siege engine, either an animal-headed battering-ram or a wooden tower. But there are serious objections to this explanation. There is no evidence for siege engines in the Bronze Age. Sieges of walled cities are often depicted in Egyptian reliefs, but the storming parties are equipped only with scaling ladders, picks, and crowbars. The Assyrians of the ninth and eighth centuries appear to have been the first people to develop battering-rams and siege-towers. Rumours of these inventions might have percolated to Ionia in the century before Homer. J. K. Anderson has no doubt that 'the Wooden Horse of the poets was suggested by tales of how the Kings of Assyria took cities by means of great wooden monsters filled with armed men'.[29] But it seems unlikely that such a crucial feature of the Troy saga would have been introduced at such a late date in the evolution of the poetic tradition. Also, the whole point of the horse is that it is a vehicle of deception not violence, that it does not batter its way into the city but insinuates itself with the help of the Trojans themselves.

There is an old Egyptian tale that recounts how Joppa was taken by an ingenious ruse. Two footmen were permitted by the citizens to carry in sacks slung between poles. They were believed to be bearing gifts, but they had soldiers concealed in the sacks, and two hundred warriors were smuggled in by this method. J. W. Jones has suggested that an early Greek bard knew a Joppa-type tale (possibly one in which pack-horses carried in the soldiers), and invented the variant of a wooden replica of the horse as the vehicle for the 'Greek gifts'. On this view the story of the wooden horse will not reflect any historical fact, but will be a pure fiction with the neat point that the horse-taming Trojans are themselves tamed by a dummy horse.[30]

Other explanations have been proposed. Ships are called 'horses of the sea' (*Odyssey* 4, 708), and Van Leeuwen in his commentary speculated that some oracle credited the capture of Troy to 'wooden horses', meaning the Greek fleet, and that this phrase was later taken in a literal sense. W. F. J. Knight supposed that the Greeks resorted to some magical device to breach the divinely protected ring-wall of 'holy' Ilion. Presumably this was merely a prelude to a more orthodox assault with scaling ladders. One ancient view was that Troy was betrayed by Antenor, and that the gate he opened to the Greeks had a painted horse on it.

One cannot but agree with W. B. Stanford's comment that 'the origin of the stratagem of the Horse is obscure'.[31] I am prepared to credit that some unusual event underlies the story – some Greek ruse, perhaps with the connivance of a Trojan traitor – but none of the suggested explanations appears convincing. Nevertheless, though we may follow Laocöon's advice not to trust the horse, the whole thrust of Greek tradition, corroborated at so many points by the data of archaeology, constrains us to allow a generous measure of historicity to the celebrated tale of Troy.

7 Ithaca

British excavations in Ithaca in the 1930s established that the island formed part of the Mycenaean world in the Late Bronze Age.[1] The main focus of occupation lay in the northern sector near Stavros and Polis Bay. Mycenaean sherds were found at six sites in this area, the largest cache coming from Pilikata at the crest of the ridge running north from Stavros. Here too were found traces of a fortification wall. W. A. Heurtley, the director of the excavation, argued for Pilikata as the probable site of a Mycenaean palace although no actual remains of such a building were found *in situ*; but if there ever was a palace of Odysseus, this eminence would have been a suitable site for it. The summit dominates the cultivable land north of Mount Anogi, and affords good views of the two sheltered havens of Phrikes Bay and Polis Bay.

A productive excavation was also carried out on the col below Mount Aetos on the central isthmus of Ithaca. Remains on the summit of Aetos had long been known locally as the 'Castle of Odysseus', and Schliemann thought that the palace might have been located here, but his excavation did not produce any confirmation of this identification. The British excavation showed that the Aetos area was an important settlement in the Early Iron Age although the site did not yield any evidence of occupation before *c.* 1200. It is possible that, as conditions became less secure during the twelfth century, the inhabitants of Ithaca withdrew from the more exposed areas in the north of the island and fortified Aetos as a refuge point. One very important result of the excavations was to establish that there was continuity of occupation in Ithaca from the Late Mycenaean period through into the Dark Age. Traditions about Ithacan participation in the

Trojan War could therefore have been preserved and handed on locally.

Immediately to the west of Ithaca lies the much larger island of Kephallinia, with Zakynthos further to the south. Four Mycenaean sites have been identified on Zakynthos, and the pottery indicates occupation during the fourteenth and thirteenth centuries. Kephallinia was also an important Mycenaean centre at this time, with at least a dozen sites, most of them concentrated in the neighbourhood of Argostoli,[2] and there seems to have been a large influx of refugees here from the mainland after the destructions at the close of the thirteenth century.

In the Catalogue, Odysseus's kingdom includes Ithaca, Zakynthos, and Samos, and his subjects are called Kephallinians (*Iliad* 2, 631–7). There is a good case for identifying Samos with the island now called Kephallinia. The ancient name survives in the town of Sami on the east coast. Odysseus's rule also extended to parts of the mainland opposite the islands, either to western Aetolia or Acarnania, or to north-west Elis, where an Ithacan called Noemòn is said to have had a stud-farm (*Odyssey* 4, 634–7). Odysseus too kept flocks and herds 'on the mainland' (*Odyssey* 14, 100). It has been a continuing necessity in the economy of the western Greek islands for the islanders to have additional pasturage on the mainland. In this connection it is interesting to observe that strong resemblances have been noted between Mycenaean pottery from Polis Bay in Ithaca and Astakos on the mainland to the east.

Ithaca is much smaller and more rugged than Zakynthos or Kephallinia, but occupies a strategic position in the sea routes of the area. A strong ruler in Ithaca could dominate local sea traffic moving along the Acarnanian coast and through the archipelago of islands to the east. He could also profitably control the sea passages that divide Ithaca from Kephallinia and Leukas. Ships coming from the Gulf of Corinth and heading north for the Adriatic tend to pass close to Ithaca. In the late Bronze Age it must have been an important staging post in the Mycenaean trade route to South Italy and Sicily. Ithaca was thus a likely base for a resourceful and mobile leader. In the power struggle in the western islands, a well-led fleet must have counted for more than a wheat-bearing plain, and so there is nothing improbable in the legend that Odysseus dominated the region from the smallest of the major islands. He could have consolidated the rule of his father Laertes, who was credited with the capture of the town of Nerikos, probably to be identified with the classical town of that name at the northern end of Leukas (*Odyssey* 24, 377–8). The tradition also preserves traces of an earlier dynasty in the names of Ithakos, Neritos, and Polyktor, recorded as the builders of a public fountain (*Odyssey* 17, 207). The Pylos tablets prove that Neritos was a Mycenaean name, and the Argive historian Akusilaos (fifth century BC) reported the tradition that Ithakos and Neritos crossed from Kephallinia to found the city of Ithaca. If Odysseus's *floruit* is put at *c.* 1200, and the founding of Ithaca at *c.* 1300, we get a chronology which is consistent with the tradition of a succession of four or five rulers from Ithakos onwards, and also with the fact that no Mycenaean pottery of earlier date than 1300 has been found on the island.

The identification of Homeric Ithaca with the island now called Itháki (or Thiáki) was challenged early in this century by Dörpfeld. From 1901, he carried out extensive excavations in the Nidri plain on Leukas in the hope of proving his theory that Leukas was really Homeric Ithaca. He discovered a number of interesting graves and traces of settlements, but the pottery and other objects recovered were nearly all of Early or Middle Helladic date. Very few Mycenaean sherds turned up, far fewer in fact than were later found on Ithaca by the British expedition. A good Mycenaean site may yet be found on Leukas, but so far the archaeological evidence lends no support to Dörpfeld.

Dörpfeld also claimed that his theory made better sense of the Homeric descriptions of Ithaca, and in particular of the statement that Ithaca 'lies furthest out in the sea towards the dark quarter' (*i.e.*, the quarter between west and north) (*Odyssey* 9, 25–6). It also enabled him to propose a solution for the problem of Doulichion, which, with the islands of Samē and Zakynthos, is said in the same passage to lie 'around' Ithaca. Doulichion, he said, equals Kephallinia, and Samē equals Ithaca. But this shuffling of the island names creates more problems than it solves. A glance at the map will show that Leukas cannot be said to have islands 'around' it, but this is a good description of Ithaca. Ithaca is also described by Homer as a 'clear' or 'conspicuous' island (*Odyssey* 9, 21; cf. 13, 234), an epithet far from apt for Leukas. Leukas, in fact, has a somewhat doubtful status as an 'island' since a long spit of sand runs across from its northern end to the Acarnanian mainland. But for the modern ship canal which cuts through this isthmus, Leukas would technically be a peninsula. However, the ancient Greeks would have called it an 'island' (since *nesos*, 'island', could be used of peninsulas as well as islands in the strict sense). It is, I think, virtually certain that Leukas is to be identified with one of the four islands named together by Odysseus, *i.e.*, Ithaca, Doulichion, Samē, Zakynthos (*Odyssey* 9, 21–4). In that case, one should follow T. W. Allen in identifying it with Doulichion.[3] How then can Ithaca be said to lie 'furthest out towards the dark quarter', with the other islands 'well away to the east and south'? The British excavations, by revealing the main Mycenaean settlement area in the north of the island, have, I suggest, given the clue to the answer. If you go to the north of Ithaca you get the impression that the island is pointing and reaching out towards the open sea to the north-west. The main bulk of Kephallinia lies well to the south, and the lofty peaks of Leukas appear to recede towards the north-east and the mainland. You seem to be standing on the north-west perimeter of the island world, and that, I suggest, is what Homer intended to convey in this much discussed passage of the *Odyssey*.

Other points in the general Homeric description of Ithaca are that it is 'low', 'not broad', and least suited of all the islands for driving horses (*Odyssey* 9, 25; 13, 242–3: 4, 607–8). Ithaca fits all these specifications much better than Leukas. Leukas, with peaks up to nearly 4000 feet, is so obviously a 'high' island in contrast with Ithaca (maximum height 2666 feet) that Dörpfeld felt obliged to render the word for 'low' (*chthamale*) as 'close to the mainland', a meaning unparalleled in Homer or ancient literature generally. Leukas is 8 to 9 miles wide for most of its length, whereas Ithaca is never more than 3 to 4 miles wide, and contracts to less than a mile at its central isthmus. Finally, there is virtually no level ground on Ithaca, while Leukas has quite extensive plains round Nidri and at its northern end. In short, there is so little to be said in favour of Dörpfeld's hypothesis, and so much to be said against it, that the traditional identification of Homer's Ithaca with the island now called Itháki must be allowed to stand.

It then becomes a matter of interest to see how far the Homeric descriptions of localities on the island are topographically accurate. Three areas in particular engage our attention: the Bay of Phorcys with a nearby cave sacred to the Nymphs, the steading of Eumaios 'close to the Raven's Crag and the Fountain of Arethusa', and the surroundings of Odysseus's palace. The descriptions of these places add local colour to the narrative, but the localities themselves are also the scene of crucial stages in the homecoming of the hero. It will be convenient to treat them in the order in which Odysseus visits them.

The Phaeacian ship that is conveying Odysseus from Scheria lands him and his treasures at the Bay of Phorcys:

> Now in that island is a cove named after Phorcys, the Old Man of the Sea, with two bold headlands squatting at its mouth so as to protect it from the heavy swell raised by rough weather in the open and allow large ships to ride inside without so much as tying up, once within mooring distance of the shore. At the head of the cove grows a long-leaved olive tree and near by is a cavern that offers welcome shade and is sacred to the Nymphs whom we call Naiads. This cave contains a number of stone basins and two-handled jars, which are used by bees as their hives; also great looms of stone where the Nymphs weave marvellous fabrics of sea-purple; and there are springs whose water never fails. It has two mouths. The one that looks north is the way down for men.

The other, facing south, is meant for the gods; and as immortals come in by this way it is not used by men at all.

Odyssey 13, 96–112
(translation by E. V. Rieu)

Odysseus is left asleep on the beach, and when he awakes he fails to recognize his surroundings, until Athena in the guise of a shepherd lad assures him that he is really back in Ithaca, and points out the main features of the spot, including the Bay, the Cave, and Mount Neriton. There is a good case for identifying the Bay of Phorcys with the bay now known as Dexia Bay, and the Cave of the Nymphs with a cave at Marmarospilia on the hillside about 600 feet above the bay. Dexia Bay is a well-sheltered cove with abrupt headlands at its mouth, and answers well enough to the Homeric description, though it must be admitted that the description is far from specific. But the case draws its main strength from the proximity of the Marmarospilia cave, which shows the unusual feature of two 'entrances' as pictured by Homer. The 'human' entrance faces north, as Homer says, and is about 5 feet high and 18 inches wide. A single large boulder, like that placed by Athena (*Odyssey* 13, 370), could block it off. Inside the entrance a ledge about 6 feet wide runs back for some 20 feet to a shelf of rock projecting like a table and pitted with basin-like depressions. The ledge is some 15 feet above the floor of the cavern, and steps lead down from it to the main chamber. This is a large hall about 60 feet across, and roughly circular with a big recess opening off to the south. Overhead, the roof curves in quite regularly like a corbelled beehive tomb, and the whole cavern is indeed 'broad and vaulted' (*Odyssey* 13, 349). As one looks up, one sees that at the apex there is a narrow vent through which the daylight penetrates. This vent is to the south of the 'human' entrance, and it does not require much imagination to see in it the 'divine' entrance of Homer. Certainly if any mortal attempted to use it, he would fall to his death on the floor of the cave. The walls are covered with fretted stalactite formations in which one can recognize the 'great looms of stone' used by the Nymphs. In short, the Marmarospilia cave answers point by point to the Homeric description, and serves to fix Odysseus's landing at Dexia Bay. Across the water the northern skyline is dominated by the broad pyramid of Mount Anogi, Homer's 'forest-clad Neriton' (*Odyssey* 13, 351). The mountain is bare of timber now, but may well have been wooded in antiquity. Mount Aenos in Kephallinia is still noted for its natural pine forests.

After stowing his goods in the Cave of the Nymphs, Odysseus is directed by Athena to seek out Eumaios 'hard by the Raven's Crag and the Fountain of Arethusa' (*Odyssey* 13, 408). To reach the swineherd's dwelling he follows 'a rugged by-way along the heights through wooded country' (*Odyssey* 14, 1–2). This implies a footpath leading from the neighbourhood of the Cave south along the eastern slopes of Mount Merovigli to the Marathia plateau. Assuming the reliability of Homer's directions, I looked for, and duly found, just such a path. I have seen no mention of it in previous topographical studies of Ithaca, but it provides a convenient route for anyone wishing to go from the Gulf of Molo to Marathia without descending to the low ground round the head of Vathy Bay, and I have little doubt that it has been in use from ancient times.

The Raven's Crag is unmistakable and unforgettable. At the north-eastern corner of the Marathia plateau the ground falls away in a sheer cliff about 200 feet high and 600 yards long. Ravens still frequent it, and it is called *Stefani tou Korakou*, 'the Crag of the Raven'. From its base a scrub-filled gorge runs steeply down to the sea, and halfway down a perennial spring, the 'Fountain of Arethusa', wells out below a rocky outcrop. The gorge thus provides rough pasturage and water for flocks and herds, and on the cliff top one of the few cottages in the south of Ithaca shelters a goatherd and his family. Here or hereabouts stood Eumaios's cottage with its encircling yard wall of rough stones topped off with wild pear (*Odyssey* 14, 5–10). Life here has not changed much down the centuries, for the present-day cottage is fronted by an oval enclosure whose dry stone wall has a covering of spiny branches. Some incidental touches confirm how precisely Homer has pictured the setting. The yard is set 'high up in a place with wide prospects' (*Odyssey* 14, 6). The site is in fact about 800 feet above sea level, and commands magnificent views, of mountains, islands, and the sea, from Leukas south to Zakynthos. 'Throw me down the great cliff,' says Odysseus to the swineherd, 'if I am not telling the truth' (*Odyssey* 14, 398–400). And when the story-telling is over for the night, Eumaios goes to keep watch over his pigs which are sleeping 'under a hollow rock sheltered from the blast of the north wind' (*Odyssey* 14, 532–3). Rock shelters answering exactly to this description may be found at the base of the Raven's Crag.

Eumaios's cottage is a key location in the plot of the *Odyssey*. Not only does it provide Odysseus with a secure base, but it is also the place where he reveals himself to Telemachos. Father and son converge on it from opposite directions, Odysseus walking, as we have seen, from Dexia Bay, and Telemachos voyaging back from Pylos. The route followed by Telemachos is designed to bring him to a landfall in the south-east corner of Ithaca. He coasted along past Elis, and then cut across the mouth of the Gulf of Corinth to the 'sharp' islands (*Odyssey* 15, 298–9). They are probably to be identified with the island still called Oxeia (the 'sharp island'), and the pyramid-shaped promontory of Kutsilaris. Kutsilaris may well have been an island in Homeric times, as the whole coastline here has been considerably extended by the alluvial deposits of the Acheloös. From here, following Athena's advice, he made for the 'first cape' of Ithaca (*Odyssey* 15, 36), probably Cape St John, the most easterly point of the island, and rowed into a cove not far from Eumaios's cottage. The most likely landing point would be at the small beach of Port Ligia at the foot of the gorge leading up to the Raven's Crag.

After reaching the cottage, Telemachos sends Eumaios to the palace to advise Penelope of his return. As noted above, the palace was probably situated close to Stavros, and so at the opposite end of the island from Marathia. Even by the most direct route, the distance would be a good 15 miles. This is consistent with the Homeric narrative, for Eumaios starts early, wastes no time at the palace, and yet does not arrive back until nightfall (*Odyssey* 16, 2 and 452–67).

There are a number of other indications that Homer envisaged the palace and chief town of Ithaca as lying in the Stavros area. From the forecourt of the palace it is possible to see two harbours, one called 'our' harbour, and the other called 'Reithron under wooded Neïon' (*Odyssey* 16, 351–3 with 473; *Odyssey* 1, 185–6). The latter harbour is said to be some distance away from the city, and it is implied that the former is quite close to it. 'Reithron' means 'torrent', and the longest stream in Ithaca rises on the eastward slopes of Mount Exogi and finds it way to the sea at the well-sheltered anchorage of Phrikes Bay. The end of its course is channelled through the centre of the village of Phrikes, which might aptly be called 'Torrent' village. It is plausible to identify Reithron harbour with Phrikes Bay, and in that case Neïon will be Mount Exogi. The other harbour will then be Polis Bay. (Aphales Bay to the north is not a safe anchorage.) It is possible to see both harbours from the crest of the ridge running north from Stavros, and the intersection of the two lines of sight at this point, now known as Pilikata, serves to pinpoint the site of the Homeric palace here in an area where Heurtley found evidence of Mycenaean occupation and fortification. In the Early Iron Age the main habitation centre lay further south on the slopes of Mount Aetos, but tradition remembered that the Bronze Age *polis* lay 'below Neïon', close to the 'ridge of Hermes' (undoubtedly the hog-backed ridge running from Stavros to Pilikata), and in sight of a harbour that is still called Polis (*Odyssey* 3, 81; 16, 471–3).

Homer's firm grasp of Ithacan topography is also apparent in his account of the ambush set by the suitors for Telemachos. Telemachos had set sail from Polis Bay on his journey to Pylos, and had gone south down the Ithaca channel. The suitors naturally assumed that he would return by the same route, and so needed a base from which they could watch and patrol the channel ready to intercept him. Such a base may easily be found at the northern end of Kephallinia just across from Polis Bay. Homer indicates its location in a passage that has generated much controversy:

> A rocky island lies in mid-channel between Ithaca and rugged Samos, Asteris by name, not a large island, and there are twin harbours in it offering a safe anchorage for ships. There the Achaeans waited in ambush for Telemachos.
>
> *Odyssey* 4, 844–7

There is only one island in the whole of the Ithaca channel, so Homer has chosen a neat and unambiguous way of fixing the area of the ambush. This is the islet, now called Daskalio, lying due west of Polis Bay and close to the Kephallinian shore. It is a limestone reef about 200 yards long by 30 wide, rocky and small indeed. Asteris, 'star-island', was an apt name for it, for in the morning sunshine it gleams brightly against the darker flank of Kephallinia. Asteris = Daskalio is a satisfactory equation, except for the 'twin harbours'. There can never have been even one safe anchorage for a Homeric longship in this small islet. The 'twin harbours' must be sought on nearby Kephallinia, and will be found there without any difficulty, as a glance at a map of the indented coastline will show. This part of the coast is also marked by a succession of elevated promontories affording excellent views down the whole length of Ithaca channel. As Homer later says when describing the routine of the patrol:

> By day a string of sentries kept watch from the windy heights; and at sunset we never slept on shore, but kept sailing the sea in our swift ship, waiting for the dawn.
>
> *Odyssey* 16, 365–8

This passage shows that he must have envisaged the patrol as based on Kephallinia, for Daskalio-Asteris rises only about 10 feet above the water, and can never have provided 'windy heights' for sentries. When taken together, the two passages give a very fair account of the location of the ambush, based on the Kephallinian shore and patrolling the channel between Daskalio and Polis Bay. Homer has taken the minor liberty of transferring the twin harbours to Asteris, thus making his description more compact, while not seriously weakening its correspondence with reality. Modern story-tellers from Sir Walter Scott onwards can be shown to have taken similar liberties with real landscapes.

Telemachos, on the advice of Athena, avoided the Ithaca channel on his return (*Odyssey* 15, 27–39). His course took him 'away from the islands', that is to say, he followed the coast of the Peloponnese as far as Cape Araxos, then struck across to Oxeia, and approached the south-east promontory of Ithaca from the east. By taking this circuitous route he avoided all risk of observation by the watchers in the Ithaca channel, and also landed close to Eumaios's cottage to join forces with his father before returning overland to the palace. His ship presumably went on up the east coast of Ithaca and slipped in to Polis Bay behind the backs of the sentries. Interpreted in this way, the movements of the various parties as described by Homer make good sense in relation to the topography of Ithaca and its environs.

As Miss Lorimer remarks, 'the story-teller who develops a complicated plot involving frequent changes of scene must, if he aims at producing an impression of reality, carry a map of operations in his head'.[4] Homer appears to have a very good grasp of Ithacan topography as he makes Odysseus and Telemachos converge from different directions on Eumaios's cottage, and brings them on to the palace. Stock descriptions of Ithaca as 'sea-girt', 'rocky', and 'rugged', and the names of prominent landmarks like Mount Neriton, were probably a long-established part of the tradition. But Homer does much more than merely repeat such details for local colour. He stage-manages the action against a natural back-drop with originality and realism, and one is driven to wonder how he could have acquired the necessary information about the terrain.

Finds of late eighth-century Corinthian pottery from Aetos confirm that by that date Ithaca was a regular port of call for shipping on its way to and from the newly established colonies in Corcyra, Italy, and Sicily. One or two fragments of Ionian pottery have even been found near Polis Bay. After 750 there must have been plenty of sailors in Aegean ports who could give a fairly detailed account of Ithaca. Homer might have derived information from this source, just as the local colour in Shakespeare's *Tempest* is said to be based on a contemporary narrative of a shipwreck on the Bermudas. But in the *Odyssey*'s picture of Ithaca, direct description and incidental allusion interlock so convincingly, and the topography underpins the narrative so realistically, that the hypothesis of second-hand information seems inadequate to explain the correspondences. Could Homer have visualized from a description the relationship between Mount Neriton, Dexia Bay, the Marmarospilia Cave, and the path to Marathia? By merely talking to sailors could he have grasped the nature of the terrain round Stavros, and correctly imagined the views from Pilikata to Polis Bay and Phrikes Bay? It seems unlikely that he could have gained such accurate and detailed knowledge of Ithaca from hearsay, and one must therefore consider the possibility that he visited and stayed on the island.

This conjecture was made in antiquity, and appears in some of the ancient *Lives* of Homer. Many modern topographers of Ithaca contend that Homer must have seen what he describes.[5] The difficulties that have been found in two passages (the general description of Ithaca in *Odyssey* 9, 21–8, and the description of Asteris in *Odyssey* 4, 844–7) are, in my opinion, capable of solution, and are not serious enough to preclude the hypothesis of autopsy. They must be weighed against the many other passages in which Homer builds up a convincing picture of Ithaca by numerous deft and detailed allusions. On balance, the Homeric account matches the realities so well that it must in all probability, I submit, be based on personal knowledge of the island.

There is nothing intrinsically improbable in this supposition. As a professional bard, Homer is likely to have travelled extensively. There is reason to think that he visited the

Troad (see p. 138). There was an ancient tradition that he competed against Hesiod in Euboea. Miss Lorimer argues that he had personal knowledge of Attica.[6] At Corinth he could easily have boarded a westward-bound ship, sailing either round the Peloponnese, or by the more direct route through the Gulf of Corinth. If he had decided to compose a large-scale poem about Odysseus, the desire to see the reputed home of the hero would have been sufficient motive for the journey.

One of the discoveries of the British excavations on Ithaca has lent unexpected support to the hypothesis that Homer visited Ithaca. Between 1930 and 1932 Miss Benton excavated an interesting site on the north shore of Polis Bay. In antiquity it had been a cave shrine, but the roof of the cave collapsed early in the Christian era, and the site was forgotten until an Ithacan called Loizos dug there in 1868 and 1873, and recovered a bronze sword and spear and a bronze tripod-cauldron. Vollgraf found some Mycenaean pottery in 1904, but Miss Benton was the first to make a thorough exploration of the site. Her finds of stratified pottery and votive offerings showed that the cave had been a centre of cult from the Bronze Age down to the first century AD. The Nymphs were worshipped there, and a fragment of a terracotta mask bore the words ΕΥΧΗΝ **ΟΔΥΣΣΕΙ**, 'A Prayer to Odysseus'. The fragment dates from the second or first century BC, and indicates that there was a cult of Odysseus associated with the cave at this period.

Miss Benton and her team also recovered the remains of twelve bronze tripod-cauldrons that must have been among the most impressive dedications in the cave. Of fine workmanship, they stood about 3 feet high; their circular handles were surmounted by figurines of dogs or horses and the legs and handles were chased with linked spirals and other Geometric motifs. They are dated to the ninth or eighth centuries, considerably later than the age of Odysseus, but earlier than the probable date of the composition of the *Odyssey*.

We do not know whether the cave was already associated with Odysseus by the eighth century, but there does seem to be some connection between the tripod cauldrons and the *Odyssey*. Among the treasures brought back from Phaeacia were thirteen bronze tripods and cauldrons presented to Odysseus by Alkinoös and his twelve peers (*Odyssey* 8, 390–1 and 13, 13–14). The number thirteen agrees exactly with the finds in the cave (twelve found by Miss Benton plus one previously recovered by Loizos). The coincidence can hardly be accidental. Was a dedication made to match a number established in the tradition about Odysseus? Or had Homer seen, or heard, of the tripod-cauldrons, and did he work the number thirteen into his narrative so that the story and the dedication would appear to corroborate each other? The second alternative is perhaps more likely. If Homer visited Ithaca he would certainly have seen the Polis Bay cave. He may even have been told that the tripod-cauldrons were the 'originals' brought home by Odysseus. With his subtle skill as a story-teller, he would have taken pleasure in weaving confirmation of such a picturesque legend into the traditional tale of the Return.

In general, close examination of what is said about Ithaca in the *Odyssey* serves to vindicate the accuracy of Homer's picture of the island. The approximate site of the palace of Odysseus could be deduced from the topographical indications in the text alone. When this internal data is compared with the archaeological findings about the Mycenaean occupation, the convergence of the two lines of evidence is very striking, and encourages belief in the essential soundness of the epic tradition.

8 On the fringes of Homer's world

Homer's world centres on the Aegean. He has a clear conception of the geography of the sea and its main islands from Samothrace to Crete. In the *Odyssey* (3, 169–73) he pictures some of the Achaean leaders deliberating in Lesbos about their passage back to the Greek mainland. Are they to risk the 'long' open crossing to the north of Chios, keeping Psyra on their left, or are they to hug the coast, passing down the channel between Chios and the mainland to Samos, and so round by the Cyclades? In response to a divine sign they opt for the more direct route and fetch up safely at the promontory of Geraistos in the south of Euboea, where they perform a grateful sacrifice to Poseidon for their safe passage of such a 'great expanse of sea'. The debate is bred out of the realities of Aegean travel in small boats,[1] and it is likely that Homer had personal knowledge of these sea routes.

Since the *Iliad* is set in the Troad, geographical information about that area is naturally quite detailed. About the rest of the coast of Asia Minor the epic tells us little, but the reference to the 'weeping Niobe', a rock formation on Mount Sipylos, is rightly taken to indicate Homer's familiarity with the area to the east of Smyrna (*Iliad* 24, 614–17).

The political geography of the Greek mainland is defined in the Catalogue and presupposed throughout the rest of the poems. Extensive knowledge of the towns, districts, mountains, and rivers is displayed. Stock epithets embody distinctive features of the landscape. Lakedaimon is 'hollow' and 'full of ravines'; Ithaca is 'rocky' and 'narrow'; Mount Taügetos is 'long', and Dodona 'wintry'. The tradition takes note of peculiarities like the junction of the clear-flowing Titaressos with the muddy Peneios (*Iliad* 2, 752–4).

For areas beyond the Aegean and its coastlands information is sparse. The interior of Asia Minor is almost a complete blank. Cyprus is occasionally mentioned (*e.g.*, *Iliad* 11, 21; *Odyssey* 4, 83), and there is an allusion to the precinct and altar of Aphrodite at Paphos (*Odyssey* 8, 362–3). 'Sidonia' is known as the homeland of the Phoenicians, whence textiles and mixing-bowls of silver are exported. This tradition may have originated in the Bronze Age: Mycenaean trade with the Levant was on an extensive scale between *c.* 1400 and 1200, but the Homeric references to the Phoenicians derive their colour from a later age.

The scattered references to Egypt are significant for the information of the tradition, as they undoubtedly reflect Greek contact with that country in the Late Bronze Age. Achilles, in the *Iliad* (9, 381–4), alludes to the great wealth of 'Egyptian Thebes' with its 'hundred gates' and its massed squadrons of chariots. This must be a memory of Thebes at the height of its glory in the fourteenth and thirteenth centuries. Mycenaean trading contacts with Egypt are certified by pottery finds at many sites of sherds dating from the fourteenth and early thirteenth centuries (IIIA 2 and IIIB 1). The legend of Menelaos's stay in Egypt and the great wealth that he acquired there is likely to be the product of such commercial contact (*Odyssey* 4, 83–90; compare p. 58 above). Later, in the Dark Age, the Greeks completely lost touch with Egypt, and contact was not resumed until *c.* 650.

The story of Menelaos in Egypt contains some circumstantial details: Helen had received a pain-killing drug (possibly opium) from an Egyptian lady, Polydamna the wife of Thon (*Odyssey* 4, 227–9). From another Egyptian lady in Thebes she had received a silver work-basket that ran on wheels and had gold inlay on the rim, and the lady's husband Polybos had given Menelaos 'two silver bath-tubs, a pair of tripods, and ten talents of gold' (*Odyssey* 4, 125–9). Such interchanges are consistent with known trade connections between the Peloponnese and the Middle East in the Bronze Age. A Fifth Dynasty Egyptian cup was found in Kythera, where a Minoan colony was established at Kastri perhaps as early as *c.* 2300.[2] The site was abandoned by its Minoan colonists about 1450, and it is likely that Mycenaean merchants from the Peloponnese then took over the trade routes leading to the Levant. A recently discovered Egyptian inscription, dated *c.* 1400, mentions Kythera and Knossos (and possibly also Mycenae, Nauplia, and Messene) in what appears to be a list of Aegean place-names, and the link can only be a commercial one.[3] Besides the celebrated gold cups of Minoan workmanship, the Vapheio tomb treasure included alabaster jars and a silver spoon of Egyptian provenance.

The legend of Odysseus's wanderings may also derive in part from memories of Mycenaean seafaring in waters to the west of Greece. Since World War II, excavations in Sicily, the Lipari islands, and the south of Italy, have added greatly to our knowledge of Mycenaean penetration into the western basin of the Mediterranean.[4] A recognized route went from the Peloponnese past Ithaca to Corfu, and then cut across the Strait of Otranto to the 'heel' of Italy. At Scoglio del Tonno (at the entrance to Taranto harbour) Mycenaean remains indicate the presence of an important trading-post continuously occupied from *c.* 1400. From there the route ran along the south coast of Italy to the Strait of Messina and through to the Lipari islands, where Mycenaean merchants appear to have established a connection with shipping from Sardinia. Copper ingots of Aegean type, dated *c.* 1200, have been found in Sardinia, but no Mycenaean pottery has yet been found so far west. The Mycenaeans also probably traded up the west coast of Italy at least as far as Ischia, and perhaps on to Etruria where Mycenaean pottery has recently been found. Another route took in the east and south-facing shores of Sicily, with an extension to Malta. There is so far no evidence of any Mycenaean presence on the south coast of France or the

Iberian peninsula, but there are slight indications of some penetration up the Adriatic.

It is evident that from *c.* 1600 Mycenaean merchant adventurers were pioneering routes that took them over 500 miles west of the Greek mainland into unfamiliar seas. It would be strange if these daring voyages left no mark on Greek legend. If we examine the adventures of Odysseus with this background in mind, we can point to one or two places where Bronze Age sea lore has almost certainly coloured the narrative.

One such place is in the sailing instructions that Circe gives to Odysseus on his final departure from her island (*Odyssey* 12, 37 ff.). She tells him that he has a choice of routes, and it has often been suggested that the passage embodies traces of an ancient Pilot or Sailing Manual. One route lay through a narrow strait between the twin terrors of Scylla and Charybdis. In the ancient world it was generally accepted that Charybdis symbolized the dangerous waters of the Messina Strait. The risks to ancient shipping were real enough, as may be judged from the *Admiralty Pilot* which even now warns that 'the currents and whirlpools, famous from antiquity, are such as to necessitate some caution in the navigation of the strait'. The Strait is narrowest at its northern end (it is barely 2 miles from Cape Peloro to the Italian coast), and from there south to Messina the currents and eddies are most marked. There is a tidal flow which changes direction four times in twenty-four hours, and attains a speed of up to four knots. Such conditions would have seemed menacing and awe-inspiring to a Bronze Age mariner from the tideless Aegean. The tidal flow and the whirlpools are related, and the admixture of waters from the seas to the north and south of the Strait often produces the effect of a boiling surface with denser water sinking and lighter water welling up from below. The passage of the Strait must have been attempted with much trepidation by Mycenaean sailors, and their feelings appear to be reflected in the Homeric description of Charybdis, which 'three times each day sucks down the dark water, and three times releases it, a terrible sight' (*Odyssey* 12, 105–6).

If one of Circe's routes lay through the Messina Strait, what of the other route which involved a passage by the Planktae, or 'wandering rocks'? Here were to be found surf, smoke, fire, and noise, an unusual combination of effects that suggests a localization in the Lipari islands (*Odyssey* 12, 68 and 202). The group is volcanic in origin, and is known to have been more active in ancient times. When Odysseus sights the Planktae, he issues an order to his steersman, the only such order recorded in all his wanderings: 'Keep the ship well clear of this surf and smoke, and make for the crag [*sc.* of Scylla]' (*Odyssey* 12, 217–20). It is not beyond the bounds of possibility that this direction might derive ultimately from ancient sailing instructions for ships making the passage from Campania to Sicily.

As Ernle Bradford has pointed out in his *Ulysses Found*, the west coast of Italy south of the Gulf of Salerno is dangerously short of harbours.[5] His view, based on much experience of small-boat sailing in the Mediterranean, is that a yacht making for Sicily is well advised to leave the coast and head due south. Its route will be sign-posted by Stromboli (3136 feet), whose summit, smoke-wreathed by day and flaring at night, has always provided a distinctive seamark for sailors. From there a choice of routes obtains: standing well off to the east of Stromboli, a boat can hold on south for the Messina Strait – the course chosen by Odysseus – or it can turn west to sail round Sicily. If it follows the latter course, it will have to negotiate the Lipari archipelago, a route with its own hazards through rugged volcanic islands. Circe's sketch of alternative routes certainly suggests a choice of passage past volcanoes or through a tidal strait, and it is a striking coincidence that the alternative passages to west or east of Sicily offer just such a choice to a ship sailing south from the Campanian coast. At this point the *Odyssey* may well be based on sailing lore going back to Mycenaean times.

To accept so much is not to agree that all of Odysseus's landfalls can be identified. There is rarely enough *distinctive* detail to make any one identification really convincing. But this has not deterred critics, ancient and modern, from proposing a wide range of localities both inside and outside the Mediterranean. For example, the ancients generally located the Cyclopes in Sicily. Euripides set the scene of his *Cyclops* on the slopes of Mount Aetna, but some modern writers have argued for the area around Trapani and Mount Eryx.[6] The only indications in Homer are that the Cyclopes lived in caves in a mountainous region, and that there was an uninhabited island off their coast (*Odyssey* 9, 116–24). Again, Calypso's island home, Ogygia, has been variously sought in Malta, Ustica, Madeira, near Ceuta by the Straits of Gibraltar, and even as far afield as Iceland.[7] Homer merely says that the island lies far away 'at the navel of the sea', and that Calypso lived in a cavern with four springs nearby (*Odyssey* 1, 50; 5, 55–74). Sometimes even the scanty Homeric clues are disregarded, as in the case of Circe's island, Aeaea. Homer says that Aeaea was 'an island surrounded by the boundless sea', and that it contained 'the halls and dancing places of Dawn and the rising places of Helios' (*Odyssey* 10, 195; 12, 3–4). This implies a location in the far east. Yet there was a tradition going back to the sixth century BC that connected Circe with Latium, and located her, not in an island, but on the promontory Cape Circeio that still bears her name.

Only the start of Odysseus's voyage can be precisely located on the map. After leaving the Troad he raided the Kikones in eastern Thrace, and was then blown by a north-easterly gale down the Aegean and out past Cape Maleia and Kythera into the wide expanse of open sea to the south and west of Crete (*Odyssey* 9, 39–81). From then on, his course cannot be charted. Kythera is the last place on his travels that can be definitely identified until he finally returns to Ithaca. Nevertheless, there are some indications that his adventures are to be thought of as taking place in the seas to the west of Greece. For instance, after leaving the island of Aiolos, Odysseus has Zephyros as a following wind and runs before it for nine days and nights before sighting Ithaca (*Odyssey* 10, 25–9). This implies that in the epic tradition Aeolia was conceived as lying a long way over open sea to the west or north-west of Ithaca. Again, on leaving Calypso's island in his makeshift boat, Odysseus keeps the Great Bear always on his left, an indication that his seventeen-day voyage to Scheria was in an easterly direction (*Odyssey* 5, 270–81). But these are only slight and general indications, and there is nothing more definite in the Homeric text. All attempts to plot the adventures along a definite course are misconceived in principle and bound to fail for lack of evidence. The story of the wanderings is not the record of an actual voyage; but on the other hand it is probably not entirely divorced from reality. Admittedly the imprint of folk-lore and fairy-tale is strongly marked; one-eyed giants, the bag of the winds, men transformed into animals – such motifs indicate that Odysseus in one sense sails in a Wonderland that never was on land or sea. But the narrative also includes some elements which can be interpreted as reflections of actual experience: the North African coast between Cyrene and Carthage *was* the home of a fruit-tree plausibly identified with the lotus; cave-dwelling pastoralists *did* live in southern Italy in the Late Bronze Age, and tribes as savage as the Laestrygonians were doubtless to be found in Corsica or on the shores of the Adriatic.

The tradition of the wanderings is complex, and certain elements can most plausibly be explained as being based on the experiences of Mycenaean seafarers in western waters. A good case can also be made out for commercial interchange between the Aegean and central and north-west Europe during the Late Bronze Age.[8] Considerable quantities of Baltic amber have been recovered from graves at Mycenae and elsewhere in the Peloponnese. The amber was probably brought overland via central Europe to the head of the Adriatic, and thence by ship. A winged-axe mould of north Italian or upper Danubian type was found in a merchant's house at Mycenae.[9] The Mycenaeans were in the market for copper, tin, and gold, and in return traded jewellery, weapons, and possibly wine. The influence of Mycenaean weapon types is clearly apparent in a bronze corslet found at Čaka (Slovakia), in a bell-type helmet found at Beitzsch (north Germany), and a flange-hilted bronze sword from Ørskovhedehus (Jutland). Analysis of the metal of the sword has shown that it was not manufactured in the Aegean, but in the shape of the tang and in the number and placing of the rivet holes it is very reminiscent of an Aegean sword type of *c.* 1400. If it was manufactured locally, as seems almost certain, we must conclude that a typical product of Aegean craftsmanship was being copied in Denmark in the fourteenth century BC.

It is possible that some vague geographical information about northern Europe filtered back along the trade routes and helped to define the traditional Greek picture of the ends of the earth. A passage in Hesiod's *Theogony* (729–45) may indicate a dim awareness of northern wastes and desolation. In Homer's land of the Laestrygones, 'the paths of day and night are close together', and a herdsman who could do without sleep could earn double pay (*Odyssey* 10, 84–6). This obscure passage must bear some relationship to the mythical portal described by Hesiod (*Theogony* 748–50) 'where Night and Day coming close together hail each other as they pass over the great bronze threshold'. The relationship is corroborated by Homer's name Telepylos, 'Distant Gate', for the Laestrygonian citadel. Both poets appear to be drawing their imagery from a traditional picture of the 'ends of the earth'. Crates of Pergamum took the Homeric passage as a reference to the short summer nights of northern Europe, and many modern commentators have agreed with this interpretation. The passage resists explanation in Mediterranean terms, and appears to suggest the early dawns and lingering twilight of midsummer days in high latitudes. Some inkling of these conditions is more likely to have been transmitted to Greek lands in the Bronze Age when trade and travel were on a far wider scale than in the ensuing Dark Age.

As a general rule in the epics detailed geographical knowledge appears to be coterminous with the areas of Mycenaean occupation, and any knowledge of peoples or places outside these areas can be related to Mycenaean trading ventures. Recent discoveries have enlarged the known area of Mycenaean penetration in north-west Greece. Fifteen years ago no certain Mycenaean settlement was known north of Ithaca, though finds of pottery on Leukas pointed to a Mycenaean presence there as well. But now the district of the lower Acheron in Thesprotia has yielded significant evidence of Mycenaean settlement. Traces of a Cyclopean wall are visible on the hill of Xylokastro, forming a small citadel from which Mycenaean sherds have been recovered. Some miles to the north, near Parga, a *tholos* tomb has been found. Further north again at Mazaraki, Mycenaean pottery and weapons were found in 1970 in a IIIB tomb.[10] But the most significant discoveries have been at Mesopotamos, where an impressive range of buildings has been unearthed on a rocky bluff overlooking the confluence of the rivers Acheron and Cocytus.[11] The buildings constitute an oracular shrine for the consultation of the dead, and date from the third century BC, but the Oracle had a long previous history. Sixth-century votives have been found on the site, and the discovery of Mycenaean sherds and a Mycenaean tomb within the sanctuary precinct makes it quite possible that the Oracle was in continuous operation from the Late Bronze Age.

The site has great interest in relation to the Homeric description of the visit to the Underworld in the *Odyssey*, Book 11. Odysseus is required to journey to the House of Hades to consult the ghost of the Theban prophet Teiresias. Circe explains that he must cross the stream of Ocean in his ship, and continues:

You will come to a wild coast and Persephone's Grove, where

> the tall poplars grow and the willows that so quickly shed their seeds. Beach your boat there by Ocean's swirling stream and march on into Hades' Kingdom of Decay. There the River of Flaming and the River of Lamentation, which is a branch of the Waters of Styx, unite round a pinnacle of rock to pour their thundering streams into Acheron.
>
> *Odyssey* 10, 509–15
> (translation by E. V. Rieu)

This is the spot where Odysseus is to dig a trench and, after due sacrifice and libation, talk with the spirits of the departed. The description is graphic: the remote sea beach, the groves of trees, and a rocky crag rising over the junction of three rivers, Acheron, Cocytus, and Pyriphlegethon. It might be expected to owe something to the scenery of an actual place, and Pausanias long ago suggested that Homer found the originals of his underworld rivers in Thesprotia, where the willow-fringed Acheron still winds its way to the sea across a broad and marshy plain. The discovery of the Oracle at Mesopotamos greatly strengthens this suggestion, for the buildings stand on a rocky bluff that rises steeply on the north bank of the Acheron at the exact point where the Cocytus flows down to mingle its waters with the larger stream. N. G. L. Hammond has made a careful study of the topography of the region, and discovered that a third stream used to flow in from the south at the same point. This stream has disappeared as a result of drainage work in this century, but the locals told Hammond that it was highly phosphorescent, and that 'between March and June there used to be a noise of subterranean waters rumbling and echoing.' The case seems strong for identifying it with Pyriphlegethon the 'fire-blazer'.[12] Drainage work has also greatly altered the appearance of the plain above the junction of the three rivers, for there used to be an extensive lake there, the Acherusian Lake, which pilgrims coming from the south to consult the Oracle would cross by boat. It seems that the river junction at Mesopotamos must be added to the list of venerated places, such as the waterfall of the Styx in Arcadia and the cave of Cape Taenaron, that have influenced poetic descriptions of the Hose of Hades.

S. I. Dakaris excavated the site of the Oracle, and has given a detailed description of the finding of the bones of domestic animals (sheep, cattle and pigs) in small pits, and also grain, libation-dishes, and urns that had once held honey (see note 11 above). He compares the ritual used by Odysseus for the calling up of the ghosts: the digging of a pit 'a cubit this way and that'; the pouring of a libation of honey-cum-milk, wine, and water; the sprinkling of barley; and the cutting of the throats of the sacrificial victims so that the blood flowed into the pit (*Odyssey* 11, 23–37). The coincidence is very close. One could argue that the Hellenistic priests knew their Homer, and modelled the ritual on the *Odyssey*. But this may be too sceptical an approach. The shrine had a long history, and tradition is likely to have been strong in regard to the solemnities of necromancy. Homer could be describing a ritual that was familiar to pilgrims in his own day. The description may even have formed part of the Odysseus legend from its inception. We know that Thesprotia had a sprinkling of Mycenaean settlements, and Odysseus was closely connected with Thesprotia in ancient tradition. There are several references to Thesprotia in the *Odyssey*, and in the epic tradition represented by Eugammon's *Telegony* Odysseus commanded the Thesprotians in a war against the Brygi. The campaign is dated after his return from Troy. In the classical period the Thesprotian royal house claimed descent from Odysseus.

The possibility of yet another link between the visit to Hades and Thesprotia arises from the actual account of the adventure as distinct from Circe's advice beforehand. As Odysseus tells it, he sailed for a whole day with a following wind until he reached 'the bounds of deep flowing Ocean', and there he beached his ship 'in the land of the Cimmerians' (*Odyssey* 11, 6–22). The Cimmerians are living people, not ghosts, but the sun never shines on their land which is always shrouded in mist and cloud. The identification of the Cimmerians was a problem for ancient, as for modern, critics, and the actual reading of the name was in dispute. Among a number of variants in the manuscript tradition is the reading 'Cheimerians', and this spelling of the name points to a possible solution. We have it on the authority of Thucydides (1, 46) that the name 'Cheimerium' was applied to a harbour and headland in Thesprotia north of the mouth of the Acheron. This suggests that Cheimerium was a district name, possibly derived from a local tribe, and if so we have further confirmation that the region of the lower Acheron furnished the setting for the adventure in the Land of the Dead.[13]

Mycenaean trade links with the central Mediterranean weakened after *c.* 1250. At this time the older cultures of Sicily and the Lipari islands were disrupted by a series of invasions from the Italian peninsula. Insecure conditions developed, just as they did in the Aegean after the fall of Troy, and, if we may believe Greek tradition, the instability produced a westwards movement of peoples. For example, Pylian comrades of Nestor were credited with the founding of Metapontum. Thucydides records the story of a detachment of Phocians on their way back from Troy who were swept by a storm to Libya, and then made their way to western Sicily where they settled near the Elymians. The Elymians themselves were said to be displaced Trojans, and it is against this background that the legend of Aeneas's wanderings took shape.

Some historical reality probably underlies these legends. The story of the Phocians shares with the *Odyssey* the motif of a storm driving ships away from Greece into the Libyan Sea. In the fragmented Mycenaean world of the twelfth century, the Aegean and Ionian seas must have been full of marauding squadrons only too ready to sail before the wind and plunder at each new landfall. In unsettled conditions, islanders take readily to piracy. Ithaca was a noted haunt of corsairs in the Byzantine Middle Ages, and may well have been so at the close of the Bronze

Age. The story of Odysseus's descent on the Thracian coast has an authentic ring about it (*Odyssey* 9, 39–61). The marauders win an initial advantage by their surprise attack, but then the natives rally and muster reinforcements, and the attackers are driven off with serious losses. It sounds like a saga fragment deriving from the same period of buccaneering and folk migration that produced the other legends mentioned above.

The exploits of the city-sackers became part of the heroic tradition. Some of their forays are likely to have followed the old trade route to the west, leading to the settlement of scattered detachments along the coast of Italy and Sicily. But this westwards movement did not, it seems, last long, and no permanent settlements of any importance were established. It was, however, a forerunner of the great colonial movement of the eighth and seventh centuries, though not comparable in weight or impetus.

The eighth-century movement was spearheaded by Euboeans, and the latest discoveries by Dr Buchner on Ischia indicate that the Euboean colony there was founded before 750.[14] In the second half of the eighth century it became a densely populated and flourishing settlement with an iron foundry, and a pottery producing a distinctive variety of Late Geometric ware. One fragment of a painted *crater* bears the inscription . . . **ΙΝΟΣ ΜΕΠΟΙΕΣΕ** ('. . . inos made me'). It is sad that the maker's name is incomplete for this inscription is claimed as the earliest potter's signature extant. This find confirms the cultural vigour of the colony, already known from items like the Ischia cup inscribed with hexameters (dated *c.* 725–700), and a vase with an unusual shipwreck scene. It has been suggested, though proof is not possible, that this scene is an illustration of the wreck of Odysseus's ship in the *Odyssey*. What does seem certain is that the Etruscans derived their knowledge of the Odysseus legend from early contacts with a Euboean colony. The Euboeans would have used the East Greek form of the name of the hero, Odysseus rather than

Olysseus (=Ulysses), and this was taken over into Etruscan *Utuse*.

Settlement on Ischia before 750 implies exploration of the Italian coast perhaps as early as *c.* 800. Information about this Euboean prospecting is therefore likely to have been circulating in Aegean ports throughout most of the eighth century. Homer, especially if he visited Ithaca, could hardly have failed to pick up some of this sailors' talk. The assumption that he did so would help to explain the incidental but convincing references to South Italy and Sicily in the *Odyssey*. Most of these relate to slave-trading between Ithaca and the territory of the Sikels (which could be either in Italy or Sicily). There is a Sikel slave-woman in Laertes's household (*Odyssey* 24, 211, 366 and 389), and the Suitors propose to sell unwanted visitors to the Sikels (*Odyssey* 20, 383). In the last of his 'lying tales' Odysseus pretends to Laertes that he is a certain Eperitus from Alybas (the old name for Metapontum), and that he had been intending to go by ship to Sikania (the pre-colonial name for Sicily), but had been driven off course to Ithaca (*Odyssey* 24, 304–7). Taken together, these references seem to imply that our poet was well informed about trading in the Ionian Sea, and in possession of geographical knowledge that had recently become available as a result of Euboean penetration into the western Mediterranean. The same hypothesis would explain the odd reference to Euboea in the Phaeacian episode. At one point Alkinoös says that the most distant place visited by his seamen is Euboea (*Odyssey* 7, 321 ff.). This remark would gain considerable point as an oblique allusion (a reference in reverse, as it were) to the remote colonial outpost of the Euboeans in the Tyrrhenian Sea.

Homer's description of the uninhabited island lying off the coast from the Cyclopes has been well characterized as a blueprint for a 'colonist's ideal landfall':[15]

> Across the bight of the Cyclopes' country extends a fertile island, a wooded island; not very far, yet not close . . . the spot

continues in solitude, wholly uncultivated, a paradise for the bleating she-goats . . . anything would grow well there in season, in the soft moist meadows behind the dykes of the silvery sea: and its vine-stocks would bear for ever. The crop to be harvested at the due time from such smooth plough-loam would be heavy, seeing that the undersoil is fat. Its haven is a natural port requiring no such gear as anchors or wraps.

Odyssey 9, 116–39
(translation by T. E. Shaw)

Though there is nothing to identify the island with Ischia, we may recall the ancient tradition that the Ischian colony prospered because of the fruitfulness of the soil. Certainly in the enthusiastic elaboration of the description we seem to catch an echo of the excitement of the eighth-century colonial movement, with bardic audiences eager to hear stories of undeveloped territories in the west.

Another allusion to early Greek colonial practice has often been noted in the Homeric account of the early history of the Phaeacians.[16] When Nausithoos led his people away from the hostile incursions of the Cyclopes and settled them in remote Scheria, 'he surrounded the city with a wall and built houses and made temples of the gods and divided out the arable land' (*Odyssey* 6, 4–10).

If, as seems likely, the *Odyssey* did not take its present shape much before 700, the early eighth-century colonists would not have known it, but they were probably familiar with earlier versions of the legend which placed the wanderings in western waters. Because of this and other legends, they were very willing to believe that their heroic predecessors had visited Italy and Sicily before them. The great wealth of Odysseus legends in Italy shows that the colonists thought of themselves as returning to areas traversed by their ancestors.[17] This belief is also responsible for the early identification of Odyssean place-names, and the location of peoples like the Cyclopes and Laestrygones in Sicily. The earliest Greek colony on the mainland of Italy was at Cumae close to the actively volcanic regions bordering the Bay of Naples. Here was Lake Avernus, later regarded as an entrance to the Underworld, and it is not improbable that the grotto of the Cumaean Sibyl was already the scene of necromantic practices when the colonists arrived. If so, it would have been natural for them to view this area (rather than Thesprotia) as the scene of Odysseus's consultation with the ghosts on the borders of the Land of the Dead. This identification would have entailed locating Circe not far to the north, for Odysseus sailed only a day's journey south from her island to reach the confines of the House of Hades (*Odyssey* 10, 507 with 11, 11). Here we may have the origin of the association of Circe with the Italian promontory that still bears her name. As noted above, this attribution is not consistent with the Homeric text, but local pride would easily overlook such difficulties. It may be supposed that similar considerations induced the early Sicilian colonists to identify their island with Thrinakia, despite the fact that the Homeric description of Thrinakia implies a small deserted island poor in natural resources, and therefore very unlike Sicily (*Odyssey* 12, 260 ff.).

Epilogue: The Homeric tradition

Before listing the Greek forces at Troy, Homer makes one of his rare personal comments (*Iliad* 2, 484–93). 'I could never attempt it,' he confesses, 'not even if I had ten tongues and a voice that never wearied, unless the Muses remembered all who came to Ilion.' He had obviously reflected on the problem of recalling the distant past. In the absence of written records, neither he nor his hearers had any sure knowledge about the Trojan War, but only hearsay information. One had to turn to the immortals, for they had witnessed the events and knew it all. So he summons to his aid the Muses, daughters of Zeus and Memory. In his own idiom the poet is making two points: first, that any one person's beliefs about the past are sketchy and fallible; secondly, that the noble tradition of narrative song has an inspiration that can raise it above the passing scene to span the centuries. Emboldened by this thought, he then proceeds to catalogue the leaders and the numbers of the ships.

In the epic tradition, the Heroic Age was an age of superhuman achievement based on superior prowess and physical strength. It is a Homeric cliché that two men 'as men are now' could not lift the boulders that the heroes flung at one another (*Iliad* 5, 303; 20, 286; *cf.* 12, 383 and 449). The Cyclopean walls of Tiryns and Mycenae are a standing proof that the men of old could indeed raise heavy masses of stone. Homer was aware, of course, of the human propensity to exalt the past, and neatly uses this trait to characterize Nestor on his first appearance in the *Iliad* (1, 245 ff.). After praising the champions of his youth, Nestor affirms that 'no mortals now on earth could fight with them'; but the tribute might stand as Homer's epitaph for the Heroic Age. Homer accepts that in olden times men lived on a higher plane of endeavour, and were closer to the gods.

Homer was not concerned to try to date the past. Even if he had wanted to do so, he could not have expressed the gap between the Heroic Age and his own day in terms of the lapse of centuries. His handling of past events was that of the dramatist rather than the chronicler, as Aristotle appreciated (*Poetics*, ch. 23). An ample setting and noble characters were supplied by the legends; he proceeded by selection and emphasis to evoke the tragedy of their conflicts.

In his sonnet *Epic*, Patrick Kavanagh has made the valid point that involvement can be intense and passionate even in such a trivial matter as a quarrel between peasants over a boundary fence:

I heard the Duffys shouting 'Damn your soul';
And old McCabe stripped to the waist, seen
Step the plot defying blue-cast steel:
'Here is the march along these iron stones'.

And he goes on to suggest that Homer by his art has magnified events of small moment:

Homer's ghost came whispering to my mind.
He said: I made the Iliad from such
A local row.
Gods make their own importance.

It is a nice notion, and one that was seriously maintained by many critics of Homer in the last century. Thucydides obviously considered it, but only to reject it as historically unsound. The poets, he allows, glorified the Trojan campaign more than its results warranted (1, 11), but at least it was no 'local row'. It was an enterprise in which all Greece took part (1, 3), and upwards of 100,000 men were probably involved on the Greek side alone (1, 10). It is interesting to see how Thucydides bases his estimate on the Homeric Catalogue (1186 ships with an average complement of 85). Unlike most modern historians he regards the total as not exaggerated, even though Mycenae seemed to him a 'little' place, and the Mycenaean world lacking in material resources.

Thanks to the progress of archaeology, we now have a much better understanding than Thucydides of the grandeur and wealth of the Mycenaean centres. Few would now downgrade the clash between Achaeans and Trojans to the status of a border raid. But where do the Homeric poems stand in our attempts to reconstruct the history of the Late Bronze Age?

In recent years widely differing assessments have been given on this point. For instance, P. Vidal-Nacquet holds that the advance of archaeology has widened the gap between Homer and the Mycenaean world. Miss Gray, on the other hand, thinks that the view of the Homeric poems as almost wholly Mycenaean derives support from the more recent discoveries.[1] I should certainly not contend that they are 'almost wholly Mycenaean'. They are concerned with events that really occurred in Bronze Age Greece, and they preserve a memory of that world that is remarkably accurate in many particulars; but they also contain important cultural elements that are undeniably post-Mycenaean. Nevertheless, the credibility of the Homeric tradition about the Mycenaean Age has, in my opinion, been strengthened rather than weakened by major discoveries in the past forty years.

The British excavations in Ithaca in the 1930s showed that the island was occupied by Mycenaeans in LH IIIB and IIIC times. The Cincinnati expedition to Hisarlik uncovered crucial evidence about the destruction of Troy VIIa. Increased understanding of the Hittite archives has thrown much light on conditions in Asia Minor from *c.* 1400 to the close of the Bronze Age. It is now possible to give a plausible account of the political background of the Trojan War with the aid of contemporary documents.

The excavation of the palace at Englianos has added greatly to our understanding of how Mycenaean kingdoms were organized, and has confirmed the Homeric tradition about Nestor's Pylos. The discovery of the Knossos helmet (1951) and the Dendra panoply (1960) have corroborated the Homeric picture of Achaean body armour. Finds of Mycenaean pottery in southern Italy, Sicily, and the Lipari islands have at least enhanced the possibility that the story of Odysseus's wanderings owes something to early Mycenaean voyages.

All these discoveries have been discussed in earlier chapters. In addition, mention should be made of the discovery in 1961 of a large Mycenaean temple (over 60 feet long and 20 feet wide), with some life-sized cult statues, on the island of Kea.[2] It was the first building of its kind to be found at any Bronze Age site in Crete or Greece. Some years later, in 1968, a similar but smaller temple, dating from the thirteenth century and containing cult statues up to 23 inches in height, was found on the citadel of Mycenae.[3] Before these discoveries, Rhys Carpenter had expressed the received opinion when he declared himself convinced that there were no separate roofed temples in the Aegean Bronze Age, and argued that Homer's references to such buildings must be post-Mycenaean.[4] In particular, Homer's picture of the temple of Athena in Troy with its seated cult statue had long been regarded as anachronistic, based on Late Geometric cult (*Iliad* 6, 297–311). These opinions will have to be reconsidered in the light of the new discoveries.

From the historical point of view, the most significant Mycenaean element in the *Iliad*, according to Page, is the prominence of names ending in -eus.[5] The tablets prove that the suffix was common in Mycenaean names, but it 'went out of use before the historical period'. Page concludes that names like Achilleus and Odysseus (and many more such as Atreus, Neleus, Peleus, Perseus, Theseus, etc.) would not have been invented by later poets or storytellers. These archaic names must early have been associated with their specific legends, and this tends to confirm that both name and legend are historical rather than fictional.

The heroic song cycles of medieval Europe have been checked against written chronicles and, under much exaggeration, distortion, and fictional embellishment, a hard historical core has been found in every case.[6] There was a Roland, Prefect of the Breton Marches, who was killed at Roncevaux in AD 778, though the attack came from Christian Basques, not Saracens. This last fact was suppressed when Roland became the prototype Crusader. In the *Nibelungenleid*, Gunther, Attila, and Theodoric were real persons, though their historical relationships have been considerably distorted, and interwoven with fictional characters like Siegfried and Brunnhilde. In *Beowulf* the royal dynasties and genealogies of Geats and Danes are in close conformity with Scandinavian written sources. Beowulf's uncle Hygelac and the Rhine-mouth raid in which he perished are independently attested. Ballads of the Kiev cycle (*byliny* = 'events of the past') still circulate orally in parts of the Soviet Union, often in regions very remote from Kiev. They refer to actual events and personalities of the twelfth and thirteenth centuries, and their scenery remains recognizably south Russian. The oldest song cycle of the Yugoslav heroic tradition is firmly anchored to the Ottoman invasion and the defeat of the Serbs under Prince Lazar at Kossovo in AD 1389. The result of the battle is correctly reported, and details like the killing of Sultan Murad by Miloš Obilič are independently confirmed by contemporary records. The main distortions occur in regard to Marko Kraljević and Vuk Branković. Both were actual people alive at the time, but Marko was far from a hero (he did not even fight at Kossovo), and Vuk was not, as the songs have it, the traitor responsible for the defeat (though he did defect to the Turkish side some years later).

By all analogy, the main characters and events of the Homeric poems should have some historical basis. We may suspect that there have been some chronological distortions – Nestor looks like an intrusion from an earlier generation of warriors – but unfortunately no independent checks are available from Greek chronicles. If anyone asserts that the Trojan War never took place, or that Helen did not go to Troy, or that City VIIa at Hisarlik was sacked by nameless northern barbarians, he cannot be proved wrong. But neither can such sceptics produce any evidence to back up what Palmer has aptly styled their 'facile and barren agnosticism'. On the other hand, those who are prepared to trust the tradition can fall back for support on the data of archaeology, and here, as I hope to have shown, the historicity of the Homeric poems has been progressively vindicated over the past hundred years.

I do not advocate a fundamentalist faith in every Homeric statement, but neither do I rule out the poems completely as evidence for Greek prehistory. The Homeric tradition was obviously not immune from exaggeration, distortion, and falsification, but it was also, I believe, safeguarded by a number of factors that did not always obtain in the case of other heroic traditions. The foundation was well and truly laid. There is reason to suppose that the first lays of Troy were sung in Mycenaean palaces by bards operating within a well-established tradition of courtly and martial song.[7] Trained in the techniques and conventions of poetic expression, their duty would be to glorify the royal house by proclaiming the 'famous deeds' of its 'great men' (*klea andrōn*). Judicious embellishment would be in order, but not barefaced falsification. The 'divine entourage' of the Olympians might be invoked to enhance the glory of the living monarch or the dead champion, but at the centre of the halo was a human face.[8] With the decline and fall of the Mycenaean world, the genealogies, panegyrics, and recitals of merit (*aristeiai*) became the precious heirlooms of refugees. The aristocratic families lost their other possessions, but they and their retainers clung to the memory of their great past. In the precarious and impoverished world of the Dark Ages, the bards were primarily the mouthpieces for a tradition that consoled noble and commoner alike as they gathered in forge or tavern, or round the hearth of some earth-floored smoke-filled hall. There were no written records to contaminate the tradition or confuse the memory of the singers. For some centuries the songs did not travel far afield, unlike the *Chanson de Roland* and the *Nibelungenlied*, which were widely diffused among peoples of very varied backgrounds and folklore.[9] From *c.* 1000 to 700 the Aeolian and Ionic colonies in Asia Minor constituted a small and close-knit world untouched by invasion and relatively immune from outside influences.

As a milieu for the propagation of heroic songs, the valleys and villages of Serbia, Bosnia, and Montenegro bear some resemblance to ancient Ionia. For many centuries after the Turkish occupation they remained politically isolated, and largely untouched by the literacy of more progressive communities. From the field studies of Parry and Lord we can derive some notion of what their traditional poetry meant to the Southern Slavs. Parry tells how an old man from Gatsko dictated to him the story of his life, and in recounting his youthful battles against the Turks used the phrase: 'Two pashas we fought and overcame,' a phrase which is a common formula in the Kossovo ballads.[10] Parry comments: 'For the people as a whole who created the verse and kept it, it is an ideal; for this man it has become a boast . . . the whole body of traditional poetry from the past brought with it the ideal of life as a whole for these men of Gatsko who have ever been renowned for their singing. So in the Greek heroic age did they sing the *klea andrōn*, the "high deeds of men".'

The comparison is suggestive. We may believe that the heroic tradition was just as closely integrated into the life of the early Ionian communities, fostering their will to survive by its patterns of loyalty and fortitude. C. R. Beye has stressed the importance of such poetry in an illiterate culture:[11] 'Not only does the poetry articulate the culture as it is, but more important, what it was, thereby giving the culture stability and continuity. Oral saga poetry for such a culture is its history and school as much as its art . . .' In Ionia, Greek oral poetry flourished, gathering new material because it was a vital art form, but also preserving in its stories a true outline of what had happened. As the servant of the community, the singer was not free to alter arbitrarily what everyone in his audience believed to have been the case. As the servant of the Muses he was inspired to use all his powers to preserve the memory of great achievements. It is tempting to speculate that Homer's respect for past realities was not exceptional, but rather the culmination of an attitude that had characterized the long line of his forerunners in the art of oral narrative song. In modern Greek oral poetry between AD 1500 and 1800 examples have been noted of a 'tendency to be truthful and accurate . . . about contemporary events.'[12] It would not be surprising if ancient Ionian bards had shown the same historical sense.

While recreating the past, Homer had also to keep in touch with his audience and their experience of a very different present. He modernized his material to some extent, just as his predecessors had done in respect of iron-working, cremation, and the use of two throwing spears. It is W. G. Forrest's opinion that 'there is little in them [the Homeric poems] of the eighth century except Homer's own genius, little except the bare bones of the story, that belongs to the thirteenth.' If this is correct, it follows that the Homeric world is largely the world of the tenth and ninth centuries, but I share the view that the centuries before and after this relatively 'dark' period contributed more to the Homeric picture.[13] I hope that the previous chapters have demonstrated that some of the furniture and much of the feel of the Mycenaean world survive in Homer. It can also be shown, I believe, that eighth-century Phoenician trading, the growth of the *polis*, and the colonial movement of Homer's own time, have coloured the poems in certain important respects.

What of Homer's own genius? Oral convention required that the singer's personality should merge unobtrusively into the stream of song, so Homer himself remains elusive. Perhaps we can most plausibly detect his hand at work in some of the elaborate similes that embellish the narrative.[14] The humbler members of his audience would respond instantly to the picture of the castaway Odysseus huddled in his bed of dry leaves:

> like a brand which a man hides under the black ashes, in a remote and lonely spot where there are no other neighbours near, saving the seed of fire that he may not have to seek elsewhere for kindling.
>
> *Odyssey* 5, 488–90

The wealthier nobles would appreciate the references to four-horse racing chariots – an eighth-century innovation (*Odyssey* 13, 81–3; cf. *Iliad* 11, 699–701). Homer, I like to think, had himself in mind when he sung of Hera speeding from Ida to Olympos:

> quick as the darting mind of a man far travelled, whose shrewd heart forms the thought 'O to be there . . . or there!', and deeply desires it.
>
> *Iliad* 15, 80–2

We can even, I believe, follow him a little on his travels, for some of his similes are tagged with proper names, a fact significantly at odds with the generic style normal in epic comparison. The Achaean assembly is moved

> like the long surges which the east wind and the south wind stir up in the *Icarian* sea [i.e., the Aegean south of Samos].
>
> *Iliad* 2, 144–6

The army musters for battle

> like the many flocks of birds, geese or cranes or long-necked swans, clamorously fluttering and settling in the meadow of *Asia* by the streams of the *Caÿster* [near Ephesos].
>
> *Iliad* 2, 459–63

Nausikaa is as tall and graceful as

a young shoot of the palm tree beside the altar of Apollo in *Delos*.

Odyssey 6, 162–3

When Menelaos is wounded by an arrow the blood stains his thighs

as when a woman of *Maeonia* or *Caria* stains ivory with purple dye to make a cheek-piece for horses.

Iliad 4, 141–2

Homer inherited a poetic language which, like the tradition, was a blend of overlapping elements, a contrived amalgam of forms and phrases deriving from successive stages in the evolution of the Greek dialects. The decipherment of Linear B confirmed the previous deductions of philology, namely, that the epic dialect is firmly rooted in the Mycenaean Age. Archaic and obsolete 'Achaean' words and inflexions are preserved side by side with the latest developments of the Ionic vernacular. Over hundreds of years successive generations of singers had built up the repertoire of stylized expressions which we call the formulaic system. Inevitably, therefore, the system reflects the speech patterns of all periods from the Mycenaean onwards. We can check the truth of this by the evidence of epigraphy only near the beginning and at the very end of the process. The development through the Protogeometric and Geometric epochs has to be inferred. Kirk has stressed the importance of the Dark Age in the forging of the formulae,[15] and I would agree that the period from *c.* 1050 to 800 was very significant in the evolution of the forms of epic utterance. This period bequeathed to Homer an instrument of expression which informs his poetry as thoroughly as previously developed forms and harmonies pervade the music of Beethoven. Like Beethoven, Homer accepted and worked within a long-established tradition, and succeeded in transcending it. That is the measure of his genius. Using phrases and word-patterns familiar within the context of his art, he rewove the old legends into majestic and harmonious compositions that expressed a vision of gods and men at once Hellenic and universal.

The songs of Homer soon rang out through the Greek-speaking world. Between 750 and 700 we can trace a revival of hero-cult at the tombs of Agamemnon near Mycenae and Menelaos at Sparta.[16] It is not possible to say whether this manifestation was caused by the circulation of the *Iliad*, or whether it merely shows that the Greeks were ripe for the evocation of the past that Homer was to provide. Be that as it may, the Homeric poems helped the Hellenes to realize their fundamental unity as a people. Homer gave definition to the Olympian pantheon, and turned the tale of Troy into a myth that Dorian and Ionian could live by. The *Iliad* and the *Odyssey* helped to shape the evolution of Greek civilization, and, as the old cliché has it, became the 'Bible of the Greeks'. Many of them had Homer by heart, and down the ages his 'winged words' have never ceased to hover on the lips of Philhellenes.

The death-defying courage of the heroes was recalled by Socrates at his trial (*Apology* 28 b–d). He imagined a critic attacking him for having worked himself into a position where he was in danger of losing his life, and then made his eloquent rejoinder:

> By this argument the heroes who died at Troy, and especially the son of Thetis, would be unworthy of any respect . . . When Thetis warned Achilles: 'My son, if you avenge the death of your comrade Patroklos by killing Hector, you yourself will die soon after', Achilles despised the risk of death, being much more afraid of life with dishonour if he failed to avenge his friend.

Socrates showed a more enlightened form of heroism – the indomitable courage of the Nonconformist conscience – but he turned instinctively to Homer's Achilles for his example of a kindred spirit. The comparison must have been much in his thoughts, for shortly before his execution it came to him in a dream that his death was to be a 'homecoming to fertile Phthia' – the Avalon that Achilles never reached (*Crito* 44 b).

Alexander the Great, it is said, took his *Iliad* with him on all his campaigns. To judge from the extant fragments of literary papyri, the *Iliad* was easily the most popular book in Hellenistic Egypt. The *Odyssey* came some way behind it, but was the first Greek work to be translated for use in Roman schools. When the Elder Cato persuaded the Senate to release the Achaean exiles, Polybius thought of applying for a further restitution of privileges. He consulted Cato on the matter, and Cato smilingly compared him to an Odysseus wanting to return to the cave of the Cyclops to fetch his cap and belt. Five years later, Polybius was standing beside Scipio at Carthage, watching the city burn. Scipio, with a strange foreboding that Rome itself might one day be sacked, turned to him and quoted from the *Iliad* (6, 448): 'There will come a day when holy Ilion shall fall.'

Cicero in his *Letters* quotes Homer forty-five times, far more than any other author. At the age of twenty-five, Julian was honoured with the purple by Constantius, and elevated to the post of Caesar of the West. As he returned in his chariot from the solemn investiture, he repeated to himself with wry foreboding a familiar line from Homer (*Iliad* 5, 83 *et al.*):

> Purple death seized him and overmastering fate.

A final example, this time from eighteenth-century England, will confirm the universal appeal of Homer at times of stress and danger. The Earl of Granville, a few days before his death, was approached by Robert Wood on state business. He was so obviously a sick man that Wood proposed to defer the matter, but the Earl insisted on hearing him, saying that it would not prolong his life to neglect his duty. Then he repeated the closing lines of Sarpedon's exhortation to Glaukos:

Man, supposing you and I, escaping this battle,
would be able to live on forever, ageless, immortal,
so neither would I myself go on fighting in the foremost
nor would I urge you into the fighting where men win glory.
But now, seeing that the spirits of death stand close about us
in their thousands, no man can turn aside nor escape them,
let us go on and win glory for ourselves, or yield it to others.

Iliad 12, 322–8
(translation by R. Lattimore)

As Wood tells it, His Lordship repeated, 'Let us go on', several times, 'with a calm and determinate resignation'.[17]

What is the secret of Homer's continuing appeal? First, I would say, he captivates us by the beauty and aptness of his diction. In his first contribution to Homeric criticism, Millman Parry wrote: 'The first impression which this use of ornamental words makes upon the reader is one of utter loveliness. They flow unceasingly through the changing moods of the poetry, inobtrusively blending with it, and yet, by their indifference to the story, giving a permanent unchanging sense of strength and beauty.' Secondly, I would point to the generous idealism of Homer's view of life. Homer 'shows us what human character can be; what men and women have to do and to bear, how great they can be; life means more, is better worth living, when one has got Homer written in one's heart'.[18] Thirdly, I would hold that the charm and nobility of the poems are constantly enhanced by 'that sweet ornament which truth doth give'. The songs of Homer are true to life. In their conception of the Heroic Age, the Homeric poems have distilled the truth of a nation's past. The tradition inherited by Homer was inherently sound. At its heart lay the valid memory of a great period in Greek history, an age of wealth, refinement, and military prowess, when the long-haired Achaeans travelled far and endured much suffering while the will of Zeus was accomplished.

Notes on the text

List of Abbreviations

AH G. L. Huxley, *Achaeans and Hittites*, Oxford 1960

AJA *American Journal of Archaeology*

AM *Mitteilungen des deutschen archaologischen Instituts, Athenische Abteilung*

AR *Archaeological Reports:* Supplement to the *Journal of Hellenic Studies*

Armour A. M. Snodgrass, *Early Greek Armour and Weapons*, Edinburgh 1964

BICS *Bulletin of the Institute of Classical Studies, University of London*

BSA *Annual of the British School at Athens*

CAH(3) *The Cambridge Ancient History*, Third Edition revised, Cambridge, 1970–
(Note: At the time of going to press, Vol. I, Parts 1 and 2, and Vol. II, Part 1 have been published, and page references to these volumes are given. In the case of Vol. II, Part 2, page references are to the fascicules separately published in advance.)

CJ *Classical Journal*

Companion A. J. B. Wace and F. H. Stubbings, *A Companion to Homer*, London 1962

CQ *Classical Quarterly*

CR *Classical Review*

DAG A. M. Snodgrass, *The Dark Age of Greece*, Edinburgh 1971

Documents M. Ventris and J. Chadwick, *Documents in Mycenaean Greek*, Cambridge 1956

EGW P. A. L. Greenhalgh, *Early Greek Warfare: Horsemen and Chariots in the Homeric and Archaic Ages*, Cambridge 1973

Essay R. Wood, *An essay on the original genius and writings of Homer*, London 1775

FFS Rhys Carpenter, *Folk-Tale, Fiction and Saga in the Homeric Epics*, Berkeley and Los Angeles 1958

GGP J. N. Coldstream, *Greek Geometric Pottery*, London 1968

GR *Greece and Rome*

GRBS *Greek Roman and Byzantine Studies*

HC J. L. Myres, *Homer and his Critics*, edited by D. Gray, London 1958

HHI D. L. Page, *History and the Homeric Iliad* (2nd printing), London and Berkeley 1963

HM H. L. Lorimer, *Homer and the Monuments*, London 1950

Hom-Myc M. P. Nilsson, *Homer and Mycenae*, London 1933

JHS *Journal of Hellenic Studies*

JRS *Journal of Roman Studies*

MH T. B. L. Webster, *From Mycenae to Homer*, London 1958

MHV Milman Parry, *The Making*

of Homeric Verse, edited by A. Parry, Oxford 1971

Mycenae G. E. Mylonas, *Mycenae and the Mycenaean Age*, Princeton 1966

PN C. Blegen and M. Rawson, *The Palace of Nestor at Pylos in Western Messenia*, 3 vols., Princeton 1966–

Problèmes *Problèmes de la guerre en Grèce ancienne*, edited by J.-P. Vernant, Paris 1968

REG *Revue des Études Grecques*

SH G. S. Kirk, *The Songs of Homer*, Cambridge 1962

TAPA *Transactions of the American Philological Association*

Totenkult *Archaeologia Homerica*, edited by F. Matz and H. G. Buchholz, Goettingen 1967–: Band iii, Kap. W: M. Andronikos, *Totenkult* 1968

Troad J. M. Cook, *The Troad*, Oxford 1973

Troy C. W. Blegen, J. L. Caskey and others, *Troy*, 4 vols., Princeton 1950–6

UMME *The University of Minnesota Messenia Expedition*, edd. W. A. McDonald and G. A. Rapp Jr., Minneapolis 1972

Introduction

1 Page, *HHI*, 137.

2 'The name *Homeros* is known to occur in Greek inscriptions from districts which were historically Aeolic, and hitherto has occurred only there.' Myres-Gray, *HC* 17.

Chapter 1

Homer and the archaeologists

1 For details see W. B. Stanford, *The Ulysses Theme* (2nd edn revised, Oxford 1963), ch. xii.

2 Myres-Gray, *HC* ch. vi, especially 105 and 112–13.

3 Data from Schliemann's own pen include: a) an autobiography in various versions (see H. Schliemann, *Selbstbiographie bis zu seinem Tode vervollständigt*, ed. Sophie Schliemann, 10th edition (Wiesbaden 1968) by E. Meyer; b) 18 diaries; c) some 60,000 letters. For critical comments on these sources, see W. M. Calder III, 'Schliemann on Schliemann', *GRBS* 13, (1972) 335–53. Calder warns that 'Schliemann created for himself in his diaries and letters a fantasy-life. His autobiography is not historical truth'. There appears to be some truth in these allegations, but Calder probably overstates his case. Biographies include: *Schliemann of Troy* by E. Ludwig (trans. by D. F. Tait, (London 1931); *The Gold of Troy* by R. Payne (London and New York 1959); *One Passion, Two Loves: The Schliemanns of Troy* by Lynn and Gray Poole (London 1967); *Heinrich Schliemann, Kaufmann und Forscher*, by E. Meyer (Göttingen 1969). The Pooles' book incorporates family papers made available by General Mélas, a grandson of Schliemann. The material, including 750 letters and memorabilia found in a locked trunk in Athens in 1965, had not previously been shown to any other biographers.

4 Appendix B in the Pooles' biography contains an outline of the subsequent history of the

Schliemann Collection. This account should be supplemented by Nicholas Adams's article 'Treasure they buried again' in *The Observer*, Magazine Section, 12 November 1972. The Collection was presented to the German people in 1881 on condition that it should remain on view for all time. After the outbreak of World War II it was dispersed and hidden at various places in Germany and Poland. Thanks to the initiative of Dr Gertrude Dorka, 400 crates of ceramics, marble idols, etc., were recovered from Schloss Lebus on the Oder and returned to East Berlin in 1946. The storage depot at Schönebeck was destroyed and everything stored there was lost. Nothing was recovered from Schloss Peruschen in Poland. At the end of the war the gold and silver objects constituting 'Priam's Treasure', packed in three crates, are known to have been reposing in a bunker beside the Zoological Gardens in Berlin. The Soviet authorities, who took over this sector of the city, say that the Treasure was no longer there when they entered the bunker on 3 May 1945. There are various theories as to what may have happened to it, but it has not been seen since, and there are grave fears that it may have been stolen and melted down. Mr Adams, however, is not without hope that in time it may 're-emerge in all its glory'. Some of the less valuable items of the Collection have been placed on display in various museums in the German Democratic Republic.

5 In Wace-Stubbings, *Companion*, 385. Cf. *CAH*(3) I, 2, 411.

6 For a sceptical view, see M. I. Finley, 'The Trojan War', *JHS* 84 (1964), 1 ff., with rejoinders *ibid* by J. L. Caskey, G. S. Kirk, and D. L. Page.

7 M. P. Nilsson, *The Mycenaean Origin of Greek Mythology* (New York 1932).

8 For a very readable history of the decipherment, see J. Chadwick, *The Decipherment of Linear B* (Cambridge 1958).

9 The date of the tablets is the date of the destruction of the Palace of Knossos, because the tablets were baked, and thus preserved, in the terminal conflagration of the building. L. R. Palmer initiated a bitter controversy when in 1960 he challenged Evans's dating of *c.* 1400 for the destruction, and argued for a date closer to 1200. The majority of scholars still support a date close to 1400. For details of the controversy see L. R. Palmer and J. Boardman, *On the Knossos Tablets* (Oxford 1963). Further discussion by S. Hood ' "Last Palace" and "Reoccupation" at Knossos', *Kadmos* 4 (1965), 16–44; M. R. Popham, 'The Destruction of the Palace of Knossos and its Pottery', *Antiquity* 40 (1966), 24–8.

10 *AJA* 65 (1961), 221–60; *AJA* 68 (1964), 229–45; *AJA* 73 (1969), 123–77; *UMME*, ch. 8.

11 Detailed reports of the Ithaca excavations will be found in *BSA* vols. 33 (1933), 35 (1934/5), 39 (1942), 43 (1948), 44

(1949), 47 (1952), 48 (1953), 50 (1955). Further information in S. Benton, 'Antiquities of Thiaki', *BSA* 29 (1927/8), and Lord Rennell of Rodd, 'The Ithaca of Odysseus', *BSA* 33 (1933).

Chapter 2

From Mycenae to Homer

1 The rise, expansion, and decline of the Mycenaean civilization is described, with extensive bibliography, in *CAH*(3) II, 1, ch. xiv (F. H. Stubbings), II, 2, chs. xxii(a) and xxvii (*fascs.* 26 and 39, F. H. Stubbings), II, 2, ch. xxxvi (*fasc.* 13, V. R. d'A. Desborough and N. G. L. Hammond). See also E. H. Vermeule, *Greece in the Bronze Age* (Chicago 1964).

2 H. W. Catling, E. E. Richards, A. E. Blin-Stoyle, 'Correlations between composition and provenance of Mycenaean and Minoan pottery', *BSA* 58 (1963), 94–115. The method has been challenged (see Millett-Catling, *Archaeometry* 8 (1965) and 11 (1969) with full bibliography to date), but apparently vindicated by G. Harbottle's neutron activation analysis, for which see *Archaeometry* 12 (1970), 23–24.

3 For Mycenaean roads, especially in Messenia, see W. A. McDonald in *Mycenaean Studies* (ed. E. L. Bennett, Madison 1964) 217–40. In Phocis, *AJA* 77 (1973), 74–7.

4 For an introduction to the archaeology of Mycenae the following works may be consulted: A. J. B. Wace, *Mycenae* (Princeton 1949); S. Marinatos and M. Hirmer, *Crete and Mycenae* (London 1960); W. D. Taylour, *The Mycenaeans* (London 1964); G. E. Mylonas, *Mycenae and the Mycenaean Age* (Princeton 1966).

5 'Tumulus-burial in Albania, the Grave Circle of Mycenae, and the Indo-Europeans', *BSA* 62 (1967). For tumulus-burials in Messenia, see *UMME*, 135–6.

6 For the destruction horizon at the end of the thirteenth century, see V. R. d'A. Desborough, *The Last Mycenaeans and their Successors* (Oxford 1964) *passim*, and *The Greek Dark Ages* (London 1972), ch. 1.

7 V. R. d'A. Desborough, *The Greek Dark Ages*, 19–20. For Messenia and Triphylia, *UMME*, 142–3.

8 For some recent discussions, see *CAH*(3) II, 2, ch. xxxvi (*fasc.* 13, pp. 3–7 and 47–50); Mylonas, *Mycenae* 224–9; A. M. Snodgrass, *The Dark Age of Greece* (Edinburgh 1971), 304–13; Desborough, *The Greek Dark Ages*, 21–3; R. J. Buck, 'The Mycenaean time of troubles', *Historia* 18 (1969), 276–98.

9 *Discontinuity in Greek Civilisation* (Cambridge 1966). Carpenter's thesis is criticized by H. H. Lamb, *Antiquity* 41 (1967), 233–4, and by H. E. Wright Jr., *Antiquity* 42 (1968), 123–7.

10 N. K. Sandars, 'The Last Mycenaeans and the European Late Bronze Age', *Antiquity* 38 (1964), 258–62.

11 The depopulation seems to have been remembered in the epic

tradition. The *Cypria* opened with an allusion to a 'plan of Zeus' to reduce the population of the earth by the Trojan War.

12 J. M. Cook, *CAH*(³)II, 2, ch. xxxviii (*fasc.* 7); G. L. Huxley, *The early Ionians* (London 1966), 23–39.

13 Desborough, *The Greek Dark Ages*, 83.

14 Snodgrass, *DAG*, 375.

15 L. H. Jeffery, *The local scripts of Archaic Greece* (Oxford 1961), 1–21.

16 G. S. Kirk, *SH* 59.

17 The collection is housed in the Widener Library of Harvard University. For the initial publication of the material, see *Serbo-Croatian Heroic Songs*, edited and translated by A. B. Lord, vol. i (Cambridge, Mass. 1953). For some striking comments on the material by Parry himself, see the extracts from his previously unpublished treatise *Cor Huso: A Study of Southslavic Song* in *MHV*, 437 ff.

18 *SH*, 57.

19 *Homer* (London 1972), 80 ff.

Chapter 3

The overlapping worlds of Homeric poetry

1 For some recent discussions of 'Homeric' architecture, see: H. L. Lorimer, *HM*, ch. vii; Wace-Stubbings, *Companion*, 489–97; D. H. F. Gray, 'Houses in the Odyssey', *CQ*, N.S. 5 (1955), 1 ff.; H. Drerup, 'Griechische Baukunst in Geometrischer Zeit', *Archaeologia Homerica* II, O, (Göttingen 1969); M. O. Knox, 'Megarons and *Megara*: Homer and Archaeology', *CQ*, N.S. 23 (1973), 1–21. Details of the Palace at Pylos in *PN*.

2 A point made by Knox, *CQ*, N.S. 23 (1973), 10–11.

3 *Mycenae's last century of greatness* (Sydney 1968).

4 R. D. Barnett, *CAH*(³)II, 2, ch. xxviii (*fasc.* 68), with bibliography.

5 The absolute dating of the reigns of the 18th and 19th Dynasty Pharaohs is currently under vigorous discussion, but the margin in dispute is only of the order of ten to twenty years. Some experts favour dates of 1290–1224 for the reign of Ramesses II, and on this basis the 5th year of Merneptah would be 1220.

6 Page (*HHI* 21, n. 1) gives a useful summary of the controversy, which is still unsettled. The Akaiwasha are distinguished from the other northern allies of the Libyans in two respects: (i) they come from the 'alien land of the Sea'; (ii) they are (almost certainly) circumcised. (i) implies that their homeland is divided from Egypt by a considerable expanse of sea, and the description favours one of the Aegean islands (*e.g.*, Crete), or even the Greek mainland. (ii) is a difficulty, perhaps magnified by our tendency to oppose Jew and Gentile in terms of 'circumcised' and 'uncircumcised'. It is a tenable supposition that some Mycenaean Greeks practised circumcision. To the Egyptians circumcision indicated a people at a higher level of culture and civilization. In the Merneptah inscription the Akai-

washa are distinguished in this respect from other northerners. It is also to be noted that among the booty captured by the Egyptians were chariots of the four-spoke type characteristic of Mycenaean lands. On balance it seems to me that the equation Akaiwasha=Achaeans is likely to be correct.

7 As early as the mid-14th century the King of Alasiya (Cyprus) is complaining of yearly sacking of cities in his land by Lukka raiders (Tell el-Amarna Tablets, I, p. 203, no. 39, Mercer).

8 Pottery of Mycenaean III C type has recently been found at Ashdod, well known in the Bible as a major Philistine city. This is yet another indication of links between the Mycēnaean world and the Sea Peoples.

9 Page (*HHI* 15 ff.) favours the identification of the Ahhijawa of Hittite documents with Rhodes. Huxley *AH* contains a clear exposition of the complexities of the Ahhijawa problem. He argues that the documents by themselves cannot show where the King of Ahhijawa lived, but when their evidence is combined with that of Mycenaean archaeology and Greek tradition we can be sure that it was at Mycenae.

10 *SH*, ch. 6.

11 This section is largely based on D. H. F. Gray's 'Metal-working in Homer', *JHS* 74 (1954), 1–15. Much relevant material also in Lorimer, *HM*, ch. III, 2, and Snodgrass, *DAG* ch. 5.

12 Lorimer, *HM*, 111, no. 2.

13 Ventris-Chadwick, *Documents* No. 290.

14 *Documents*, p. 330.

15 Snodgrass, *DAG*, 248.

16 Edition of *Odyssey* by W. B. Stanford (London 1947), *ad loc.* Gray, *JHS* 74 (1954), 4.

17 For this section I have chiefly consulted: Nilsson, *Hom-Myc*, ch. III, sect. 2; Lorimer, *HM*, ch. II, 1; T. J. Dunbabin, *The Greeks and their eastern neighbours*, *JHS* Suppl. Paper No. 8 (1957), 35–43; Coldstream, *GGP*, 380–1, 386–90.

18 Stanford, *Odyssey*, *ad loc.*

19 For a fine Phoenician bronze bowl of 8th–7th century date from Olympia, see Dunbabin, *op. cit.*, Plate VI–VII.

Chapter 4

The picture and the record

1 M. I. Finley, *The World of Odysseus*, rev. ed. (London 1956), 86. An Appendix (not in the first edition) gives reasons for Finley's belief that the tablets 'reveal a world altogether unlike the Homeric, and contribute little to our understanding of the world of Odysseus'.

2 *CAH*(3)II, 2, ch. xxxix (b) (*fasc.* 22, p. 25).

3 *HHI*, 186.

4 Compare the appeal of Tuthalijas IV to his nobles, summarized in *HHI*, 109, especially the passage: 'Lords who command my troops and charioteers and strongholds, stand by with loyal hearts; as you love your own wives and your own children and your own homes, even so

love your King's commands and practise them well.'

5 The progress in his field may conveniently be judged from *AR* 1959–60, 27 ff., 1964–5, 32 ff. (espec. p. 44), 1970–1, 33 ff. The evidence for Mycenaeans in Western Asia Minor is summarized by Mellink in *AJA* 75 (1971), 168–9.

6 The fundamental publication is M. Ventris and J. Chadwick, *Documents in Mycenaean Greek* (Cambridge 1956). J. Chadwick and S. Dow have recently reviewed the progress of Linear B studies, with extensive bibliography, in *CAH*(³)II, 1, ch. xiii. Sharply contrasting views of the relevance of the tablets to Homer may be found in T. B. L. Webster, *Companion* 452–62 (receptive), and M. I. Finley, 'Homer and Mycenae: Property and Tenure', *Historia* 6 (1957), 133–59 (sceptical).

7 See *Documents*, 108. One celebrated tablet (*Documents* No. 53) is headed: e-re-ta pe-re-u-ro-na-de i-jo-te=Rowers to go to Pleuron. The words if written in Homeric Greek would form the second half of a hexameter.

8 For a selection of the most significant tablets, see *Documents* Nos. 56–60. This type of tablet is fully discussed by M. Lejeune in *Problèmes de la guerre en Grèce ancienne* (ed. by J.-P. Vernant, Paris 1968).

9 *E.g.*, both are used of Odysseus in *Odyssey* 20, 194. *Cf.* Alkinoös who *wanassei* (*Odyssey* 7, 23) and is *basileus* (*Odyssey* 7, 55).

10 M. Lejeune, 'Le DAMOS dans la Société mycénienne' *REG* 78 (1965), 3, notes that *wanax* is applied to the Pylian monarch and to certain deities as in Homer.

11 C. G. Thomas, 'The roots of Homeric kingship', *Historia* 15 (1966), 393.

12 Hector is not said to possess a *temenos*, but one of his Maeonian allies, Iphition, has one (*Iliad* 20, 391). *Cf.* also Achilles's sarcastic question to Aeneas whether the Trojans have promised him a *temenos* if he wins the duel (*Iliad* 20, 184–6). In the *Odyssey* Laertes owns an estate, perhaps gained as a reward for military successes (*Odyssey* 24, 205–8 with 24, 376–8).

13 *Iliad* 18, 550; *Documents* No. 152. Homer also uses *temenos* in the later sense, *e.g.*, *Iliad* 8, 48, of the precinct of Zeus at Gargarus on Mount Ida.

14 See, *e.g.*, the controversy between M. I. Finley, *Historia* 6 (1957), 133–59 and L. R. Palmer 'The Mycenaean tablets and economic history', *Economic History Review* 11 (1958–9), 87–96.

15 *CAH*(³)II, 1, 620.

16 W. Ridgeway, 'The Homeric Land System', *JHS* 6 (1885), 319–39.

17 *CAH*(³)II, 1, ch. xxii(a) (*fasc* 26 p. 18): *Cf.* Finley in *Economic History Review* 10 (1957), 139: 'We must imagine a situation in which officials, soldiers, craftsmen, herders and farmers all held land (or worked on the land) on condition that they rendered either appropriate services or quotas of products'; Nilsson, *Hom-Myc.* 238: 'a kind of loose feudalism'.

18 Webster, *Companion* 456, notes that it can be paralleled from Knossos tablet As 821; *cf. Documents*, 168–9, on *themis* and *opa* as feudal dues.

19 For which see *Documents*, 123.

20 *CAH*(3)II, 1, 619.

21 *Documents*, 92–105, espec. 103 ff.; *MH*, 114–28; Gray, 'Mycenaean names in Homer', *JHS* 78 (1958), 43–8.

22 *MH* 116.

23 Agelaos: *Iliad* 8, 257; 11, 302. Deukalion: *Iliad* 13, 451; 20, 478. Laodokos: *Iliad* 4, 87; 17, 699.

24 For detailed discussions of the Greek and Trojan Catalogues in the light of post-war archaeological discoveries see Page, *HHI*, 118 *ff*.; Huxley, *BICS* 3 (1956) 19–30; R. Hope Simpson and J. F. Lazenby, *The Catalogue of Ships in Homer's Iliad* (Oxford 1970). See also Kirk, *CAH*(3), II, 2, ch. xxxix(b) (*fasc.* 22, p. 20). G. Jachmann, *Der Homerische Schiffs-Katalog und die Ilias* (Cologne 1958) is very sceptical about the historicity of the Catalogue.

25 C. M. Bowra, *Homer*, 90 f., notes that 'the kings of Uganda kept official singers who recalled their descent for thirty generations; the Maoris remember in detail the voyages that brought them from Tahiti to New Zealand between c. AD 825 and c. AD 1350.'

26 The Boeotians have 50 ships, each holding 120 men (*Iliad* 2, 509–10).

27 Page, *HHI*, 10–17, 147–9.

28 'The Mycenaean Documents' in *UMME*, 100 ff., espec. 109 (*ai-pu*) and 113–14.

29 Even if we allow that Thruon may be indirectly authenticated, it must be remembered that Homer's Thruon commanded a ford on the Alpheios (*Iliad* 2, 592; *cf.* 11, 711), and was therefore, in Chadwick's view, well outside the frontiers of the Pylian kingdom revealed in the tablets. See *UMME*, 109 and Fig. 7–1.

30 The 'Hither Province' interpreted as the region between the sea and Mount Aigaleon.

31 The 'Further Province' centred on the Pamisos valley to the east of Mount Aigaleon.

32 *Cf.* Hope Simpson and Lazenby, *The Catalogue of Ships in Homer's Iliad*, 86–7.

33 Lines 853–5 are almost certainly a late interpolation, and are here excluded from the enumeration of place-names.

34 For this section I have chiefly consulted: Lorimer, *HM*, 103–10; Mylonas, *Companion*, 478–88; Andronikos, *Totenkult*; Snodgrass, *DAG* 140–97. D. C. Kurtz and J. Boardman, *Greek Burial Customs* (London and Ithaca, N.Y. 1971).

35 Lines 334–5 refer to the bringing of the bones of the cremated dead home to their families at the conclusion of the campaign. They were rejected in antiquity by Aristarchus, who pointed out that no attempt is elsewhere made to bring remains home. They are generally thought to be an Athenian interpolation based on Attic custom, as argued by F. Jacoby in *JHS* 64 (1944), 37 ff.

36 *E.g.*, Eëtion, father of Andromache, was cremated in his armour (*Iliad* 6, 416 ff.) The ghost of Elpenor pleads for similar rites, and for the raising of a mound near the sea with an oar set in it, and this is duly done. (*Odyssey* 11, 74–8; 12, 11–15).

37 The translation is that of R. Lattimore. The treatment may have been a form of 'elementary embalming' in view of the long time the corpse was exposed on the bier, according to Mylonas, *Companion*, 479.

38 See map (fig. 68) in Snodgrass, *DAG*.

39 Homer never explicitly describes inhumation. Some of his phrases like 'go below the ground', 'the earth shall hold', have been taken to *imply* inhumation. But this is by no means a necessary inference, since such phrases could apply to the burial of the urn holding the ashes.

40 For this and other possible examples, see Andronikos, *Totenkult*, 104–5.

41 *Dendra*, I, 73 ff., 108 ff.

42 For a detailed account, with fine illustrations, see V. Karageorghis, *Salamis in Cyprus* (London and New York 1969).

43 J. N. Coldstream, 'Cypro-Aegean exchanges in the 9th and 8th centuries BC', *Acta of the 1st International Cyprological Congress* (Nicosia 1972), 21.

Chapter 5

Weapons and warfare

1 The fundamental work in English is Lorimer *HM*. See also Stubbings in *Companion* 504–22; Snodgrass, *Early Greek Armour and Weapons* (Edinburgh 1964), *Arms and Armour of the Greeks* (London and Ithaca, N.Y. 1967). *Problèmes de la guerre en Grèce ancienne* (Paris 1968), edited by J.-P. Vernant, contains important contributions by G. S. Kirk on 'War and the warrior in the Homeric poems', M. Lejeune on 'La civilisation mycénéenne et la guerre', P. Courbin on the archaeological evidence for warfare in Mycenaean and Geometric times, and M. Detienne on the history of the war-chariot.

2 J. A. Charles, 'The first Sheffield Plate', *Antiquity* 42 (1968), 278–84.

3 *phasganon* was the Mycenaean word for sword; in the tablets it appears in the plural as *pa-ka-na* in tablets listing swords.

4 'Euknemides Achaioi', *Mnemosyne* 14 (1961), 97–110.

5 The epic occasionally refers to greaves of tin, *e.g.*, *Iliad* 18, 613; 21, 592.

6 No specimens of greaves have been recovered from Greek lands between *c.* 1150 and *c.* 700 with the sole exception of a bronze pair from a 9th-century Athenian grave: preliminary publication in *Archaeologikon Deltion* 21, 2 (1966). Snodgrass, *DAG*, 333, regards them as an import from barbarian Europe.

7 In the second edition of his *Homerische Waffen* (Vienna 1901), 102 ff.

8 *PN*, vol. 2, 44–5, and Plates 16, 17, A, M. For twelfth-century specimen, *AM* 75 (1960), 44, Beilage 31, 4. For a recent and

full discussion, with catalogue of remains and representations, see J. Borchardt, *Homerische Helme* (Mainz 1972), 18–36 and 78–81.

9 Many critics think that Book 10, the Doloneia, was not part of Homer's *Iliad*, but was added later, but this does not affect the point of the argument here.

10 I owe this example to the important pioneering study *Oral Traditions* by J. Vansina (trans. by H. M. Wright, Harmondsworth 1973), 45.

11 According to Gray, *JHS* 78 (1958), 47, 'The Periphetes episode is a homogeneous piece of fourteenth- (or even fifteenth-) century tradition'. His father's name Kopreus is attested as Mycenaean by the tablets.

12 N. M. Verdelis, 'Neue Fund von Dendra', *AM* 82 (1967), 1–53.

13 *gualon* means literally 'hollow (thing)'. In view of *Iliad* 15, 529–33, which gives the pedigree of a 'corslet fitted with *guala*', the term should probably not be confined to the main 'shells', but extended to cover all the curved attachments of a Dendra-type suit of body armour. Weapons pierce *guala* to wound abdomen (*Iliad* 13, 506–7), and shoulder (*Iliad* 5, 98–9).

14 *to-ra-ke* (*thorakes*) occurs on the Pylos tablets with an appropriate ideogram. The ideograms on the Knossos tablets differ somewhat from the Pylian ones, one in particular closely resembling the Dendra suit. Ventris and Chadwick, *Documents*, p. 376, make the interesting point that 'such body-armour may have been restricted almost entirely to charioteers, for whom the absence of a shield made it a necessity'. A. Severyns, 'Homère et l'histoire', *Antiquité Classique* 33 (1964), 336, suggests that the *teuchea* which 'rattle' when a hero falls may originally have been the separable pieces of a Dendra-type suit. *Cf. Iliad* 4, 420.

15 Explicit: *e.g.*, *Iliad* 13, 372, 398. Implicit: in epithets like 'intricate' (*poludaidalos*), 'glancing' (*panaiolos*), 'glittering' (*phaeinos*), 'newly-wrought' (*neosmektos*); also in statements that the corslet shatters a weapon (*Iliad* 17, 606–7), or is fitted with 'plates' (*guala*) (*Iliad* 5, 99; 13, 507).

16 A corslet fitted with plates has a history of three owners (*Iliad* 15, 530ff.). *Cf.* the pedigree of the boar's tusk helmet.

17 Miss Lorimer, writing before the Dendra discovery, could find no satisfactory explanation for either *mitra* or *zoster* (*HM*, 245–50).

18 Paris, *Iliad* 3, 328–38; Agamemnon, *Iliad* 11, 15–46; Patroklos, *Iliad* 16, 130–44; Achilles, *Iliad* 19, 369–91.

19 Kirk, *SH*, 190–1. See also Webster, *MH*, 167–8.

20 W. E. McLeod, 'An unpublished Egyptian composite bow in the Brooklyn Museum', *AJA* 62 (1958), 397 ff.

21 Quantities of *agrimi horn*, presumably raw material for composite bows, are listed on a series of tablets from the Arsenal

building at Knossos. (*Documents*, pp. 301–2). This particular type of entry has not been found on the Pylos tablets, but bow-makers are included among a list of tradesmen on a Pylos tablet, *Documents* No. 52.

22 Lorimer, *HM*, 276–7.

23 This is the view of Stubbings, *Companion*, 520.

24 Snodgrass, *Armour*, 142–3.

25 The series of Pylos tablets covering chariots is unfortunately incomplete. One group lists wheels, but the main inventory has not been recovered. Pylos tablets En 421 and 809 mention the chariot-maker of the *Lawegetas*.

26 *The Decipherment of Linear B*, 108 with fig. 14. The Homeric word for 'charioteer' (*heniochos*) occurs on one of the tablets, presumably designating the driver as distinct from the warrior.

27 Homer, *Iliad* 9, 383–4, attributes very large chariot forces to the Egyptians.

28 O. R. Gurney, *The Hittites* (Harmondsworth 1952), 49. Lorimer, *HM*, 323.

29 *Greece in the Bronze Age*, 261. See also M. A. Littauer, 'The military use of the chariot in the Aegean in the Late Bronze Age', *AJA* 76 (1972), 145–57.

30 For the Mycenaean sherds, see Lorimer, *HM*, Pl. II, 3, and Snodgrass, *Armour*, Pl. 20. H. Catling, 'A Mycenaean puzzle from Lefkandi in Euboea', *AJA* 72 (1968) thinks that the two Mycenaean fragments probably come from the same vase. The men in the chariot are well-armed and appear to be galloping into battle. They wear the same type of 'hedgehog' helmet as the foot-soldiers on the Warrior Vase.

1 *Armour*, 159 ff., 433. P. A. L. Greenhalgh, *EGW*, gives a typological analysis of the representation of chariots in eighth–seventh century Greek art which appears to refute Snodgrass's theory.

32 *E.g.*, 2, 466; 8, 59; 11, 47–8; 15, 258; 20, 157. The battle in Bk. 11 has most references to chariots – 15 to separate chariots, and 4 to chariots *en masse* in about 500 lines. By contrast, the battle in Bk. 13 (over 800 lines) has only 2 references to chariots.

33 Ajax because of his huge shield, and Odysseus because Ithaca was unsuitable for horses.

34 *Cf.* also 5, 835 ff. It is interesting that the chariot of Diomedes is involved in all these incidents, and that he wins the chariot race in Bk. 23.

35 Glaukos kills a Greek as he mounts his chariot in 7, 13–16, and Hector kills two in a chariot in 5, 608.

36 *FFS* 33. *Cf.* Snodgrass, *Armour*, 160: 'To suppose that warfare was actually carried on in this manner at any time seems curious.' Kirk, *Problèmes*, 111, n. 49: 'nothing that Anderson (see note 38) says removes the impossibility in practical terms of many of the equine circumstances described in the Iliad.'

37 Diodorus Siculus, Bk. V, 21, 5 (Loeb, vol. iii, 155). *Cf.* Bk V, 29, 1 on the Gallic use of chariots. At the battle of Sentinum

in 295 BC Gallic chariots put Roman cavalry to flight (Livy, x, 28).

38 'Homeric, British and Cyrenaic Chariots', *AJA* 69 (1965), 349–52.

39 *PN*, Pl. 123. G. Rodenwaldt, *Der Fries des Megarons von Mykenai* (Halle 1921), reconstructed one of the Mycenaean frescoes to show an 'archer' dismounted from a chariot and about to shoot. The chariot faces away from the conflict.

40 In contrast to *Iliad* 11, 47–52, where men-at-arms advance on foot ahead of the charioteers.

41 In the 'Pylian epic', *Iliad* 11, 748, he is credited with the capture of 50 chariots. In *Iliad* 23, 306 ff., he gives detailed advice on racing technique to his son.

42 Illustrated in Lorimer, *HM*, fig. 47.

43 Published with photographs by G. Buchner and C. F. Russo, *Academia dei Lincei: Rendiconti* 10 (1955), 215 ff. For the latest review of the literature, see *A Selection of Greek Historical Inscriptions*, edd. R. Meiggs and D. Lewis (Oxford 1969), No. 1. I follow the reading and interpretation of D. L. Page, *CR* 6 (1956), 95 ff. Kirk, *SH*, 283 f., writes: 'The Ischia reference must either be to the Iliad or to a separate Pylian poem perhaps used by the main composer of the Iliad.' For a more sceptical interpretation, see Stubbings in *Companion*, 536. He makes the interesting suggestion that *depas*, the word used for Nestor's cup in the *Iliad*, may mean 'mixing-bowl', a sense which in fact suits the context better than 'cup'.

44 Greenhalgh, *EGW*, *passim*, contends: (i) that chariots were used for racing and for funeral processions in Greek lands in the eighth century; (ii) that they were not used in warfare at this time; (iii) that the Knights in the pre-hoplite period were not true cavalrymen, but rode on horseback to battle accompanied by mounted squires, and then dismounted to fight on foot; (iv) that this practice continued in the seventh and sixth centuries, along with the use of hoplite infantry and genuine cavalry; (v) that the Homeric language for chariot fighting, and some incidents in the poems, indicate (a) that epic bards of the eighth century had no personal experience of chariots in warfare, (b) that the bards deliberately archaized the battle scenes to include chariots, knowing only the bare fact that chariots, like bronze weapons, had been a standard feature of Late Bronze Age fighting, and (c) that 'war-chariots' are disguised Geometric cavalry.

I would accept contentions (i), (iii) and (iv), and there is some truth in v(b), but I would reject (ii), v(a) and v(c) as inherently unlikely.

45 Strabo 448, on the Artemis temple dedications at Amaranthos in Euboea.

46 There is no certain reference to cavalry in the Homeric poems. The many references to 'driving horses', 'fighting from horses', etc., are all to be understood of

horses-cum-chariots. See E. Delebecque, *Le cheval dans l'Iliade* (Paris 1951). *Iliad* 11, 150–1, 'foot-soldiers slew foot-soldiers, knights [*hippeis*] slew knights', is sometimes taken as a reference to cavalry, but there is no reason why *hippeis* should not bear its normal Homeric sense of 'one who fights from, or drives, a chariot'. The same observation applies to *hippeus* in the cheek-piece simile (*Iliad* 4, 142). Riding is occasionally mentioned, (only in similes), *e.g.*, *Iliad* 15, 679–84; *Odyssey* 5, 371.

47 'Reflections upon Epic Warfare', Presidential Address by General Sir John Hackett, *Proceedings of the Classical Association* 68 (1972).

Chapter 6

Troy and the Trojan War

1 Coldstream, *GGP*, 376, says that 'the earliest datable vases . . : are bird-kotylae of Rhodian type, *c.* 720–700; but some sherds with semi-circular decoration may be older.'

2 W. Leaf, *Troy: A Study in Homeric Geography* (London 1912), 24. This book, and Leaf's *Strabo on the Troad* (London 1923), may still be consulted with profit for the topography of Troy and the Troad.

3 *Odyssey* 14, 474 recalls a marsh close to the walls of Troy. Achilles's fight with the river god (*Iliad* 21, 200 ff.) is a good example of fiction based on fact. The lower plain of the Skamander is subject to severe flooding in the rainy season. Augustus's daughter Julia was nearly drowned crossing the river.

4 The Sigeum ridge was probably the site of the earthwork of Herakles from which the gods on the Achaean side watched the battle. South and east of Rhoeteum stands the prominent hill Kara Tepe, probably to be identified with Homer's Kallikolone which served as a grandstand for the gods favouring the Trojans (*Iliad* 20, 144–52). For the most recent discussion of the topography and identifications see J. M. Cook, *The Troad: an archaeological and topographical study* (Oxford 1973), 110–13, 165–9.

5 It is hard to see why Cook, *Troad*, 171, stigmatizes the beach at the north end of the Trojan plain as 'an impossible camping site'. The alternative which he appears to favour, without actually committing himself, is Besika Bay, but this hypothesis raises many more difficulties than it solves.

6 Cook, *Troad*, 186–8, puts the best possible construction on it. It may be thought to solve some of the problems inherent in Homer's account of the Trojan campaign. But the placing of ancient Troy here comes up against the extremely damaging fact that the site has no major remains of any consequence, while Hisarlik is one of the major Bronze Age sites of the Aegean.

7 *Fair Greece! Sad Relic: Literary Philhellenism from Shakespeare to Byron* (London 1954). There is a very full treatment of the his-

tory of the controversy, with notices of all the most important travellers and their works, in Cook, *Troad*, 14–51.

8 For a detailed account of the springs, see Cook, *Troad*, 140 ff., who describes them as 'perhaps the most celebrated of all the curiosities of the Troad'.

9 Maclaren did visit the Troad in 1847, and in 1863 produced his *The Plain of Troy described*.

10 For an appreciation of his archaeological work, see Cook, *Troad*, 35–6.

11 D. B. Monro, edition of *Iliad ad loc*, following Virchow, is more definite than the facts warrant. See Cook. *Troad*, 291–3.

12 Leaf, *Troy*, 50. He is suitably cautious about the twin springs at the source of the Skamander.

13 Leaf, *Troy*, 166, and Schliemann, *Troja*, 64.

14 'Homeric epithets for Troy', *JHS* 80 (1960), 18.

15 Leaf, *Troy*, 157.

16 *HHI*, 101 ff. *Cf.* Huxley, *AH* 32 ff. These reconstructions depend for much of their detail on the then generally accepted dating of the relevant documents of Tuthalijas (the 'Annals of Tuthalijas') and Arnuwandas to the second half of the thirteenth century. Recently, however, this dating has been challenged, and a much earlier dating proposed. See H. Otten, 'Sprachliche Stellung und Datierung des Maduwatta-Textes', *Studien zu den Bogazkoy-Texten* 11 (1969); O. R. Gurney, *CAH* (3) II, 1, 678; Ph. H. J. Houwinkten Cate in *Bronze Age Migrations in the Aegean*, edd. R. A. Crossland and Ann Birchall (London 1973) 147–53. The proposed up-dating has not by any means been generally accepted; see, for instance, A. J. Mellink in *AJA* 75 (1971), 168–9.

17 *Mycenae*, 217.

18 *E.g.*, Hammond, *CAH*(3)II, 2, ch. xxxvi (*fasc.* 13 pp. 23–4 and 48); Stubbings, *CAH*(3)I, 1, 246–7; Mylonas, 'Priam's Troy and the date of its fall', *Hesperia* 33 (1964), 352–80. There is a good summary of the controversy by J. Wiseman, *Arion* 4 (1965), 700 ff.

19 *Troy* IV, 12 (*c.* 1240); *CAH*(3), II, 2, ch. xxi (*fasc.* 1, p. 14) (*c.* 1250); *The Mycenaean Age* (Cincinnati 1962), 15 and 27–8 (*c.* 1270–1260).

20 A. Furumark, as reported by C. Nylander, 'The fall of Troy', *Antiquity* 36 (1963), 7, thinks that some of the Troy VIIa sherds are III C, differing in this from the excavators.

21 N. K. Sandars, 'From Bronze Age to Iron Age: a Sequel to a Sequel' in *The European Community in Later Prehistory* (C. Hawkes, *Festschrift*, edited by J. Boardman, M. A. Brown and T. G. E. Powell) (London 1971) 6–9 and 17–18.

22 P. B. S. Andrews, 'The falls in Troy in Greek tradition', *GR* 12 (1965), 28–37.

23 Homer, *Iliad* 21, 441 ff., traces the wrath of Poseidon to this event.

24 The arguments for a close affinity between Greeks and Trojans are well summarized by C. H. Whitman, *Homer and the Heroic*

Tradition (Cambridge, Mass. 1958), 27–30.

25 Page, *HHI*, 66–70.

26 F. Schachermeyr, in his *Poseidon und die Enstehung des griechischen Götterglaubens (Munich 1950), 189 ff.*, argued for Troy VI as Priam's Troy.

27 Leaf, *Troy*, Appendix D, lists thirteen passages from the *Iliad* alluding to what he calls the 'Great Foray', and reconstructs the course of the raid, 242–52.

28 There is a good discussion of Virgil's account by R. G. Austin in *JRS* 49 (1959), 16–25.

29 J. K. Anderson, 'The Trojan Horse again', *CJ* 66 (1970), 22–5.

30 J. W. Jones Jr., 'The Trojan Horse: Timeo Danaos et dona ferentes', *CJ* 65 (1970), 241–7, argues that the story of the capture of a fortress by pretended gifts was traditional, but that the horse is not traditional, and that the first inventor of the story may have thought of a horse because the Trojans worshipped horses. Nilsson, *Hom-Myc.*, 256, noted the Joppa parallel.

31 Edition of the *Odyssey*, on 8, 492.

Chapter 7

Ithaca

1 For a complete list of the excavation reports, see p. 201, n. 11. The topography of Homeric Ithaca was controversial in the ancient world, and there are echoes of the controversy in Strabo's *Geography* and Porphyry's *Cave of the Nymphs*. In modern times a good foundation was laid by Sir William Gell in his *The Geography and Antiquities of Ithaca* (London 1807). R. Hercher was very influential in propagating undue scepticism about the *realien* of Ithaca (*Hermes* i, 1866). After one day's walking in the vicinity of Vathy he became convinced that any identification of individual Homeric sites was 'antiquarian hallucination'. Dörpfeld's theory that Leukas was ancient Ithaca created bitter controversy from the time of its propagation early in the 1900s. His *Alt-Ithaka* (Munich 1927) contains the definitive statement of his position. A. Shewan listed 35 objections to it in his forceful article, 'Beati Possidentes Ithakistae', *Classical Philology* 12 (1917), 132–42. The traditionalist position is supported with a wealth of first-hand information about Ithaca by V. Bérard, *Les Navigations d'Ulysse*, I (Paris 1927), and by Lord Rennell of Rodd, *Homer's Ithaca: A Vindication of Tradition* (London 1927). See also Pavlatos, *The true Ithaca of Homer* (in Greek) (Patras 1901), and Thomopoulos, *Homeric Ithaca* (in Greek, with a German summary) (Athens 1908). There is an excellent summary of the main points in the controversy by Stubbings in *Companion*, 398–421.

2 See S. Benton, 'The Ionian Islands', *BSA* 32 (1931–2), 213–46.

3 *The Homeric Catalogue of Ships* (Oxford 1921), 87.

4 *HM*, 497–8.

5 *E.g.*, D. T. Ansted, *The Ionian*

islands in the year 1863 (London 1863), 233; Thomopoulos (*op. cit.* in n. 1), 235–6; Lekatsas (a native of Itháki), *Ithake* (in Greek) (Athens 1933), 63.

6 *HM*, 436–7.

Chapter 8

On the fringes of Homer's world

1 Wood was present at a consultation on precisely this question on H.M.S. *Chatham* in 1742 (*Essay*, 40–1).

2 A marble cup inscribed with the name of the Sun Temple of Userkaf (2494–2487): *CAH*(3) I, 2, 180. For an estimate of the date of the first Minoan colony, see *Kythera*, ed. J. N. Coldstream and G. L. Huxley (London 1972), 276.

3 *Kythera*, 33.

4 See W. D. Taylour, *Mycenaean Pottery in Italy and adjacent areas* (Cambridge 1958); T. J. Dunbabin, *The Western Greeks* (Oxford 1948).

5 *Ulysses Found* (London, 1963), 120.

6 See, *e.g.*, L. G. Pocock, *The Sicilian Origin of the Odyssey* (Wellington 1957).

7 Malta: Bradford, *Ulysses Found*, chs. 26, 27; Ustica: Breusing, *Die Lösung des Trierenrätsels* (Bremen 1889); Ceuta; Bérard, *Les Navigations d'Ulysse*, vol. iii, 220 ff.; Teneriffe: Hennig, *Geographie des Homerischen Epos* (Leipzig 1934); Iceland: Pillot, *Le Code secret de l'Odyssée* (Paris 1969).

8 For a summary of the evidence see my chapter 'Ancient Explorers' in *The Quest for America* (London 1971), espec. 74–6.

9 F. H. Stubbings, *BSA* 49 (1954), 297–8.

10 *AR* 1970–1, 18.

11 S. I. Dakaris, 'The Dark Palace of Hades', *Archaeology* 15 (1962), 85–93.

12 *Epirus* (Oxford 1967), 63–9.

13 G. L. Huxley, 'Odysseus and the Thesprotian Oracle of the Dead', *Parola del Pasato* 13 (1958), 245–8; N. G. L. Hammond, *Studies in Greek History* (Oxford 1973), 452–6.

14 'Recent work at Pithekoussai (Ischia), 1965–71', *AR* 1970–1, 63–7.

15 G. S. Kirk, *Myth* (London 1970), 165.

16 See, *e.g.*, J. M. Cook in *BSA* 53–4 (1958–9), 12 ff., 26 f., for the parallel between Scheria and Old Smyrna.

17 E. D. Phillips, 'Ulysses in Italy', *JHS* 73 (1953), 53–67; J. Bérard, *La Colonisation grecque de l'Italie méridionale et de la Sicilie dans l'Antiquité* (2nd edn., Paris 1957).

Epilogue

1 P. Vidal-Nacquet, 'Homère et le monde mycénien', *Annales* 18 (1963), 703–19. D. H. F. Gray, *Fifty years (and twelve) of classical scholarship* (Oxford 1968), 46.

2 Details in *Hesperia* 33 (1964), 326–35.

3 Details in *Antiquity* 43 (1969), 91–7; 44 (1970), 270–9.

4 *FFS*, 27–8.

5 *HHI*, 196–7.

6 See further C. M. Bowra, *Heroic Poetry* (London 1961), ch. xiv; Rhys Carpenter, *FFS*, 38–44; M. I. Finley, *JHS* 84 (1964), 1–9.

7 T. B. L. Webster, *MH*, 129–35.

8 For the 'divine entourage', see G. M. Calhoun, 'Homer's Gods: Prolegomena', *TAPA* 68 (1937), 11–25.

9 For reflections on this factor, see Kirk, *JHS* 84 (1964), 12 f.

10 *MHV*, 389–90.

11 *The Iliad, the Odyssey, and the Epic Tradition* (London 1968), 203.

12 Bowra, *Heroic Poetry*, 511–12.

13 W. G. Forrest, *The Emergence of Greek Democracy* (New York 1966), 62. For the alternative view, see Snodgrass *DAG* 389.

14 For the significantly high proportion of linguistically late elements in the Homeric similes, see G. P. Shipp, *Studies in the Language of Homer* (2nd edn., Cambridge 1972), 208–22.

15 *SH*, 133 ff.

16 J. M. Cook, 'The cult of Agamemnon at Mycenae', *Festschrift for A. Keramopoulos* (Athens 1953), 112–18; 'The Agamemnoneion', *BSA* 48 (1953), 28–68.

17 Wood, *Essay*, p. vii.

18 T. R. Glover, *Springs of Hellas* (Cambridge 1945), 84.

Index